BLISTER

KJ KALIS

Published by:

BDM, LLC

ALSO BY K.J. KALIS:

1

As the last test round exploded out of the barrel of Morgan's gun, she held her position then slowly lowered the pistol and stuck it back in her holster. Flipping the switch to slide the target back to the bench, she could hear the clatter of the wires and wheels moving above her even through her ear protection. Staring at the target, she nodded, seeing small groups of threes and fives that penetrated the paper target leaving perfectly round holes. No scatter shot there. Exactly what she wanted. Pulling the target off of the clips, she crumpled it up, turning behind her and tossing it into the closest wastebasket. She picked up the half-used box of ammunition she'd just bought and walked towards the exit.

"How'd it feel?" Duncan said, coming out of the office, leaning his arms on the counter. Morgan heard the tap of toenails on the floor. The first weekend she and Danny had been back in Tampa from West Virginia, they'd found Bo at the local shelter. He came out from behind where Duncan was standing, trotting toward her. He was brown and white with a sweet disposition except if delivery people brought something to the front door. No one would be interested in breaking into her house after all the growling and barking from behind the door. It was good protection. Morgan felt his hot breath on her fingers and then a kiss from Bo's tongue. He laid down on the floor next to her, putting one paw on top of her shoe as she talked to Duncan.

"The new trigger is much better. It's a lot more reactive. I think we've got it dialed in," she said, reaching for the gun case she'd left on the counter while she was it. She slid her pistol out of her holster, keeping the barrel pointed towards the floor, checking to make sure it was completely empty before putting it back in the gun case. That was the thing about gun safety — it was a zero-sum game. She knew she had to be careful every single time, just like everyone that came to Duncan's range. Duncan didn't have any patience with sloppy gun handling. Luckily, Morgan had learned her fair share of safety at the police academy, but that seemed like a lifetime ago.

"Anything else I can get for you?" Duncan asked, turning towards the cash register.

Morgan shook her head, "No, that's it for today."

Morgan had met Duncan a few months before when they'd moved back to Tampa from West End, West Virginia. He was the gunsmith and owner of Oceanside Gunsmithing and Range. Going to the range was new, at least since she'd come out of witness protection. Before West Virginia, the Sons of Goliath, and what they'd done to her family, Morgan had always used the police department's range and their gunsmith, but now she was on her own. One of the first things she'd done when she got back to Tampa, other than adopting Bo, was to purchase a new pistol, a nice, mid-sized nine-millimeter. It wasn't as large as her duty weapon, which made it easier for her to conceal it. With the addition of the new trigger assembly that Duncan installed, it shot nearly as smooth and a lot more accurately.

Reaching down to scratch Bo's head, Morgan could hear

Duncan poking away at the cash register. It wasn't as old as some of the cash registers Morgan had seen gathering dust in her grandfather's basement, but it certainly wasn't the newest variety, either. More than once, she'd caught Duncan hitting it, trying to get it to do something thinking that it would cooperate with a little physical punishment. It never worked. Morgan stood up, smiling, watching Duncan in his newest wrestling match with the register. While he figured out how to get it to do what he wanted it to do, Morgan turned and walked over to the shelf of gun parts and lube that were nearby, glancing at the items stacked on the shelf. She heard Bo get up and follow her, standing right behind her left knee. He'd come with the name Bo, but she probably could have easily have called him Shadow. Everywhere she was, he followed.

Turning towards Duncan, Morgan looked at him. He was as close to a friend as she'd had since they moved back to Tampa. The first time she'd come to the range, asking about buying a gun, he'd eyed her up with some suspicion. Halfway through the visit, after Duncan had told her about his time as a tank commander with the Army Rangers, Morgan understood why. Combat veterans seemed to have a sixth sense about them, much like police officers. After all, their lives depended upon their ability to discern if someone was telling the truth or not and if they meant them any harm. Duncan was no different, even if he was just a civilian now.

"Did you get it to work?" Morgan said, looking at him.

"Yeah, just barely," he grunted, rubbing his beard. "It's forty-five bucks for installing the trigger and another fifteen for the box of ammo. You want to pay now or you want to put it on your tab?"

"You can put it on my tab."

Duncan shook his head, "I guess I should've asked you that before I spent the last five minutes wrestling with this stupid cash register. I'm thinking about going back to an old-fashioned cash box instead of this contraption."

"Well, I'm not that great with technology, but Danny is. If you decide to upgrade your register, let me know and I'll have him come in and help you get it set up."

"Will do. Kids always seem to be better with technology than us old guys. Anything else I can get for you today?"

Morgan reached over to the gun case, wrapping her fingers around the handle when she looked up at Duncan, "No, I'm good." She paused for a second, catching his eye, "Have you seen Paul DeLuca around? I usually bump into him every week or so, but I haven't seen him recently."

Duncan's range attracted an eclectic group of people — everyone from moms who wanted to learn how to shoot to veterans who just wanted to keep their skills sharp. Paul was one of the latter, an older guy with the fluff of gray hair on the top of his head and a set of square shoulders he held proudly. He had small eyes that seemed to bore through whoever he was talking to, but Morgan had found him to be calm and relaxed once she'd gotten to know him a bit. "You didn't hear?"

"Hear what?"

Duncan shook his head, "I guess I should've told you. Paul's been gone for the last week or so. Katrina tried to commit suicide. She's been at St. Anne's ever since."

"His granddaughter?" A tingle ran up and down Morgan's spine. Katrina DeLuca was one of the things she and Paul discovered they had in common. Katrina was one of Danny's few friends at school. They were both seniors at Palm Coast High School. Katrina was one of the few people that Danny had been able to connect with since he started back there a few months before. Morgan pressed her lips together. She'd thought on their way back to Tampa that Danny would have an easy time adjusting to their previous life. After all, they'd only been in witness protection for a couple of years. She'd wrongly assumed that his former friends would be glad to see him and happy to have him back. Their response had been anything but that. Apparently, two years was a long time in the culture of a high school. The people he'd counted on before they'd left to go into hiding didn't want to give him the time of day. Katrina DeLuca was one of the few exceptions to that rule. For a couple of days, Morgan was wondering if he was interested in her, but Danny quashed any of her questions about that.

"Yeah. Danny didn't tell you?"

Morgan shook her head, "No, I guess I missed out on that piece of information. Maybe he doesn't know?"

Duncan looked right at her, narrowing his eyes, "Now, don't feel bad about that. You know how kids are. They forget to tell you the most important things."

Morgan's mind was racing, "Suicide? I'm just trying to wrap my brain around that. I know Paul better than I know Katrina — she's been over at our house once or twice just for a minute — but she doesn't seem like the kind of kid that would try to kill herself."

"I have to say I don't know her, but knowing Paul, I can't imagine what he's going through. It's awful. I know a lot of combat veterans struggle with that, too."

Before Morgan could ask any other questions, the phone on the counter rang. As Duncan reached to pick it up, Morgan waved at him, walking out of the range, her mind racing. One of Danny's friends in a coma? How was that possible?

The hair on the back of Morgan's neck stood up as she walked to her truck. What had really happened to Katrina?

2

As Morgan got her gear loaded into her truck, the thought of Katrina in the hospital wouldn't leave her. During her time as a detective with the Tampa Police Department, she'd gone to training after training on suicides and suicide prevention. Suicide was an epidemic in adolescence, one made worse by social pressures, social media, and the constant rush of uncontrollable hormones.

Heading back to her house in Palmetto Harbor, Morgan's mind raced. The people at the range had become like a miniature family to her since she got back. It was one of the few things that was keeping her sane. She kept the windows rolled down as she drove, feeling the wind blowing through her hair. She hadn't had it cut in months, so it was getting long, pushing just past her shoulders, the blonde finally starting to look more natural after she'd had to strip the black dye off of it from when she was in hiding in West Virginia. As she glanced in the rearview mirror, she saw that her face had taken on the look of a woman native to Florida — slightly tan, but not enough to make her look like she'd spent any time laying outside by a pool. Morgan shook the thought off. She was definitely not that kind of person.

Bo stepped from the back seat to the front as she drove, curling up in a tight ball as she headed home. Her mind circled back to Katrina and Paul. No wonder she hadn't seen Paul at the range in the last couple of weeks. Morgan knew he was a devoted grandfather. He loved to go to all of the grandkids' events and he and his wife still hosted Sunday dinner every week for the family.

Thinking about Katrina and Danny, she felt the muscles in her back tense up. What happened? Danny hadn't mentioned anything to her about Katrina. Was it possible he didn't know? Morgan shook her head as she pulled into her driveway. The gossip ran through the high school faster than water over Niagara Falls. The only place she thought the rumor mill was more active was in the police department, but she didn't have much contact with them anymore. For a minute when she got back to town, she considered reaching out to her old chief to see if she could get her job back, but for some reason, she hadn't, at least not yet.

Pulling in the driveway, Morgan shut the truck off and let Bo out. He ran over onto the lawn, did his business, and then trotted inside the garage, waiting by the back door. Morgan unloaded her range bag and pistol case and unlocked the back door, letting Bo in. She did a quick walk-through of the house, making sure nothing was out of place. It was a strange habit she developed once they moved back to Florida; as if she was expecting Leo McDaniel or one of his gang members to be waiting to ambush her inside. She did it even though she knew it wasn't a possibility anymore. Leo McDaniel was dead. But even though he was no longer alive to haunt her, she still had a hard time thinking that someone wasn't lurking around the corner. A memory from the last conversation she'd had with Blake Hayes, the US Marshal that had been her lifeline in West

Virginia, rattled through her head. They'd stood in the parking lot of the apartment she rented for two years while she and Danny lived in West Virginia, the engine running on her truck, the vehicle packed with the few belongings they decided to take back with them to Florida. Blake handed her a thick manila envelope, filled with the documents they'd need to reestablish their old identities. He looked at her, his lips pressed together, the muscles in his face tense, "Morgan, you know I don't agree with you leaving our protection. Even with Leo McDaniel gone and a bunch of his guys awaiting trial, you know they will regroup. And since you're still alive, there may still be a bounty on your head. Honestly, I have no idea how that works within the gangs when the person that puts the bounty out is dead. That said, you'd better be careful."

She hadn't talked to Blake since.

Standing in the kitchen, Morgan realized Bo had disappeared. He was probably curled up on her bed, taking a nap. She checked to make sure he had food and water and then grabbed her car keys again. Locking the door behind her, Morgan ran out to her truck and jumped in, sending a quick text to Danny, "I heard Katrina's in the hospital. I'm going to check in on her and her grandpa. Back later."

"Okay."

Pulling the truck out of the driveway, Morgan grimaced. Okay? That was all she got? Morgan shook her head a little. Teenagers. Checking the time, she realized there were a few hours to go before Danny got home. He'd drive himself. Once they'd gotten back from West Virginia, Morgan was able to collect Peter's life insurance. Her husband had provided for them well. According to the financial consultant she'd hired to help her with the money, she'd never have to work a day in her life again if she didn't want to. She was still wrestling with that part, but she had already bought Danny a car, a used copper-colored sedan with relatively low mileage. He needed to be able to get himself back and forth to class and baseball practice without her constantly hovering over him even though she still wanted to protect him.

A lump formed in her stomach. If there was one thing she'd realized when she got back to Florida it was that her life had gotten very small. Without her work at the police department, she no longer had the daily camaraderie of other people to work with, their crass jokes and comments keeping even the worst murder scenes somehow tolerable. She might not have her work, but at least she could be herself again and not the black-haired Maddie Franklin she'd been while she was in hiding. Her mind returned to Katrina. As Morgan jumped on the freeway, heading for St. Anne's Medical Center, she realized that Paul and Duncan were some of the few friends she had.

The drive to St. Anne's took just a couple of minutes once she was on the freeway. As she pulled up to the complex of buildings, Morgan scanned the area. She hadn't been there in a few years, not since before she'd left for West Virginia. She pulled the truck over to the side, swallowing. The last time she'd been at the hospital was when she followed the ambulance carrying Peter's lifeless body to the morgue.

Morgan glanced down for a second and then scanned the parking lot. There were signs for visitor parking that pointed her towards the underground garage. She felt her body tense. There was no way she was parking in the underground garage. Thoughts of the trailer Leo McDaniel had locked her in surfaced. She pushed them away, refusing to think about them and what it had been like to be trapped in the dark for days on end. She felt her heart skip a beat as she looked around. Behind the hospital, there was a large, open parking lot. Choosing the open lot, she found a spot in the back. The longer walk into the building was worth not having to be in a small space.

Just inside of the hospital, Morgan heard the doors slide close behind her, the sound of their movement just above a whisper. Cool air descended over her. To her right and left there was a long, open reception area, peppered with couches and chairs up against a full wall of glass, televisions bolted near the ceiling. A few people were sitting either by themselves or in small groups. She couldn't hear any voices. It was as quiet as a church on Sunday. A woman behind the guest relations desk in front of her stood up, wearing a red blazer and a nameplate that read Marianne. "Hello, can I help you?" she said.

Glancing at Marianne and the man sitting next to her, she guessed that they were at least in their eighties, both of them with thick, gray hair. Good for them, Morgan thought. At least they'd found something productive to do with their time. That might be more than she could say about herself right now, she realized. "I'm here to see Katrina DeLuca, please. Can you tell me what room she's in?"

Marianne sat down at the computer in front of her, typing in Katrina's name. "She's in the pediatric intensive care unit. The PICU. Are you family?"

"No."

"I'm sorry, but the hospital policy is that unless you are family, the ICU doesn't permit any visitors. I can give you a number to call —"

Morgan didn't wait for Marianne to finish her sentence. She pulled her wallet out of her pocket and opened it up, flashing the detective's badge Blake had returned to her before they traveled back to Tampa. "I need to see her, please."

The color drained from Marianne's face; as if she was shocked that a police officer would need to interview someone in the hospital. "Of course, officer. I'm so sorry."

Morgan almost corrected her. She was a detective, not an officer, or at least she had been. Almost correcting her, Morgan stopped at the last second. She couldn't push the ruse too far. If the badge did its job, that was fine. But if Marianne called the department, Morgan could end up in trouble, that was for sure. She held her breath for a second, waiting for Marianne to react.

"Go down to the end of this hallway, make a left-hand turn. You'll see a bank of elevators. You'll want to take those elevators to the third floor and follow the signs to the pediatric intensive care unit. The sign will read PICU. There is a buzzer outside the door. Just tell them who you are there to see."

Morgan nodded, shoving her wallet back in her pocket. "Thank you, Marianne. Have a good day."

Morgan took a deep breath as she turned away. Hospitals always made her a little nervous. As she walked to the elevators, she realized she was chewing her lip. Coming back to Tampa had been great — no more cold, slushy West Virginia weather. She liked being back in the sunshine, but there was some downside. The memories of the time she had right before witness protection surged into her mind. Her heart started to beat a little faster as the elevator doors slid open and she stepped inside, pressing the button to go up. She stared at the floor, trying to ignore the fact that it was a small space.

Morgan blinked as the elevator doors closed. The memories of Peter and seeing his body rushed into the emergency room were almost more than she could take. She remembered following the ambulance as close as she could, barely getting inside the door before the doctor on duty came out to tell her that Peter was gone. She knew the paramedics had brought him in as a favor to her rather than just declaring him dead on the scene. In some ways, she wished they hadn't.

Hearing the elevator beep as it arrived on the third floor shook Morgan out of her thoughts. The doors slid open and Morgan stepped out into a wide, white hallway. There was a bank of windows in front of her, a couch and some chairs set up to try to look friendly and inviting, magazines scattered on a coffee table nearby. She nearly rolled her eyes. There was nothing about a hospital that was inviting or welcoming, no matter how they tried to dress it up. Looking both ways, she saw the door to the PICU. Just as Marianne had described, there was an intercom system next to it. She pressed the buzzer.

"Can I help you?" a woman's voice came through the intercom.

"I'm here to see Katrina DeLuca." Morgan glanced up at the ceiling, seeing the glass globe of a surveillance camera. She pulled her wallet out of her pocket again and held her badge up. There was no response from the person on the other side of the intercom. The door simply buzzed open.

As Morgan walked inside, she was surprised at how dark it was except for the nurses' station. To her right, there was a long bank of computer monitors bolted to the wall, behind a counter, bed numbers and the patient's vitals giving the nurses and doctors a steady stream of information, but beyond that, the hallway was dark. There were at least four nurses huddled in front of computers and three white-coated doctors. Morgan stopped for a second. She felt her heart tighten in her chest. Part of her was glad that she came to the hospital. Part of her wasn't.

"You're looking for Katrina DeLuca?" A nurse with a long ponytail wearing navy blue scrubs leaned toward her over the counter.

"Yes."

"She's in bay five," the nurse pointed.

Morgan gave the nurse a quick nod and walked down the hall. The shadows were long as she peered into each room. Some of the rooms had the curtains closed, but one had the curtain open, a crib inside, a pale mother sitting next to it, glancing Morgan's way as she passed. Following the numbers down the hallway, Morgan stopped just outside of bay four, taking a deep breath. A small girl, maybe four or five years old was in the bed, sound asleep, hooked up to monitors, wearing an oxygen mask on her face. Morgan knew anyone younger than eighteen would be in the pediatric intensive care unit, but seeing their small bodies was something else entirely. Morgan's breath caught in her throat. She knew she could turn around and walk out of the hospital. Paul would never know whether she came to visit or not, but something in her gut told Morgan that she needed to. She needed to figure out what happened to Katrina; if nothing else to put her mind at ease about the high school Danny was attending. Based on what she knew about the DeLuca family, none of it made sense. Sighing, she took a couple of steps forward and then stood in the doorway of bay five.

The small room where Katrina DeLuca was laying was filled with equipment. There was a small lamp on in the corner of the room casting a yellow glow over the bed. It smelled like the plastic of latex gloves and gauze. Morgan saw the shock of Paul's hair from behind him. He was turned towards his grand-daughter, holding her hand. "Paul?"

Paul's head whipped around. He seemed surprised someone was calling his name. He stood up and walked toward Morgan, wrapping his arms around her in a hug, "Morgan? What are you doing here?"

The two of them stood at the foot of Katrina's bed for a moment before Morgan answered. Katrina's eyes were closed, her body limp. A ventilator was breathing for her, quiet beeping in the background. There were two tall stands of IVs, the banks of pumps pouring medication into Katrina's body. Morgan felt the bile rise in the back of her throat as she looked back at Paul, "Duncan told me about Katrina. I thought I'd come by to see how you are holding up. What happened?"

Paul shook his head, shoving his hands in his pockets and looking at the ground, "Honestly, I don't know. She was found behind the wheel of her car in the driveway. They said they think she tried to kill herself, but there weren't any drugs or anything in her car, no empty bottles or notes." As he looked up at Morgan, she noticed his eyes were filled with tears, "This isn't the Katrina I know, Morgan. There was nothing wrong with her. Why would she do this?"

Morgan reached out and squeezed his arm, "I don't know. I just wanted to come by and see if there's anything I could do to help. Katrina's been nice to Danny since we came back into town."

The two of them stood in silence for a second, the only noise in the room the machinery keeping Katrina alive. Morgan watched her for a moment, her chest rising and falling rhythmically, the lines on the monitor next to her bed following her heart rate in red and green and blue. Although Morgan wasn't a doctor, her vitals looked stable. At least that was good news. "What's the prognosis?"

Paul shook his head. "The doctors aren't saying much. Part of the problem is that they don't know what she took. They've run a bunch of toxicology screens, but nothing has come back. Until they know what's in her system, there's not a lot they can do for her other than help her body heal and hope it does it on its own. She's been in a coma since they got her here." He looked down at the floor, "I'm hoping time doesn't run out on her before they figure out what happened."

Morgan blinked, sadness filling her chest. "Are you here by yourself?"

"Yeah. My son and daughter-in-law, they've been here almost non-stop. I told them I would take the dayshift for them. They'll come tonight as soon as they get off of work. My daughter-in-law has been texting me about every hour to see if there's been any change." Paul looked at the ground again, "It's so sad, Morgan."

The heaviness in the room was palpable. It was as if a cloud had descended into the space they were standing in, the air heavy. A second later, Paul drew in a sharp breath. "You said you might be able to help?"

"I guess that depends on what you need help with."

Paul walked over to a little dresser that was next to Katrina's bed and opened the drawer. From inside, he pulled a silver laptop and handed it to Morgan. "Her mom brought this up to the hospital. She thought it would be good if Katrina had her computer handy when she woke up. I've been on it a couple of times, trying to see if there was any information on there that would help the doctors figure out what happened to her, but a lot of it is technological mumbo-jumbo. I don't understand it very well. I asked my son about it, but they're so upset about Katrina that he doesn't even want to look at it. I think it's too hard for him. But I don't know, Morgan, I feel like there might be something on there that could help. Can you look at it?"

"Sure, but I can only do the basics with computers, if you know what I mean." Morgan glanced around. There was only one chair in the room. "Is there a place we can go and sit so I can take a look at this?"

"Yeah, for sure. There are some couches by the elevators."

Morgan followed Paul out of the room, instantly grateful to get out of the small space. As they passed the nurses' station, Paul looked at the same nurse that had let Morgan in, "I'll be out by the elevators if you need me."

The nurse nodded, "Okay, Mr. DeLuca. I'll come get you if anything happens." Morgan wondered how many times a day the nurses heard the same thing. She sighed.

The door slid open and closed behind them as they left the PICU. Morgan followed Paul down the hallway towards the elevators by the windows. Outside, the sun had come out, the brief afternoon clouds that were so common to Florida's tropical climate pushing back off the coast and out to sea. Paul sat down on a chair and Morgan sat on the couch next to him as he handed her the computer. As she opened the laptop, she noticed it was password enabled. "Do you know the password?"

"Yeah, luckily Katrina's mom made her give them all of her

passwords. It's 7735." As Morgan glanced at the screen, she realized Katrina's parents had been smart. She'd been so busy getting her and Danny set up in Tampa that things like knowing his passwords had kind of slipped her mind. She made a mental note to ask him for a list.

As the computer opened up, Morgan stared at it. There were a few icons on the left side of the screen and a line of them at the bottom. Morgan opened up Katrina's email and started going through them. There wasn't much to be seen — notifications about some sales at clothing stores, a few emails from her teachers at school, and a few forwards from her friends. Morgan realized there probably wouldn't be much there, or at least not what she was looking for. Most of the kids tended to do everything on their phones except for homework.

Frowning, Morgan opened up the search browser and found the option to view Katrina's search history. "Have you taken a look at what she was searching for on the Internet?" Morgan asked, trying to be gentle. Her police training kicked in, speaking slowly and softly to Paul, although she knew he'd hate that she was being careful around him.

"What's that?"

Morgan tilted her head to the side as she waited for Katrina's history to load. "The computer keeps track of what Internet sites she's visited." What Morgan didn't say is that typically people who are contemplating ending their life frequently go to websites to get information on how to do it. It was the dark, scary side of the online world, one that should never be available to anyone, but the reality is that it was. There was evil around every corner, it seemed.

Staring at the screen, Morgan looked through the list that had populated. Most of the places Katrina had searched on her computer had something to do with school, including a couple of searches for nearby universities, and shopping. Typical teenager stuff. Morgan frowned. There were no indications that she'd been looking at drugs or ways to kill herself. She realized that if Katrina was looking at colleges, she was probably thinking about her future, not ending her life. Morgan checked the dates, wondering if maybe Katrina had scrubbed her history before she got sick, erasing the sites she'd been searching. Scrolling through the list, Morgan noticed there were months of Internet searches on her computer. If she had scrubbed her history of sites about suicide, she would have had to remove sites individually. That seemed a little too meticulous for someone who was thinking about ending their life. A knot formed in her stomach. Something wasn't right, that was for sure. "Paul, when did this happen?"

He pushed his hair off his forehead, leaning back in the chair. "It was last week. My son found her in the driveway when he got home from work. She was barely breathing. They rushed her here. The doctors haven't been able to do much — just stabilize her, I guess."

Morgan frowned. She stared at the computer again and then noticed there was an icon in the lower left-hand corner she didn't recognize. She clicked on it and waited for it to open. It asked for a password, the entire screen blank except for the request. Morgan turned the computer towards Paul. "Any idea what this is?"

Paul shook his head, "No. Like I said, I'm not good with computers."

As Morgan spun the display back towards her, she stared at the screen. Normally computer programs were more than happy to tell you who owned the software or the name of the company. For some reason, all this one wanted was a password. Other than that, it was a dark purple screen with no other writing or logos on it. One of the last trainings Morgan had gone to before she left the police department was on technology. The speaker that came in to train them talked about how many encrypted applications were being launched each year.

They numbered in the thousands, and many of them were not meant for the greater good. A tingle ran up her spine. Morgan wondered if that was what she had stumbled upon.

Morgan closed the window for that application and opened another. It was similar except it had two cartoon people kissing in the corner. Was Katrina using dating applications? That didn't seem to make any sense. She was still in high school and as pretty as she was, she had her pick of boys. Looking at Paul, she closed the lid to the laptop, "Was Katrina dating anyone?"

He shook his head, "No, at least no one that the family knew about. Did you find anything?"

Morgan tilted her head, "No, nothing obvious. There are a couple of applications on here that we need passwords for to get into, but I suspect they're the kind of sites that Katrina didn't give her mom access to."

A flash of concern ran across Paul's face, the muscles along the side of his jar replying, "What are you saying?"

Morgan knew she needed to choose her words carefully, "There's a lot of dark stuff out on the Internet now. Katrina has a couple of sites on her computer that I'm not familiar with. That doesn't mean there's anything wrong with them, but they don't look to be standard sites."

"And you think that might have something to do with her being sick?"

Morgan noticed that Paul didn't say that Katrina tried to kill herself. It was like it was too much for him to deal with. "It might, but I can't get into these sites. I'm not a tech expert."

"Can you take the computer home to Danny? Could he help? You know, those kids are all on the same sites together."

Morgan paused for a second, pressing her lips together. "I can, but are you sure that would be okay with your son and daughter-in-law? I mean, they don't know us." Morgan realized no one knew them that well since they'd only been back in town for a couple of months.

Paul nodded. "I'll make it okay with them. Don't you worry about that. You just take that computer and see if you can figure out what happened to my granddaughter." He put his hand on Morgan's wrist. "Listen, I can tell by looking at you that you have more of a story than you've told me, but I think whatever it is you've been through, that'll help you figure out what happened to my Katrina. You'll help my family, right?"

Morgan licked her lips. Pretty much everyone at the range knew she was a former police detective and that she no longer worked for the department, but no one knew why. At that moment it felt like Paul was looking right through her. Her stomach lurched. Morgan swallowed, "I'd be happy to take the computer home to Danny to see what he can figure out, but I can't make any promises. You understand that, right?"

"Yeah, of course. Just let me know what you find out, okay?"

Just then the nurse with the ponytail came out of the PICU and walked towards Paul. "The doctors are starting to make their rounds if you want to come back to Katrina's room, Mr. DeLuca."

Paul stood up, staring at Morgan. "I'm not expecting anything. Just do what you can, okay?" He pointed toward the PICU, "I gotta go."

Morgan nodded, still sitting on the couch holding Katrina's computer, the weight of it heavy in her hand. Questions were surging through her mind. What were the applications on her computer? Where did they lead? Morgan stood up and walked to the elevator, leaving the hospital with more questions than answers.

3

By the time Morgan left the hospital, she realized it was time to go meet Amber. They'd arranged coffee dates in the afternoon every couple of weeks since Morgan got back into town. Amber D'Amico was one of the few people from the police department that was interested in talking to her now that she was out of hiding.

The Beachline Coffee Shop was in a strip center just down the road from the police station where Amber worked. They'd been there enough times that the staff had started to wave when they walked in the door. Amber was there already by the time Morgan walked in. She was sitting at the corner table just like usual, the smell of freshly roasted coffee hanging in the air. Approaching the table, Morgan realized there was another woman with Amber. A wave of tension flooded over her.

Amber stood up and gave Morgan a hug, wearing wide-leg navy blue pants, chunky heels, and a sleeveless top that had embroidery around the neck. She certainly didn't look the part of a detective, more like a marketing executive out to lunch with an important client, although Morgan knew she was one of the best in the department at what she did. The woman sitting next to her seemed to be a little bit older than they were, her mousy brown hair pulled back from around her face. She had on a white blouse and a red jacket, her fingers wrapped around a mug in front of her.

Amber looked at Morgan, "I want you to meet Dr. Sylvia Knapp. She's the county coroner and a very good friend. We've worked on a lot of cases together. I thought maybe the two of you should meet."

Morgan eyed both of them with a little bit of suspicion, feeling unsure of herself. "It's nice to meet you," she said, reaching out her hand. Morgan glanced back at Amber, searching her face, wondering why she'd brought Sylvia. Why did she want them to meet?

Morgan slid down into a chair against the wall across from Dr. Knapp. Amber was still standing up, "Morgan, you want coffee?"

"Yeah, that would be good." Morgan started to get up, "I can get it."

"Naw, I'm already up and you got it last time. I'll be right back."

Morgan watched as Amber walked away, the fabric of her tailored pants swishing around her ankles, leaving them in the wake of her lemon-scented perfume. Morgan turned to Dr. Knapp, her mouth dry. "I heard there was a new coroner." It came out more awkwardly than she wanted it to.

"Yeah, that would be me. I've been here for just over a year. Came in from the southern part of Georgia."

Morgan waited for a second, unsure of how much Sylvia knew of her story. That had been happening to her a lot lately. Anyone who talked to her for more than a couple of minutes would realize there was a gap in her timeline of living in Florida. Most of the time, she just told people she went to West Virginia for work, but then she came back. The lie was running thin.

Before Sylvia could ask Morgan anything about herself, Amber was back, carrying two heavy mugs filled with coffee, setting one down in front of Morgan. "Morgan, I know it was a bit of a surprise to bring Sylvia here, but I wanted you to meet her. She's new to town, too."

Morgan grimaced. Other than the two years away, she wasn't exactly new to town, but Morgan swallowed, trying to accept Amber's help as gracefully as possible. Graceful was not something she did well. "Yeah, we were just talking about that."

Over the next couple of minutes, Amber led them in a casual get-to-know-you discussion about all the basics. Sylvia talked about her kids, who were both in their thirties and what they were doing. Her son was an engineer and her daughter had just finished her residency as a pulmonologist. "I got divorced about ten years ago," Sylvia said, looking down at the table for a second and then back up at Morgan. "Best and worst time of my life, that's for sure. Now, I live alone, except for my cat, Peaches. It's just nice to have some other noise in the house when you're all by yourself."

Morgan nodded, remembering how many nights she'd sat in the little apartment she and Danny shared while they were in hiding, the only noise the tick of the ductwork as it blew hot air into their apartment, the occasional groan of a water pipe in the wall adding to the noise. That's what she liked about having Bo around. When she was home, he was constantly by her. Not to say that it didn't become aggravating at times when she was trying to walk someplace and he nearly tripped her, but it didn't matter. She was grateful for what he'd brought into their life. "I get that. When I got back into town, Danny and I got a dog the first weekend we were here. A boxer. His name is Bo."

Sylvia cocked her head to the side, "Amber said you'd recently relocated into the area. She said she's known you for a long time."

Morgan shot a look at Amber. "Yeah, my son and I — we've

only been back in town a couple of months. Used to live here though..."

Amber leaned across the table closer to Sylvia, her voice low, "Sylvia, this is Detective Foster. I'm sure you've heard about her."

Sylvia's eyes got wide, "Oh! I'm sorry. I didn't realize."

Morgan fought off the urge to beat Amber senseless for outing her secret. Morgan wanted to bolt from the coffee shop and never return. She took a breath in and then swallowed, looking back at Sylvia, "Yes, I don't generally talk about it," she said, glaring at Amber, "but my son and I were in the witness protection program for the last couple of years. Some bad stuff happened at work."

Sylvia nodded, "I know all about it. I've been doing case reviews with the gang unit. I heard about the Sons of Goliath and that one of the detectives had disappeared out of town. I just didn't put it together that it was you. When they heard Leo McDaniel had been killed, the unit actually went and got a cake and sent a piece over to the lab for me. They were so happy about it, I think they celebrated for a week. Congratulations."

"I don't know if congratulations are in order when you have to kill someone. There was no choice." Morgan glanced away for a second, the memories of seeing Leo McDaniel hold a knife to Danny's neck rising in her mind. She did what she had to do, that was for sure. At that moment, she'd been pinned between two of his men that were coming up the steps and Leo holding Danny on the other side of the room. Now, they were all gone even though Blake Hayes still insisted there was danger for her. Morgan wasn't sure that was actually the case.

Pushing the thoughts out of her mind, Morgan looked back at Amber and Sylvia, "Enough about me. I actually have a question for you. Either of you hear about an attempted suicide at Palm Coast High School? Katrina DeLuca?"

Amber shifted in her seat, "Yeah, I heard about it. That's the one where the girl was found in her car sitting outside her house?"

Morgan nodded, "That's the one."

"We don't have a lot to go on as far as I know. She's still in the hospital, right?"

"Yeah. I'm friends with her grandfather, Paul. I just came from there. She's in a coma. The doctors can't seem to figure out what she took."

Amber frowned, "I remember hearing Ben Acosta talk about it. He said there was no note and no bottles of alcohol or pills nearby. I think they just rolled up on the scene and sent her off to the hospital. I'm not sure how much follow-up he's done."

"Wait, Palm Coast is the local high school, correct?" Sylvia asked.

Amber nodded.

She shook her head, her face taking on a stony expression. "That's not the only suicide."

Morgan held her breath, staring at Sylvia for a second. "What do you mean?"

Sylvia took a sip of her coffee before continuing, "Yeah, there've been a couple of other bodies from that same school. Both girls. I can't exactly remember their names at the minute, but I know I have the information back at the office." She glanced at Amber, "I'm sure you have those files too, right?"

Morgan pressed her palms into the table and leaned forward, "Are you telling me there's a suicide cluster at the same high school where my son goes?" Everything in Morgan wanted to drive straight to the high school and get Danny out of there. She set her jaw and stayed put.

Amber cocked her head to the side, "I don't know if I would call it a cluster just yet —"

Sylvia shook her head, "I'm sorry, but I have to disagree.

The CDC considers three or more attempted suicide within thirty days at any one given location a cluster. Technically, I should be calling them, but I've tried that before and they aren't exactly, how can I say it, helpful. They make me do a lot of paperwork and don't give the community any help."

Morgan leaned back in her chair for a second. It was bad enough that Katrina was laying flat on her back in a coma over at St. Anne's. Morgan had seen the look of weariness on Paul's face. She couldn't imagine what Katrina's parents were going through. To think there were two other families that were going through the same thing was just unbelievable.

A quiet settled over the table for a second, the three women lost in their own thoughts. Amber was the first one to speak. "I don't have kids, but honestly, I can't imagine."

"You said Ben Acosta was assigned to the case?" Morgan asked.

Amber nodded. Morgan remembered Ben from the time before she left the department. He'd been a brand-new detective around the time that the problems with the Sons of Goliath cropped up. She didn't know a lot about him. "Does he have any leads?"

Amber shook her head no, "Not that I know of. In our last case review meeting, he said he'd marked the case as solved. He felt like they were clear-cut suicides -- nothing to look into. I didn't put together that they were all from the same high school until Sylvia just said something about it. Incredible."

Something in Morgan shifted knowing there were more bodies. She swallowed. She had to remember she wasn't a detective anymore. "Don't you think there has to be something more to this than just a coincidence?"

Sylvia nodded, "I don't care what Ben says. I do. The odds of three young women trying to take their own lives within such a short amount of time that all go to the same high school —

that's just not normal. That's why the CDC calls three or more a cluster."

Amber tilted her head to the side, "I can ask Ben about it, but he's pretty stubborn. If he's decided that there's nothing left to look at, then he won't do it."

Morgan leaned forward again, licking her lips, "Any chance I can get a look at the files?"

Amber and Sylvia looked at each other. Amber looked back at Morgan, "You know what you're asking me to do?"

"I do." For a second, Morgan felt bad for bringing it up, but if the detective assigned to the case wasn't going to do anything about it, someone had to. "Listen, I told Paul that I would see what I could find out. He gave me Katrina's laptop to go through. I'm assuming Ben already did that. But if there's any other information linking the cases together, I'd like to know."

Amber didn't say anything for a second. Morgan stared at her, waiting to see what she would say. Amber was right and Morgan knew it. Morgan didn't have any right to look at any of the case files in the department. Those were considered confidential and only for law enforcement review. But technically, Morgan hadn't resigned and she hadn't quit. For a while, the department still paid her while she was in protective custody during the trial. Afterward, the payments just stopped coming, a letter arriving through the Marshal's office in West Virginia that said they'd put her on non-pay status. "You know, I didn't actually resign or quit, so technically it wouldn't be a violation."

Amber laughed, "And technically, I'm not sure the brass would look at it that way." She sighed, "Let me see what I can do. I'll call you later on."

The women sat there for a few more minutes, finishing the last drops of coffee in their cups. Although Morgan wasn't sure why Amber had brought Sylvia to the coffee, walking out of the shop, she was glad she did.

By the time Morgan got home, it was nearly time to make

dinner. Going into the house, Morgan brought in the laptop that Paul had given her and set it on the counter. Bo met her at the door sniffing her legs as if asking her where she'd been while she was gone. She squatted down, scratching the spot right behind his ears. He squinted and panted. Standing up, she opened the door to the backyard to let him out and then refilled his food and water for him taking a walk through the house to make sure everything was in place. It was. Just as she let Bo back in, she heard a noise at the garage door. Turning, she saw Danny, his backpack on his shoulders, staring at his phone. "Hey, how was your day?" she said, reaching into the refrigerator.

"All right. Fall baseball practice starts next week."

"That's exciting."

"Maybe." Danny pulled the backpack off of his shoulders and tossed it on one of the chairs at the kitchen table. He slumped down into the chair next to it, staring at his phone then setting it down and looking at Morgan. "Did you go to the range today?"

"Yeah. Duncan got the new trigger installed on my pistol and wanted me to come in and try it out. You should come with me next time. I know he'd like to see you." Morgan pulled a skillet out of the cabinet next to the stove and set it on a burner, trying to not ambush Danny with the information she had. He was a little like his father that way. Working up to something seemed to get her better results than pouncing on him as soon as he walked in the door. "Hey, I heard something's been going on with Katrina DeLuca. Did you hear anything about that?"

"You know, it's weird. I texted her a couple of days ago and didn't hear back, but then somebody said she's been sick. Haven't seen her since. Did you run into her grandpa?" He said, chewing on his cuticle.

Morgan pressed her lips together. Danny was seventeen years old and he should be able to handle the information she had to give him, but part of her wondered how he'd react. Losing his father and the trauma of what they'd gone through in West Virginia had been a lot. Morgan had insisted when they got back that he got started with a counselor. Now knowing what was going on with Katrina, it made her even happier to know that Danny's weekly appointment with Dr. Solis was coming up. Morgan walked out from behind the kitchen counter and leaned against it, getting a little closer to him so she could watch his expression. "Yeah, as a matter of fact, I did talk to him, but it wasn't at the range. It was at the hospital."

"The hospital? Is Katrina okay?" Danny's dark eyebrows furrowed.

Morgan shrugged her shoulders, "They don't know. Apparently, she tried to commit suicide last week. Her dad found her sitting in her car in the driveway when he got home from work. She was barely breathing, but they got her to the hospital in time." Morgan stared at the floor, letting the words settle. "Danny, she's in a coma."

The color drained from Danny's face. He pushed his hair back off of his forehead and held his hand there for a second as though he was getting a splitting headache. "Are you kidding me? I didn't hear anything about that. No one knows at school?"

Morgan waited for a second before responding, thinking. From the look on Danny's face, he was shocked, but he was under control. That was a good sign given everything he'd been through before they got back to Tampa. "I'm not sure what the principal or guidance counselor at school knows. But Paul is really upset. The thing is, the doctors don't know what she took, so it's been very hard to treat her."

"Is she going to die?"

Morgan almost smiled. Although Danny was approaching adulthood, he still had the urge to blurt out whatever was on his mind, much like children did. "Honestly, I don't know. But Paul, he wanted me to ask you a favor."

"Of course! Anything!"

Morgan pointed to the counter, "He sent home Katrina's laptop with me. I did a quick search through her history and her email, but I couldn't find anything. We're trying to see if there's any information on her laptop that might give us a clue to either what happened or to what drugs she took. The thing is, there seems to be a couple of programs on there that I don't recognize. I was wondering if maybe you could take a look at them?"

"Sure." Danny glanced at the computer and frowned for a second, then stood up. "Let me just go get a power cable for it. I'll be right back."

Morgan sighed, realizing Danny took the information about Katrina much better than she'd expected him to. She watched as he walked down the hallway and disappeared into his room, wondering if she should tell him about the other two girls that made up the suicide cluster Sylvia was concerned about. Palm Coast was a giant high school, with more than three thousand kids in it. With Danny being a new student, it was likely he hadn't even heard about them. The group he traveled in was small, just a couple of kids he'd gotten to know over the last few months. She was sure it would get bigger throughout the year as he got to know the other boys through baseball, but for right now, she wasn't sure there was any point in telling him about the other two girls, at least not until she got more information.

Morgan walked back around the kitchen counter and turned on the burner under the skillet. After visiting Paul at the hospital and learning of the other victims, her stomach felt heavy. She didn't feel like cooking. All she wanted was answers. Luckily, Danny didn't seem to care all that much about food. Morgan threw together grilled cheese sandwiches and had them in the pan by the time he walked back into the kitchen with the power cable.

They worked in silence. A couple of minutes later, Morgan

set a sandwich and some chips in front of Danny as he stared at the computer. Bo laid down near him, waiting for a handout. Morgan didn't ask him any questions. He didn't like to be disturbed while he was trying to figure things out. As she was just about to sit down in front of her own sandwich, she heard a knock at the door. Bo took off, barking and growling, his nails scratching at the tile floor.

Checking through the side window, Morgan glanced to see who it was. Amber. She opened the door, grabbing Bo by the collar as she did, "What's going on?"

"I've got something you're gonna want to see," Amber said, frowning.

"Come on in."

Just inside the front door, Amber kicked off her heels, Bo sniffing around her and then checking her shoes. "Danny and I were just in the kitchen. He's taking a look at Katrina's laptop."

"Hey, Danny," Amber said, setting a large leather tote bag down on the nearest chair.

"Hi," he said as he chewed a bite of his sandwich. He didn't look up.

Morgan turned to Amber, crossing her arms in front of her chest, "Did you find something? I didn't expect to see you this soon."

"Maybe. When I got back to the office, I checked on those files we talked about at coffee. Since there haven't been any leads in longer than thirty days in a couple of the cases, they've already been categorized as cold or closed."

Morgan blinked, "Cold? Really? It hasn't been that long. Has Ben already given up on them?"

Amber shrugged her shoulders, "It kinda seems that way."

Morgan felt heat surge through her body. How Ben could give up on the cases, she didn't know. Were they really that cut and dry? The memory of seeing Katrina hooked up to a million

machines in the hospital lurked in her mind. She tried to shake
it off. "Okay, so what did you find?"

"Well, I did a search for any incidents tied to the high
school and the surrounding area in the last six months. I
figured that was a long enough time span. Just like Sylvia said,
there have been a couple of other suicides. Could very well be a
cluster. All girls. All either juniors or seniors." Amber pulled
files out of her tote bag. By looking at the embossed leather,
Morgan was sure it had cost her half a paycheck. Amber had
expensive taste, that was for sure. She passed the files to
Morgan. "Sarah Poole and Maisie Hill. I brought you copies of
both of those files. I also included one for Katrina DeLuca.
Maybe if you look at the three of them together, you'll see
something we missed."

"I'm sure if you had the cases, you wouldn't have missed
anything," Morgan grunted.

"Probably, but you know how the other detectives can be
when somebody questions their work."

"True."

Morgan set the files on the counter and flipped through the
pages glancing at them. There wasn't a ton in any of them, just
some pictures and a few forms and statements that had been
filled out. Maybe there was something there. Maybe there
wasn't. "Thanks. I'll take a look at these. I'll let you know if I
find anything."

"I appreciate that." Amber picked up her bag and slung it
on her shoulder again. "I feel bad. We should've picked up the
fact that there was a cluster happening at the high school. Not
sure how we missed it."

"Probably because you're buried in paperwork and don't
have enough help, like usual."

Amber nodded, "That's true. I guess that part of the job
hasn't changed since you left."

For a minute, Morgan thought that Amber was about to ask

her if she missed working for the department or if she'd consider coming back. She held her breath, but the question didn't come. For that, she was grateful. She wasn't sure she had an answer.

"Listen, I gotta go," Amber said, checking her watch.

"Hot date?" Morgan said, following her to the door.

"How I wish," Amber chuckled, sliding her feet into her heels again. "Gotta open the door for the exterminator."

Morgan nodded. "I'll let you know if I find anything."

"Thanks," Amber said, stepping outside into the late afternoon sunshine. "And Morgan, be careful. I have no idea what we're up against. If you need anything — anything at all — just let me know. I'll bring back up."

"I appreciate that. Have fun with the bug man."

4

By the time Morgan walked back into the kitchen after locking the door and watching Amber pull out of the driveway, Danny had already finished his sandwich, his hand absentmindedly crawling on the table, reaching for a chip. His eyes never left the screen. "Did you find anything?"

"Not yet. I'll let you know."

It was as close to a polite brushoff as Morgan was going to get. She decided not to press her luck. Her stomach lurched. What if Danny found something? What if it put him in danger? Morgan swallowed. It wasn't like she was in a position to help – she didn't have the same tech skills he and his friends seemed to have. She glanced at the floor, the gnawing in her stomach receding a little bit. The odds that Danny would put himself in danger were small, but there. She'd tackle any issues if they got there, like she always did. In the meantime, she needed his help.

Turning toward the counter where Amber had left the stack of files, Morgan sat down on one of the two counter stools and grabbed her own sandwich, taking a bite, wiping her fingers on her pants. She flipped open the file for Sarah Poole. The image of her dead body was the first thing she saw, a wave of nausea crashing over her. She was too young to be dead.

Swallowing, Morgan looked away, scanning the initial information that was listed next to her picture. Sarah was a junior at Palm Coast High School. Flipping the page, Morgan saw she was involved in a bunch of different activities and had a 4.0 GPA. She was involved in everything from the physics club to the swim team and cheerleading. "Busy girl," Morgan muttered.

After getting a handle on the basics of the case, Morgan turned back to the picture Amber had included. It looked like her body had been discarded at the beach. The images in the file showed a blonde girl laying on her back in the sand, her eyes open and vacant, staring at nothing, her arms limp, her hair in a tangle. The lower part of her body was wet from the tide coming in and then retreating. Her makeup seemed to be smeared, a gray pallor over her face, her mouth slightly open as though she'd struggled to get her last breaths. Morgan closed her eyes for a second, hearing Danny get up from the table. She pulled one of the other reports to the front of the file, covering up the image. It was bad enough she had to see them. Danny had seen enough trauma in his life. He certainly didn't need to see a young girl his age dead at the beach. Morgan pushed her sandwich away, the nausea getting stronger, her stomach tightening. She started reading through the report.

"Victim was found at six a.m. by a runner on the beach who called it in and stayed with the body until the police arrived. The purse of the victim was found approximately a hundred yards up the beach. Based on her driver's license, the victim was initially identified as Sarah Poole, seventeen years old, a junior at Palm Coast High School. A note found in her pocket read, 'I can't do this anymore.' See attached exhibit."

Morgan flipped through the file and looked at the picture of the note that had been included. The paper looked wrinkled, the ink slightly smeared from getting damp in the surf. She continued reading the notes, "Victim transported to the morgue where she was pronounced DOA. Family was notified, identified and the body was released. No drugs or alcohol found at the scene. Based on the evidence, the case is considered cold/closed."

It was signed by Ben Acosta.

Morgan shuddered. Maybe it was a suicide, maybe it wasn't. Her heart skipped a beat. Whatever the case was, she needed to know if Danny was safe at school -- for that matter, if any of the kids were.

Morgan pushed the file for Sarah Poole aside. She flipped open the next file Amber had brought her, pushing the one for Katrina DeLuca underneath that. Morgan could go through Katrina's file later, but she already knew most of the important points from talking to Paul at the hospital.

Opening the next file, she saw the victim's name was Maisie Hill. Morgan stared at her picture. Maisie's body was slumped in the corner of what looked like a pile of straw. Morgan frowned, her chest tightening. The environment where her body was left seemed strange. Where was she? Morgan flipped over to the report, running her finger down the page, reading, "The body of Maisie Hill was found at Gulf Shores Stables in a stall not occupied at the end of the north aisle next to the tack room." A horse barn? Morgan pressed her lips together. She pulled her phone closer to her and did a quick search, locating the stable complex on a map. Calculating the distance, she saw it was about a half-hour ride from the school. She cocked her head to the side. For a teenager with a car, half an hour was nothing. She continued reading, the knot in her stomach and growing with every word. "Nothing remarkable at the scene. Was left undisturbed by the owner of the stable who found her during early morning feedings. A backpack was found nearby. Contents are listed below.

A note was found crumpled in her hand that read, 'I'm tired of life.'"

Morgan shook her head, her stomach tightening. No wonder Ben had played these off as suicides. Each of the girls had a note on them. That explained why paramedics had pronounced them and Ben had moved on with other cases. And Sylvia didn't have any reason to look any deeper or do an autopsy. She had no reason to with the lack of additional evidence from Ben. Heat started to burn in Morgan's face. Still, Ben didn't have any questions? He wasn't concerned by anything at the scene? It seemed unbelievable that he wouldn't do any deeper digging. From she could see he had simply taken the information and written the report. Nothing more. Morgan closed the cover of the file and stood up, shoving balled fists in her pockets and staring at the ceiling. Sure, there were some cases that were just that obvious. But these? Even if they were suicides, the lack of paperwork in the file told her that Ben hadn't made much of an effort, if any at all to think of an alternate theory. Something didn't seem right, but she didn't have time to deal with it at that moment. The knot in her stomach grew. Morgan glanced down at her phone. "Danny? I hate to break you away from your project, but we gotta go."

"Are you sure?" he mumbled. "I was just getting somewhere with Katrina's computer."

"Yeah, I'm sure. Grandma and Grandpa are expecting us."

What she really wanted to say is, "They are expecting to see you." Morgan still wasn't too sure about the family scene since they'd returned.

Morgan walked down the hallway to her bedroom and changed out of the t-shirt she'd worn to the range that morning, leaving her jeans on, choosing a red blouse with a V-neck and slipping into a pair of sandals. She grimaced in the mirror as she walked by, running her fingers through her blonde hair, stopping for a second to add a sheen of lip gloss. The blouse and shoes were new, replacements for clothes she'd had when they lived in Florida before, but there was something about them that just wasn't comfortable. They didn't fit what she'd been through. Morgan looked down for a second, thinking about putting her t-shirt back on, but she didn't. Walking out of the bedroom, she realized with any luck, they'd be in and out of Peter's parents' house in an hour. She wanted to get back and keep going through the files, but it was Peter's dad's birthday, and her mother-in-law, Heidi, had texted earlier that week to see if she and Danny would like to come by to have a piece of cake. She didn't, but saying no wasn't exactly an option. They were Danny's grandparents after all.

Five minutes later, she and Danny were in the truck, headed to Charles and Heidi's house. Morgan glanced at Danny, who was staring at his cell phone, pecking away with his thumbs. He was clearly sending a text to someone. "Did you find anything on Katrina's computer that would explain what happened?"

Danny glanced up, "Not yet. You're right, though, there is some strange software loaded on her machine. Haven't seen it before. I'm talking to Brantley about it right now."

Morgan furled her eyebrows together and gripped the wheel of the truck a little harder, "Who's Brantley?" She wasn't sure how comfortable she was with other kids in the school knowing what was going on with Katrina.

"We're in the same programming class together. The thing is, he knows everything about tech. Probably going to go to college on a scholarship for computer science. I'm asking him about it. If anybody knows what it is or can figure it out, it's him."

Morgan nodded, "Okay, but try to keep it quiet. I'm not sure how much information Paul wants to get out." The truth was that if there was something more to this cluster of deaths, Morgan didn't want to alert whoever was responsible, but she couldn't make the words form in her mouth. Danny had been through too much and all she had at the moment was a gut feeling, nothing more.

"I will, Mom. Don't worry. Brantley's a vault."

Morgan didn't say anything else for the rest of the drive to Charles and Heidi's house. Her mind was teetering back and forth between the pictures of the bodies she'd seen just before they'd left, the beeping and whirring of the machines that were keeping Katrina DeLuca alive, and the inevitable lump in her stomach that formed every time she needed to see Peter's parents.

It had always been this way.

Even when Peter and Morgan were dating, Morgan had never really felt part of the family. Charles and Heidi were stiff at best, people that followed the rules no matter what. Straight-laced. They weren't sure they liked the idea of their son dating a cop. Morgan had always assumed that Charles and Heidi thought that officers should be men.

And then Peter had been killed because of Morgan.

Turning down their street, she felt the lump in her stomach grow even bigger. They'd never talked about it — there wasn't time after Peter died between her interviews with the US Marshals, the District Attorney, and getting put in protective custody. Before they'd left for West Virginia, Morgan had only seen them at the memorial service for Peter. It was small, just Morgan, Danny, Charles, and Heidi, and four US Marshals plus a priest. Morgan knew deep inside of her that Charles and Heidi blamed her for Peter's death. Maybe they were right. But, while she was to blame, it wasn't her fault. Leo McDaniel was the one that had killed their son, not her. Somehow knowing that didn't make her feel any better, though.

Pulling up in front of their house, Morgan noticed there were cars lined up and down the street. She swallowed. She had no idea there were going to be other people at the party, but it made sense. She and Danny had been gone for the last couple of years. Life had moved on. Throwing the truck into park and turning it off, Morgan glanced at Danny, "Let's go."

Stepping onto their manicured lawn, Morgan paused for a second, slamming the door and locking it behind her, sucking in a deep breath. The files sitting on the counter were eating away at her. She glanced over at Danny, "We don't have to stay too long if you don't want to."

The truth was, it was Morgan who didn't want to.

"That's fine, Mom. I've got studying to do anyway."

Morgan nodded, feeling the knot in her stomach ease just a little bit knowing that Danny's homework would provide her with a way of escape.

Walking up the front sidewalk, Morgan noticed Heidi and Charles' home was impeccably kept, as usual, a white stuccoed home with a red tile roof and arching doorways. It had been built in the 1970s, but each year, Charles and Heidi made a list of improvements they wanted to make to the house. It was always well-maintained, clean, and perfectly decorated. Inside and out, it looked more like a model house than a home. Morgan could hear voices in the backyard, so she headed down the side of the house, Danny behind her. When she got to the gate, she opened the latch, and let herself in, holding it open for Danny. There were probably twenty people milling about, the small yard dotted with clusters of people talking and laughing, drinks in their hands, smiles on their faces, next to pots filled with colorful flowers. The women were dressed in an array of white pants and sundresses, the men in shorts and polo shirts, each piece of clothing carefully pressed. Must be the neighbors and their golf buddies, Morgan thought, swallowing. The space seemed to shrink around her even though they were outside. She put her hand back on the fence, fighting off a wave of dizziness She reminded herself she was outside and not trapped in the trailer again. She sucked in a sharp breath.

Danny stopped, looking at her, his eyes wide, "Mom, are you okay?"

Morgan nodded, "Yeah, I think I just haven't had enough to drink today. Just got a little lightheaded for a second," she lied. The last thing she wanted to do was to admit that facing down her in-laws was throwing her for a loop. She just couldn't be that weak.

Swallowing, Morgan started moving forward, weaving her way through the throngs of people huddled at the back of the house. At the center of the hubbub were Charles and Heidi. Charles was just over six feet tall, with a thick tuft of gray hair on his head, perfectly combed away from his face. He had on a pair of khaki shorts and a red polo shirt with the emblem from a golf club on it. Heidi had on a pale pink floral dress cinched at the waist with a wide belt, silver sandals and a sweater over her shoulders. Morgan tried not to shake her head. After living in West Virginia for a couple of years, the idea that people got cold when the temperature hit seventy seemed a bit ridiculous. They all needed to live through a winter in West End. It would toughen them up.

"Morgan! Danny! Glad you could make it!" Charles boomed.

Morgan shuddered.

She stood back, watching Danny greet his grandparents. They each hugged him, patting him on the back. Charles smiled, giving Danny a once-over. As soon as they were done, Danny stepped away and stared at his phone. Morgan stood off to the side watching them. Parties were not her thing. They never had been. But now, after what she'd lived through in witness protection, always avoiding large groups — or at least as many as she could avoid — even a simple birthday party seemed strange to her. "Happy birthday, Charles," she said, her voice low.

"What? No hug?"

Morgan walked the two steps forward to close the distance and gave him a hug. Charles was the life of the party. He always had been. He and Heidi loved their country club life, going to parties and club meetings and restaurants with their group of cronies. Tightness traveled across Morgan's back. It was not her thing. Never would be. She stepped back, staring at them, her mind elsewhere, thinking about Paul sitting and holding Katrina's hand at St. Anne's. Here she was, watching other people laugh and joke and eat cake while Katrina could very well be dying in the hospital. It didn't seem right. They needed answers and they needed them soon.

After a minute of small talk with Charles and Heidi, Morgan drifted away, letting some of their friends take her spot. She found Danny inside by the buffet table, holding a plate with a piece of cake on it. "Want some?" he asked, shoving a giant bite in his mouth.

Morgan shook her head. She pulled her phone out of her pocket and checked it, just as Danny did the same. His head snapped up, staring at her. "I just got a message from Brantley. He wants to come over and take a look at the computer. Do you think we can...?"

"Yes." Without saying anything more, Morgan headed for the front door, avoiding the throng of people crowded in the backyard. As she put her hand on the knob, she turned it, pulled it open and slipped outside. It felt like she had been let out of jail. She jogged to the truck and got in, checking over her shoulder. Danny was right behind her. Luckily, they parked on the street far enough away that no one in the backyard could spot them as they left. Not that she cared, at least not that much. She just didn't want to have to deal with the feigned hurt of her in-laws who would surely call or text the next day saying that she and Danny didn't stay long enough at the party. They seemed to care about Danny, but Morgan couldn't tell if it was because Danny was one more thing to brag about, or if it was genuine. Morgan shook her head. Charles and Heidi were nice people, but they'd made no effort to understand what she and Danny had been through. None. Until they did, it would be hard to move forward.

Charles and Heidi's house was on a street that connected on each end to a main road, so as Morgan pulled away, she didn't have to pass their house again. That was good. The last thing she needed was Heidi running out into the street and flagging them down. Even if Morgan had taken the time to explain to them that Danny's friend was in the hospital and needed help, she wasn't sure they would understand. They were immersed in their own world and rarely popped their heads up to see what anyone else was doing. Glancing over her shoulder in the direction of their house, Morgan realized she was gritting her teeth. She blinked, forcing herself to relax, taking in a deep breath. They just weren't her kind of people. Not before, and not now.

5

By the time Morgan and Danny got back to the house, there was a car sitting out front. Danny leaned forward, squinting, "I think that's Brantley," he mumbled, practically jumping out of the truck before she had a chance to put it in park.

Leaving Danny to his own devices, Morgan pulled the truck in the garage and opened the back door, disarming the alarm system. Bo came scampering out, sniffing around her legs and banging his hip into her calf. It was his way of looking for attention. Just as she bent over to scratch his back, Bo spotted Danny and Brantley walking up the driveway. He took off, barking. Morgan could hear Danny calling to him, "It's okay, boy. This is Brantley. He's supposed to be here."

Morgan stood by the tailgate of the truck, waiting for Danny and Brantley to get closer to the house. She watched them as they walked, Danny's loping stride very different from Brantley's clipped steps. Brantley was maybe five and a half feet tall with a thin build. He was exactly the kind of kid that Morgan pictured to be a computer expert — curly dark hair, glasses, and ghostly white.

"Mom, this is Brantley. Brantley, my mom."

"Nice to meet you. Thanks for coming over."

"No problem." Morgan raised her eyebrows. Brantley's voice was a deep baritone. It was not the voice she expected out of the small body that carried it. Not saying anything else, she followed the boys into the house, whistling for Bo, who ran up the driveway, holding a Frisbee in his mouth and shaking it as he loped along.

Inside, Morgan watched as the boys settled down at the kitchen table as she walked through the house. Everything was as it should be. Walking back into the kitchen, Morgan saw Danny push Katrina's laptop towards Brantley. Seeing they were settled in and knowing there wasn't anyone else in the house, she grabbed the three files that Amber had left for her and pulled a yellow legal pad out of the kitchen drawer as well as a pen. She felt her chest tighten. There had to be answers inside the files. There had to be something Ben had missed.

Walking to the family room, she set the files down on the coffee table and turned, going to the bedroom. In the bathroom, she stripped off the red blouse and kicked off the sandals into the corner by the toilet, feeling like a chameleon shedding her skin. Pulling on a t-shirt and replacing her jeans with a pair of leggings, Morgan walked back into the family room. The boys were huddled over Katrina's laptop, talking quietly between the two of them. Bo had taken a spot nearby. Morgan went into the family room where she'd left the files and the notebook and sat down on the floor. She worked best when she had a place to spread things out. Seeing her, Bo came over and laid down next to her.

The only file Morgan hadn't looked at yet was Katrina's. She opened it up, spreading the papers on the floor, making sure she didn't mix them in with the files for Sarah Poole and Maisie Hill. There were no crime scene pictures in this file, at least not of her body. Flipping through the pages, Morgan noticed there were a few images of Katrina's car and its placement in the driveway, as well as the interior. Morgan squinted, staring at them. The interior of the car looked pretty clean. She spotted a cup from a local take-out place, a red straw sticking up from the inside, a backpack and a purse on the passenger side of the car, and what looked to be a blanket or a towel laying on the back seat. Morgan frowned, shuffling the pictures. The exterior of the car was undamaged, a late-model gold sedan with matching bumpers. It looked like a car that maybe Paul had owned previously and had given to Katrina to drive while she was in high school. It certainly wasn't a new vehicle.

Morgan shuffled the images. On the passenger side, the windows were up. The driver's side was different. The side window was open; as if Katrina had rolled it down for someone, but the passenger window in the back seat was closed. Morgan stared at the pictures. That could be something, or it could be nothing. Maybe Katrina was just driving home with the windows open after spending a long day cramped in the air-conditioned classrooms at the high school. Danny was always complaining that the school smelled funny. It was possible Katrina drove home with the window open just to get some fresh air.

Pushing the pictures off to the side, Morgan went through the other forms that were included in the file. There wasn't much. There was a description of what they'd found at the scene, a copy of the report from the paramedics, and then a statement from Katrina's dad. All of it was exactly what Paul had told her. There was nothing remarkable except for the fact that there was no note and the doctors couldn't figure out what was wrong with her. Their only working theory was that it was a suicide, just like Sarah and Maisie.

Morgan stared at the pile of papers again, then closed the file, opening the ones for Sarah and Maisie next to each other and laying them on the floor. Her eyes went back and forth over the pictures of their bodies. The girls looked similar. They were wearing jeans and tight T-shirts. There was nothing remarkable there. Morgan checked their home addresses to see if they lived near each other. After mapping them, she realized the girls seemed to live on all sides of the district. It wasn't as if they all lived in the same neighborhood. She stared at the ceiling for a second, sighing. There was no link, at least not one that was obvious. Maybe Sylvia was right. Maybe the only next step was to reach out to the CDC to get some extra counselors at the school. The files Amber had brought her seem to be a dead-end. Frustration filled Morgan as she stared at the back wall of the family room, her eye catching a picture of her and Peter and Danny together. Her heart sank. Were Katrina's parents feeling the same way? Did they have the heaviness of loss hovering over them? Morgan didn't want anyone else to have to live with grief if they didn't have to, but on the face of it, there was nothing notable about their deaths other than the knot in her gut. But Morgan knew a gut feeling wasn't evidence.

Morgan was just about to reach for her phone and text Amber to let her know she was done with the files when Danny's voice interrupted her, "Mom? Can you come take a look at this?"

Morgan got up off the floor and walked over to the kitchen table, the tile cool on her bare feet. The boys were still huddled in front of the computer, Brantley pecking away at the keyboard, scarcely looking up. "What is it?" she frowned.

"Brantley thinks he found something."

As Brantley started to speak, he twisted the computer toward her. On the screen was the first piece of software that Morgan had found that she'd been unable to open. It was basically a blank screen with a login box in the middle of the page and no other information. "I haven't actually seen one of these before as a stand-alone," Brantley started, pointing at the screen, "but, I think I know what this is. There are a bunch of encrypted messaging apps that are becoming more and more popular. I think this is one of them, but like I said I haven't seen this particular software before."

"Encrypted messaging? What's that for?" Morgan asked.

Brantley cleared his throat, "Well, this all started a while back, with video games. The video game designers put a messaging option on their platforms. That way you could talk to the other people you're playing with. It was designed for team games. You know, coordinating strategy and all that. The thing about it is the messages disappear as soon as they're read."

Morgan crossed her arms in front of her chest, "Like they disappear completely? No record of them?" As the words came out of her mouth, she realized she had heard about encrypted messaging before. She'd been on a case before she left the department — a drug case — where the buyers and sellers would arrange for a meet using the encrypted messaging app on a video game they liked to play. It made prosecuting them nearly impossible. Hours of stake-outs and tails finally brought the drug ring down, but any communications the buyers, sellers, and suppliers had disappeared into thin air. The messages simply couldn't be recovered.

Brantley nodded, "Yeah. They disappear completely. The thing is, some coders have separated the applications out from the video games. Now people use them for other reasons." He raised his eyebrows as he said the words.

Morgan didn't need an explanation. Disappearing messages would be ideal for criminals and even for people who were having illicit affairs. "So, if you think that this is an encrypted messaging app, why would Katrina have this on her computer? Are kids at the high school using this type of technology?"

"Maybe. I guess I don't have an exciting enough life to need to use one of these, though," Brantley chuckled. "Do you have any idea what her password is?"

"No, I don't. But what good would that do for us if we can access her messages?"

Brantley bit his lip for a second, "Well, if I can get into her account, I can at least see who she was talking to. Maybe not who they are exactly, but their screen names. A lot of these programs keep address books so you don't have to continue to look for people you've talked to before. I've been testing some software that might be able to recover the messages. I designed it to work with corporate platforms as a side project. I'm not sure it would work, but I can give it a try if you want."

Morgan glanced at Danny who shrugged. She looked back at Brantley, "All right. I'm game. Danny said you know your stuff."

Brantley stood up, gathering up the laptop underneath his arm, "Danny, I'll text you as soon as I know something. Other than the fact this is Katrina's laptop, am I looking for anything in particular?"

Morgan looked at Brantley and then Danny. They were too young to have to deal with the reality of life, but it seemed like technology had sped everything up for their generation. She looked at Brantley, "Yes, there is one thing. See if you can figure out who would want Katrina dead."

6

C andace Shaner was ready for work. Dressed in a light blue skirt, white blouse, and matching blue jacket with a heavy gold chain around her neck, her matching heels made clicking noises on the tile as she walked over to the French press to pour her first cup of coffee. There was good coffee at the office and she had an assistant who knew how to brew it, but she liked to have her first cup at home before going into work. She glanced around the polished kitchen. The things that she needed for the day were lined up on the counter — her keys, her cell phone, which was fully charged, her black tote bag, her planner, and a protein bar for her lunch.

Sitting down at her computer at the spacious center island of her home, she felt the granite countertops cool against her fingers. She opened her laptop, hooking her heels behind the footrest on the stool, reminding herself to sit up straight. She hated slouching. If someone slouched it said that they were lazy. If a person couldn't be bothered to sit up straight, then what else would they let slip? She'd never hired someone who slouched in their interview. She never would.

Going through the emails that had accumulated the night before in her BioNova Pharmaceuticals account, Candace saw some reports that had come in from the development side of the business, a new campaign that the marketing director wanted to launch, and an email from the man that was running the funding for their expansion projects. They were just about ready to start a major capital raise, on the hunt for almost a billion dollars to build a new plant overseas to manufacture new drugs that were in the final phase of clinical trials. With any luck, those drugs wouldn't be the only ones new to market.

Candace marked a few of the emails for reply, deleted a few others, and forwarded a few on to her assistant for scheduling. That done, Candace took a sip of her coffee, the bitter roast filling her mouth and throat. There was nothing like the first sip of coffee in the morning. It reminded her that it was a new day and that anything was possible.

And anything was possible when you were the CEO of a major pharmaceutical company and had billions of dollars at your fingertips.

Checking her schedule, Candace noticed that her assistant had already been into her calendar that morning, making adjustments to her appointments for the day. Once she got to the office, it would be in back-to-back meetings with very few breaks. She glanced at the protein bar on the counter. Most days, she was so busy there was no time to eat. Other days, when she just couldn't stomach another dry bar, she'd have her assistant order in Ahi tuna salad, no dressing, and a bottle of sparkling water. To some, Candace knew that her discipline seemed over the top. And yet, she was the CEO of BioNova and they weren't. She smiled thinking about it. She'd been able to achieve her dream. If others got stuck along the way, that was their problem.

Hearing rustling, Candace glanced behind her. "Good morning, Justin."

Candace's son, Justin, slunk into the kitchen, his head inside the pantry, looking for something to eat. "Good morning. Do we have any cereal?"

"Yes, but I'm not sure it's the kind you like. There's some Kashi on the second shelf toward the back."

Justin grunted, "I'll pick up something on the way to school. I can't eat that tree bark you like."

Candace raised her eyebrows. He was dressed nicely enough, wearing a pair of jeans and a new t-shirt she'd gotten for him. She would prefer if he'd wear polo shirts to school, but that didn't seem to be an option. Candace frowned. At least he was wearing a shirt with just a brand logo on it and not some horrible ratty piece of fabric with an obnoxious saying or graphics on the front.

She twisted on the stool and looked at him. He needed a haircut, but he didn't seem to be in the mood to receive her opinion on anything, including his hair. "I don't feel like I see you anymore, honey. How are things going at school?"

"Everything's okay, Mom. Just like usual. I don't really have anything to say." The words came out muffled. He'd found some stale candy at the back of the pantry and was eating a chocolate bar. It looked like one she'd brought home from the company Christmas party the year before.

Candace grimaced. Justin was more like her ex-husband than she would have ever thought. She shook her head for a second, realizing even though he'd been out of the picture for nearly a decade, apparently, his genetic code was alive and well inside of Justin. Justin hadn't even seen him in a couple of years, the last time when her ex flew him to Germany to spend the summer with him and his latest girlfriend. "Are you going to the lab today?"

Justin glared at her, "Yes, Mother. You know I go to the lab every day after school. That's why you gave me the internship, remember?" His tone was anything but friendly.

Candace pressed her lips together. The last thing she wanted to do was get into an argument with Justin before he left for school. They'd done that too many times. It ended up being a distraction, Candace spending the rest of the day sending apologetic texts to him, trying to get him to respond. He rarely did. Justin was the only person in her life that she would chase after like that. There had to be something to what people said about being a parent, she realized. It was a thankless job.

Not willing to take the bait, she looked at him, "Well, I hope you have a good day. If I have time, I'll try to stop down at the lab while you're there later."

Justin didn't say anything. He just turned on his heel and walked out of the kitchen, still eating the chocolate he'd found. Candace made a mental note to have the grocery service include some less healthy options. Perhaps if there was a little more sugar laying around the house, his mood would improve. She glanced up at the ceiling for a second, changing her mind. It wouldn't.

7

Every single day of school seemed longer than the last, Justin realized when he checked his cell phone for the millionth time. It was just about twelve-thirty. With his internship and his status as a senior at Palm Coast High School, the guidance counselor had tweaked his schedule with a little nudge from his mother to get him out of the building at one every day so he could spend from two to five working at the lab. At least his mom had done that much for him. Other than nagging him and putting a roof over his head, that was about the extent of his appreciation and interest in her.

Justin slumped in his seat. His chemistry teacher, Mr. Wagoner, was droning on about balancing reactions, his marker screeching across the whiteboard in the chemistry lab. Nothing in the science wing had been updated for at least ten years. Justin tried not to roll his eyes. Mr. Wagoner was teaching old news, stuff that Justin had known when he was in middle school. He didn't even bother studying for any of the tests, but managed to ace them all.

He shifted in his seat, pushing the fluff of brown hair away from his eyes. As he did, he saw two of his classmates —

Courtney Reece, a pretty girl with dark brown hair, shiny in the light glinting in from the windows outside, and Tony Barnes glancing at each other. Justin watched for another minute, noticing Courtney and Tony smiling at each other every time Mr. Wagoner turned his back. Courtney had her cell phone on her lap, underneath her desk. She glanced down at it and then back at Tony, her long eyelashes practically touching her cheeks.

Justin looked away, a knot forming in his stomach. He'd talked to Courtney before. He'd even looked her up online, thinking maybe they could be friends or maybe more. She was all smiles and white teeth. She was smart too, one of the best students in chemistry, next to him of course. And now it looked like she was interested in someone else.

The bell rang while Mr. Wagoner was in the middle of writing another formula on the whiteboard. A few of the students were busy scrawling it into their notebooks, but Justin got up and walked out. Being in high school felt like being in jail. Everything was controlled — when he could go to the bathroom, when he could eat, where he had to sit — everything, except for the work that he did at the lab. That was really his focus, his passion.

By the time the end of the day rolled around, every inch of Justin felt pent up, like he was ready to explode. He never showed it on the outside, walking calmly to his car and getting in. At least now he'd have a chance to go and get some real work done.

ARRIVING at the BioNova Pharmaceuticals lab entrance, Justin pulled his ID out of the glove compartment. The car was a lease, a silver sedan with leather seats and a high-end speaker system, definitely the nicest in the high school parking lot. His mother had given it to him on his sixteenth birthday, "Now, don't you worry. Once the lease is up, I'll take you with me and you can choose whatever kind of car you would like to have. By that time, you'll be ready to go to college," she said, beaming at him.

He couldn't wait.

The best part about going to college would be not having to live under his mother's roof anymore. A couple of times he had considered reaching out to his dad and going to live with him in Germany, but he didn't really like Germany all that much, and he'd only seen his dad a handful of times since the divorce. Justin sighed. It could get cold there and there was no telling which girlfriend his dad would be dating at any given time. He really preferred hot weather. His mom had been all over him to start working on his college applications, and he would, soon, but he was still trying to figure out where he wanted to go and how far he could really get away from her.

Pushing the thought away, he slid out of the sedan, clipping the ID badge to the bottom hem of his T-shirt. That was one of the bonuses of working in the lab, there was no dress requirement for interns.

Walking to the door of the lab building, he pushed it open, the entryway white marble and walls, brightly colored paintings on the wall. Who the artist was, he had no idea. He was sure his mother had paid some fancy commercial designer to find paintings that would inspire her researchers. That would be just like his mom, he grimaced, running his ID through the scanner and nodding at the security guard at the front desk.

Once he was logged in, Justin walked to the bank of elevators on his right, his tennis shoes squeaking on the polished marble floor. He pressed the button for the fourth floor and waited, crossing his arms in front of his chest. He wasn't sure who would be in the lab today, but he was sure that Dr. McCall would have a list of tests for him to run.

As the doors opened to the fourth floor, Justin stepped out.

There were a couple of other lab technicians standing in the hallway, two women with black hair tied neatly behind their necks, the hem of their skirts just hanging below their lab coats. They were leaning against the wall talking to each other. He gave them a quick nod. They nodded back. Pretty much everyone he worked with was at least ten years older than him. All of their undergraduate work had been done, many of them already possessing their Master's degrees and a few of them working on their Ph.D. programs, running trials through BioNova. That was one of the things he really liked about working at his mom's company — everybody was smart. It wasn't like when he sat in school all day long and the teachers had to stop and wait for people who simply couldn't grasp the most basic concepts. It made the day long and boring.

Stopping at door 410, Justin scanned his badge again, the door buzzed open.

Dr. Andrew McCall's lab stretched out left and right in front of Justin. It was a large room that had been dedicated to the development of anesthetics. People were always having surgery, they always needed to be knocked out, and Dr. McCall was coming up with new ways to make surgery safe and easy. On the first day of his internship, Dr. McCall had taken Justin into his office, positioned in the back corner of the lab, a large space with a long desk and a view out onto the manicured landscaping beyond the building. He told Justin to sit down, "The work we do here is critically important, Justin," he began, crossing his ankle over his knee and leaning back in his chair. "Literally thousands of people have bad reactions to anesthesia every year. It kills some of them. The work we're doing is to stop those reactions and make surgery even safer. With any luck, we'll be able to develop processes that can be used in less developed countries and even in field medicine. So, when I ask you to do something, you can't be sloppy. You have to follow all of our procedures. Lives could depend on it."

Working in the lab was one of the few places Justin didn't mind a few rules.

The next couple of hours went by quickly. Dr. McCall wasn't there to supervise, but he had sent Justin data he wanted double-checked. Although Justin would have preferred to be working on actual samples, he knew that crunching the data after the experiments was an important part of what they did.

After a couple of hours of looking at numbers, Justin's eyes began to swim. He stood up, stretching, staring around him. There was only one other lab tech working, but she was on the other side of the room and hadn't bothered to come over to talk to him while he'd been there. That was typical. Everyone seemed to do their own thing. It was one of the things he loved about scientists. They didn't spend a lot of time worrying about socializing. They were there for the work. That was good. It fit his personality. Being in the lab was nothing like being at Palm Coast High School. The people at the lab treated him with respect, not like he was strange because he happened to be gifted in the sciences and probably smarter than all of them put together.

Justin shrugged, trying to get the tension out of his shoulders. He'd sent Dr. McCall an email with the findings, noting specific areas they could tweak in the Alpha-7 batch of the newest anesthesia drugs they were testing. They were on their seventh iteration of the compound formula they were working on and it was showing some promise.

As Justin stood and stretched, he thought about the original meeting where they had started working on the formula for AnoVest. He remembered Dr. McCall talking about the goal for the drug, "What we want to happen here is with a very small dose, someone will fall asleep for two to three hours and then wake up on their own, with no neurological or gastrointestinal side effects. If you're familiar with twilight sleep, we want it to be like that, just deeper. Now, you might be wondering about the application and its uses. Myself, the executive team, and the marketing department -- we've talked about the need for a drug that can be safely used in outpatient clinics. Think about procedures like cosmetic surgeries and simple surgical repairs —for instance, broken noses and wound cleaning — but the reach is even farther than that. If you are working as a physician in a third-world country or on a battlefield, you don't have access to things like ventilators or monitors that would be required for deep anesthesia. Certainly, some of the more well-developed field hospitals have that, but that's not what I'm talking about. Folks, I'm talking about a tent in the middle of nowhere where a local doctor is just trying to save lives. Lots of times, people need deep anesthesia, but there's nothing that'll work short-term to put them under that doesn't require ventilation. That's what we're working on developing. According to the projections by the marketing and sales department, the need for this is staggering. The US military could be one of our biggest clients, so we've got to get this right. I need your best work on this."

Justin remembered the excitement in the room. It was palpable. The work had started six months before. Dr. McCall had two other teams working on the same problem. They were developing a Beta batch and a Charlie batch. It had become something of a competition between the teams to see who could come up with the best formula.

Staring across the room, Justin realized he still needed to feed the mice and clean their cages. It was the only job in the lab that Dr. McCall made the interns do that no one else helped with except on the weekends. He didn't mind. Walking over to the line of cages, Justin took a look at the small white lab mice that were running around. They weren't involved in any of the experiments at the moment. Justin pulled the trays out from underneath the cages, put in clean paper, replaced their water and gave each cage some food. As he did, he glanced over his shoulder, seeing the other lab tech wave. She had a backpack on. Justin checked his watch. It was well after five. His mom had never stopped by, but that was okay. Probably better.

With the cages cleaned, Justin glanced around. There was no one else in the lab. Dr. McCall's office was dark. He was out at a conference or meeting with someone. It had said in the email, but Justin didn't pay attention. All he knew was Andrew was out of the office. He must've taken a team with him because it looked like the lab was abandoned. Usually, there were other people hanging around, but not today.

Justin licked his lips, shoving his hands in his pockets underneath the lab coat. He was all alone with access to the entire lab. A tingle of excitement ran through his body. It didn't look like anyone else would be in, at least not until the morning. Justin pulled his phone out of his pocket, checking the notes for his latest formula. He'd been working on his own drug; one that would do exactly what Dr. McCall had asked them to do — put people to sleep for a few hours. He knew if he could find the formula it would be a big win for his college applications. Not to mention he'd be able to take credit for it at the lab, maybe even come back and work for BioNova after college, but not as a lab tech, as a fully accredited researcher. His mind drifted for a second, imagining himself at a conference wearing a white lab coat embroidered with his name on it, striding out onto a stage to present his findings, the roar of applause at the end as everyone understood his groundbreaking developments.

Justin narrowed his eyes, walking over to one of the supply cabinets. There was a whole bank of them in the lab, each with glass doors and fully temperature controlled. A couple of them held test tubes of compounds they were testing. Two more of them held supplies, the raw materials they used to mix their potential drug cocktails with. Surprisingly, for all of the procedures at the lab, none of them were secured. Why that was the case, he wasn't sure. He'd asked Dr. McCall about it one time, but he just shook his head and said they went through too many materials in order to have to log everything. Things were just moving too fast. Justin wasn't sure that was the actual answer. The budget for BioNova's research division was in the hundreds of millions of dollars each year. Certainly, some of it had to be chalked up as waste.

Putting his hand on one of the doors, Justin pulled it open, feeling a little tug from the seal giving way, the cool air drifting down in front of him, soaking into his pants. Glancing at his phone again to check the items he'd need, Justin shoved it back in his pocket and then grabbed three different containers, balancing them in his hands. Going to one of the work tables, he set them down and put them in a row, checking their labels. The last batch of sample anesthesia he'd made seemed to be a bit too strong. When he'd tested it, it definitely worked, but the problem was the people he tested on didn't wake up again. Inside of him, he wanted to feel bad about that, but for some reason, he didn't. If he could have told them beforehand what he was doing and why, he would have explained they were contributing to science.

As Justin set up a test tube and a scale to measure out the chemicals, he knew there was more to it, though. He'd only tested the compound on girls from his school. He'd been nice to them, but they hadn't given him the time of day. They treated him just like everyone else, even Katrina. She'd seemed nice at first, even talked to him when he stopped by her locker between classes, but she hadn't given him any attention after that, simply saying she had to get to class. It might've been true, but it didn't feel that way.

Justin shrugged his thoughts off. He would get the formula right. That was his goal, and he would get what he wanted. He always did. Focusing, he carefully measured the drugs into a test tube swirling them around so they fully dissolved. Walking back to the storage cabinets, he found a bottle of glycerin he'd hidden in the back. It was the perfect carrier for his transdermal delivery process. His idea was that eventually, his drug could be administered through a dermal patch. He knew dermal patches were inexpensive to manufacture, could carry very specific dosages and were stable in all types of weather and even during shipment. It was ideal for the application Dr. McCall was interested in.

Maybe, if he could get the formulation right, it would get his mother off his back as well.

Justin added the glycerin to the test tube, stirred it and then waited, checking his watch. He knew by his previous experiments it would take about ten minutes for the compound to adequately soak into the glycerin. While he was waiting, he went over and found a dropper, the kind they used on the mice for administering the drugs, long and thin with black markings on the side. From the back of the lab, he put a single mouse in an isolation cage and brought it over to his work table, setting it down. He stared at the mouse as it ran around the inside of the cage. Some of the lab techs had named them, thinking they were cute little pets, but Justin didn't see that as a good idea. In his mind, the mice were just like any other piece of equipment in the lab. They had the same value as a test tube or a microscope. They were just another way to get the work done.

His stomach started to flutter. It was always exciting when he got to test something he made. The timer on his watch went off. Justin gave the new compound a new name in his notes, noting the exact amounts he'd used for this version, which he named R-5. he pulled on a pair of rubber gloves. The last thing he wanted to do was end up with the compound on his own skin.

Inserting the dropper into the test tube, Justin drew out a small amount of his newest mix. He only needed a single drop for the test. Opening the wire mesh cage door at the top, he pulled out the mouse he'd selected for the experiment. He or she, Justin didn't know which but it was an active little creature, running all over the cage, trying to climb the sides as he attempted to catch it. "Come on," Justin grunted, finally grabbing the mouse in his hand. Pulling it out of the cage, he used his fingers to part the white fur on its back, lifting the dropper above it. He watched as a single droplet rested on its skin. Justin carefully put the mouse back in the cage, waiting and watching.

Setting another timer, he knelt down on the floor, eye-level with the mouse. The creature was still running around in its cage, as though nothing had happened. That was good news. It went over and got a drink of water and then nibbled some of the pellets from the dispenser. Then it ran to the corner of the cage and sat and waited. Justin stared, not taking his eyes off of it. A second later, the mouse took a few steps forward and stumbled, laying down on its belly. Squinting, Justin could see it was still breathing. That was a positive sign. The other mice hadn't lived this long. Justin assumed that it was because of the amount of drug he administered compared to their body weight, but he discovered in his other experiments that it had something to do with the cocktail itself.

Exactly a minute and a half later, the mouse lay on its side. Justin looked at it again, seeing the rise and fall of its chest. It was just asleep, that was all. Justin shot up as if electricity had surged through his body. He looked around the lab, wishing there was someone to celebrate with, but the whole lab was empty. Looking through the cage again, he stared at the mouse. Its breathing had gotten slower, but it was still alive. Adjusting the proportions seemed to have worked.

Convinced that his experiment was a success, Justin walked to the back corner of the lab where an incinerator chute had been installed. It was just a metal door in the wall with a sign on it, the drop leading into the basement and directly into the flames that ran all day long, every day. He reached into the cage, the body of the mouse still warm, picked it up by its tail and dropped it in.

Tossing his gloves in the same chute, Justin walked back to the lab table, pouring the mixture he'd created into a small bottle. Capping it, he shoved it in his pocket. He heard the lab door open, the click of heels on the tile. He whipped around, his heart pounding in his chest. "You scared me. Don't sneak up on me like that."

"Sorry. I just wanted to check and see if you were still here. Security said you hadn't left the building yet," Candace smiled.

"Yeah, I was just trying to finish something." Justin looked away. Why she was here, he didn't know. The lab was his world, not hers. She needed to stay up in the executive suites where she belonged, bossing everyone around.

"What are you working on?"

He sighed, "If you have to know, I was just cleaning out the mouse cages. I just have this one left to finish," he lied. His mother would never understand what he was doing. More importantly, he didn't want her to know until his experiment was successful. Then, he'd present his findings to her and Dr. McCall, and show them how much they'd underestimated him, how much they'd limited him to analyzing data and going to meetings instead of putting his talents to work. They didn't need a fully staffed lab in order to solve their problems. They only needed him.

"Okay. Will you be leaving soon? Do you want to stop for dinner somewhere with me?"

"No. I have homework to do. I'll see you later."

Justin walked away with the mouse cage, stopping at the back, making an entry in the log, a false one, that one of the mice had died during the day. No one would care as long as it was in the book. Glancing over his shoulder, he saw his mother leave, the light blue outfit she'd worn to work that day retreating to the lab door, it opening and closing quietly, the click of her heels leaving the lab. Setting the empty cage back on top of the other ones, Justin felt for his pocket, the bottle of his newest compound warm against his skin. He smiled. It was almost time to try it.

8

A fter seeing Danny off to school and taking care of a few things around the house, Morgan sat down with the files Amber had left her again. She'd been up late the night before after the party at Charles and Heidi's house. Hours of work and nothing...

Morgan checked her phone. Still no guilt-inducing text from them, but it was early yet.

She could feel the fatigue in her bones. She flipped open the files and went through them for what felt like the millionth time. Nothing had changed. The connections were still loose at best. All three girls went to Palm Coast High School. The girls were all upperclassmen — a mixture of juniors and seniors. They were all pretty with long hair. Morgan shook her head. Based on what she saw, the information described nearly every high school girl in America.

She leaned back in the chair at the kitchen table, crossing her arms over her chest. Maybe Paul didn't know Katrina as well as he thought he did. After all, teenagers kept secrets. It was part of the process of growing up and separating from their parents. Maybe Katrina had been depressed or anxious and just couldn't handle it anymore. It happened frequently to kids that were getting ready to leave the house. They just couldn't figure out how they were going to make the leap between high school and college or into the work world. It seemed too overwhelming. Morgan pressed her lips together and shook her head. Something about the whole situation still didn't make any sense.

Most of the time when kids became depressed or anxious, they were lacking support in their life. That was certainly not the case for Katrina. From what Paul had said, the entire family was involved in raising her. Paul had talked about their Sunday dinners each week and how the kids all spent time together, even though they were teenagers, Katrina and her cousins meeting at a local burger place or spending a night together watching a movie.

Morgan slammed the covers of the files closed so hard it rattled the wooden table. Her gut told her there was something in those files, but she just couldn't see it. The noise woke up Bo, who was sleeping in the corner. "Come on," she said to him, walking to the back door and picking up a leash, "Let's go get some fresh air."

As soon as Morgan opened the door to the truck, Bo jumped in, settling himself on the front seat. Morgan checked to make sure the door was locked then backed out of the garage.

Outside, the day was getting warmer by the minute, the bright Florida sunshine casting sharp shadows over everything as she drove. She rolled her window down, letting the wind blow through the car. Maybe getting out of the house would give her some new perspective.

Pulling up at the dog park, Morgan chose a spot near the gate and turned her truck off. Morgan sat for a second, staring at the fence in front of her, lost in her thoughts. Bo's whining interrupted. "Okay, okay. I'm getting out," she said, clipping a leash to his collar.

The Palisades Dog Park was not much more than a large fenced-in area with some beat-up grass and a few water dishes and spigots available for thirsty dogs. Morgan didn't know who maintained it. It could have been the city or the county or a private club. All she knew was that she paid ten dollars for a year when they'd joined and Bo got to run around with his friends. As she opened the gate, it creaked, the wire fencing attached to the wooden rails dragging on the ground. It was hastily made, but at least it kept the small dogs from running out into the street.

There were only a couple of other people at the park. She gave them a wave as she let Bo loose. He galloped off to go see the other dogs. A woman wearing running shorts and a tank top was in the back of the park, throwing a Frisbee to her yellow Lab. Morgan leaned against the fence, watching Bo as he joined in the game.

Usually, Morgan enjoyed her time at the dog park, but today didn't feel the same. Thinking about Katrina and the other two girls hung heavy over her. When she was a detective, she'd had cases like this one before, where she could almost feel there was a connection to a bigger issue, but couldn't get to it. It eluded her for some reason. She remembered another detective, an old guy who'd been with the department for nearly forty years giving her some advice one afternoon when she was pouring over files at her desk, "Morgan, there are just some cases you know in your gut involve a crime, but it's entirely another thing to be able to prove it."

And that was the problem.

As much as she wanted to be able to call Paul and tell him there was something to the case, and as much as her gut told her there was, she had no leads. For that matter, she wasn't really even a detective anymore, though she knew there was part of her that liked feeling part of things again. She shifted against the fence, watching Bo for a second. The other dog he'd found to play with had moved on from the Frisbee and they were now playing a game of tug of war with a thick rope someone had left on the ground. She felt like she'd been playing her own game of tug of war with the files Amber had brought her. It would be easy to text Amber and have her come and get the files and forget all about it. She'd done what Paul asked, after all. She'd poured over them. There just didn't seem to be anything there.

Morgan stared at the ground for a second, kicking a little piece of gravel with the toe of her shoe. There was a faint smell of salt in the air. The wind had shifted and was now coming in off the bay. Morgan glanced up at the sky. It was early for afternoon storms, but she could almost feel them in the air, gathering off the coast.

In her back pocket, Morgan felt her phone buzz. She pulled it out, looking at it. It was a message from Danny. "I just heard at school that Katrina's doing bad, really bad. Isn't there anything you can do?"

"Did Brantley find anything on her computer?"

"I don't know. I'll check."

Morgan shook her head and stared at the ground again for a second, a lump forming in her throat. She couldn't imagine what the DeLuca's were going through. A wave of nausea washed over her. Katrina was too young to lose her life.

A minute later, Bo came trotting up to her, his pink tongue hanging out of his mouth. The woman who'd been throwing the Frisbee followed, her own dog following along. Morgan looked up, waiting for the woman to speak. Morgan hadn't seen her before.

"Your dog really loves to run," she said.

Morgan looked at her. The woman's white tank top barely

concealed her cleavage, her pink neon shorts showing off tanned legs. "Yep."

"I haven't seen you here before. I'm Marcy. This is Griffin."

"Morgan. This is Bo."

By the time the words came out of Morgan's mouth, Bo laid down on the ground, his tongue hanging out, touching a patch of dirt. Morgan walked over to the nearest water dish, turned on the spigot and rinsed it out, getting water for both of the dogs. Bo and Griffin took turns lapping it up, the water soaking into the dry ground on either side of it. The last thing Morgan wanted to do was get into a long conversation with someone. She had too much on her mind.

"THERE AREN'T TOO many people here during the day. You must have a flexible work schedule," Marcy said. She was standing close to Morgan, a little too close.

Morgan took a step closer to the dogs hoping Marcy didn't follow. "You could say that," Morgan mumbled. If only she knew, Morgan thought.

"I'm a journalist. I work the evening shift."

"Really?" Morgan tried to sound polite.

"Yeah, for Channel 8 News."

Morgan knew Marcy was doing two things -- fishing for information about Morgan's life and sharing her thin grip on fame at the same time. Unless she recognized Morgan, of course. Morgan pushed the thought away. It was nothing but paranoia. Marcy continued chattering, "You know, I've been tracking this really interesting story. Nobody's really talking about it, but there was an unsolved murder about twenty years ago, a young girl that disappeared and then was found in a field a couple of days later. Maybe you've heard about it? We've covered it extensively," she quipped, barely taking a breath. "I've been trying to track down some leads in my free time. It's hard with work, you know, but if I can make something of it, maybe I can help bring the criminals to justice."

Morgan looked at Marcy and blinked. Everything in Morgan wanted to scream at her, to tell her that solving a crime just wasn't that easy and there were always victims that needed help. It was like Marcy was trying to impress Morgan or something. She pressed her lips together, swallowing. "That sounds interesting." Morgan looked down at her cell phone, "Listen, I'm sorry, but I gotta go." Without saying anything else, she bent over and clicked the leash back on Bo's collar, clucking to him to get him to follow her to the gate. As she closed it behind her, she heard Marcy call out, "Hope to see you and Bo again sometime!" she chirped.

Morgan lifted her hand in a half-wave and didn't say anything. She loaded Bo in the truck and closed the door behind him, getting in and leaving the windows up, turning on the air conditioning. As she pulled the truck out of the lot, she realized that Marcy was doing something she wasn't and that was tracking sources. Morgan licked her lips and glanced down at her phone. At the next red light, she opened it up, calling Amber.

"What's going on?"

"Just leaving the dog park with Bo. I got accosted by a blonde who wanted to tell me all about her job as a TV anchor. Said she works for Channel 8."

Amber giggled, "Channel 8? Let me think... That wasn't Marcy Goodin, was it?"

"Oh, I bet it was. She told me how she was following up on some twenty-year-old murder case so she could break her career wide open."

Amber groaned, "You're kidding me. Have you seen that show?"

"No. I try to stay away from the local news."

"It's so annoying — they all wear coordinated outfits. If the women wear yellow dresses, they have the male anchor wear a yellow tie. So dumb!"

Morgan just shook her head, "Listen, I'm calling for a favor. I've been going through those files you gave me."

"Did you find anything?"

"Not yet. I have Katrina's computer, but I'm still waiting to hear back on it. The one thing that I don't have is contact information for Sarah Poole and Maisie Hills' parents. Can you get that for me?"

"Are you planning on visiting them?"

Morgan heard typing in the background, "Yeah. I thought I'd give it a try. I'm sure Ben has already interviewed them, but what can it hurt?"

"Who are you gonna tell them you are?"

The question hung heavy in the air. Morgan couldn't exactly tell them she was a detective. "Your best friend. Think that'll work?" Morgan said sarcastically. But Amber was right. Who was she going say she was? Pulling into the driveway, Morgan pressed the button for the garage door, "I'll just tell him I'm friends with the DeLuca's. Hopefully, that will get me in the door."

"Sounds like a plan. I'll send you those numbers. I've got them right here. Gimme a sec."

"Thanks."

By the time Morgan got inside the house, her phone had pinged. Amber had already sent the numbers for the parents. Looking at them, she decided to reach out to the moms. Maybe if she said she had a senior at the high school, that would buy her some goodwill. She tapped on the first phone number Amber had sent, for Sarah Poole's mom, Dorothy.

"Hello?" the voice sounded muffled and soft.

"Is this Dorothy Poole?" Morgan asked, moving from the garage inside the house.

"It is. Speaking?"

"Dorothy, my name is Morgan Foster. I got your number from a friend. I have a son at the high school. I was wondering if I could meet with you about what happened to your daughter?" As the words came out of Morgan's mouth, she knew they were abrupt. The woman had no idea who she was. Morgan waited, not saying anything. It would have been so much easier if she could still say she was with the department. The affiliation tended to open a lot of doors, although it did slam some as well.

"Why?" Dorothy sounded annoyed.

Morgan swallowed, her heart beating a little faster in her chest. "Well, like I said, I have a son who's a senior at the high school. I feel really bad about what happened to your daughter and Maisie Hill. I'm also very good friends with the DeLuca family. You might not know this, but their daughter is in the hospital. They think she tried to commit suicide, but they have no idea what really happened to her. I was hoping you might be able to shed some light on the situation."

More words came out of Morgan's mouth than she would've liked, but she felt like she owed Dorothy Poole an explanation.

"I guess. When do you want to meet?"

"As soon as possible."

There was a pause for a second. Morgan could hear mumbling in the background; as if she was with another person. "Well, Lisa Hill, that's Maisie's mom, she and I are at the cemetery right now, visiting her daughter. You can come here if you like."

Morgan blinked. "That's fine. Just tell me which one."

"It's the Western Gulf cemetery, just off of Third Avenue. How long will it take you? We both have appointments we have to get to."

Morgan did a quick calculation in her head, chewing her lip. The cemetery wasn't too far from where she lived. "Give me ten minutes. I drive a blue truck. How will I find you?"

"Our cars are parked in the back of the cemetery. We both have silver minivans."

"Okay. I'm on my way."

Morgan took a second to make sure Bo was settled, locked up the house, and then ran outside and jumped into the truck. It was dumb luck that she was able to meet with both moms at the same time.

Backing out of the driveway, the tires on her truck squealed a little as she stepped on the gas. The drive to the cemetery would more likely take fifteen minutes, but not if she drove fast enough. She felt her pocket for a second, remembering she had her wallet inside. At least if she got pulled over, she could show her badge.

Racing down Gulf Shores Avenue, Morgan passed a couple of cars, laying on the horn when one refused to move over. The truck was moving so fast that the strip centers and restaurants were merely a blur as she passed them. Morgan was focused on the road ahead of her, both her hands on the steering wheel. As she glanced at them, she saw her knuckles were white. She took a deep breath in, nearly having to slam on the brakes to avoid running a red light. She needed to calm down. But something inside her told her this was the first good lead she'd had since she found out about Katrina. Maybe the moms would be able to shed some light on what had happened to their daughters, beyond what Ben had written in the reports. There had to be something more, she knew it.

Eight minutes later, Morgan pulled into the cemetery, passing a black hearse and a group of people standing around a tent erected in the middle of the grass, their clothes an array of navy blue, black and gray. She saw one of them glance at her as she drove by, then look at the ground again. A cemetery was a difficult place to be. She felt her heart skip a beat. Peter had been buried at a cemetery around the corner. She'd never been there to visit him, not since the hasty funeral with the US

Marshals before she and Danny left town. She knew there were some people that found going to the cemetery comforting; as if their loved one was still somehow there. That wasn't her.

Driving around a couple of curves, Morgan spotted the two silver minivans parked close to each other at the back of the cemetery, just as Dorothy had described. Morgan slowed down a little, not wanting to drive up on the two women too abruptly and spook them. After all, they didn't know her. Pulling the truck in behind their vehicles, she threw it into park and then got out, scanning the area around her to see if anyone else was watching them. Other than the two women and their minivans, the cemetery was quiet.

Morgan stopped for a second, looking around her. There were stands of trees that were manicured and trimmed, landscaping beds that looked like they had been recently mulched, the musty smell of the shredded bark in the air. There were no headstones sticking up out of the ground, just flat markers identifying each site, the bright colors of flowers poking up out of the grass where families had left them behind for their loved ones. There were a couple of wreaths off to her right, leaning back, looking a little worse for wear after being out in the wind and the rain.

Morgan set off across the grass, carefully avoiding stepping on any of the graves. Why, she wasn't sure. It wasn't as if the person buried below would mind. It was probably more out of respect for Dorothy and Lisa. As she made her way to the women, they had their backs to her, one of them with her arm around the other, both of them stooped and huddled together as if they were facing a storm. Morgan paused for a second looking at them and then started to walk toward them slowly. She'd have to tread carefully. People who were grieving shut down easily. They had no patience for others who didn't understand their pain. That was something she'd run across many times in the police department. "Slow and steady wins the race," she muttered to herself as she got closer.

Not wanting to startle the women, she called out when she was about fifteen feet away, "Dorothy?"

The woman on the right turned toward her. She had brown hair caught up in a ponytail, wisps of it escaping around her face. She was wearing an oversized t-shirt and a pair of leggings and flip-flops with a light jacket on top. Her skin was pale. She wasn't wearing any makeup. The woman next to her turned as well, her face red, holding a tissue up to her nose. The two of them looked like they could be sisters, with the same brown hair and pale skin, although Lisa Hill was more slight than Dorothy Poole. "I'm Morgan. We spoke on the phone a few minutes ago?"

"Yes. It's nice to meet you. This is Lisa Hill."

Morgan moved a step closer, staring at the women. Both of them looked like the life had been drained out of them, their lips devoid of color, red rings and black circles around their eyes. "Thank you for taking the time to meet me. I appreciate it, especially on such short notice." Morgan glanced at the ground, realizing they were standing at the foot of Maisie Hill's grave. "I'm very sorry for your losses. It's just tragic."

Dorothy furrowed her eyebrows, seeming to ignore Morgan's condolences. "You said that you're a friend of the DeLuca's? I don't know their daughter. What happened to her?"

Morgan spent the next minute explaining the situation and how she knew Paul, giving them an overview of Katrina's condition. She saw the women glance at each other, as though the story sounded way too familiar. When she was done, Lisa Hill looked at her, "I don't understand. Why would Katrina's granddad ask you to look into this?"

Morgan sucked in a breath, "You could say I have some experience. I used to work as a detective." The words came out in a tumble. As much as Morgan didn't like talking about her past, it was probably the only way she was going to get these grieving moms to talk to her.

Lisa squinted, "But you don't anymore?"

Morgan cocked her head to the side, "It's a long story, one we don't have time for. Let's just say one of the cases I worked on went south. Now, can I ask you a couple of questions about your daughters?"

Morgan watched them for a second, wondering if they would accept her explanation without any more questions. She held her breath. If they didn't, she would either have to spend valuable time explaining to them about the Sons of Goliath and how she'd ended up in witness protection, or they would close the door on her entirely and she'd never find out what happened to their daughters or to Katrina. Her heart clenched in her chest. Based on what Danny said, time was running out.

Nodding toward the grave in front of them, Morgan looked at Lisa, "I'm sure you were already interviewed by the detectives, but I just want to see if there is anything that you've thought of since then?" She knew for a fact that Ben had already interviewed them but based on the paperwork in the files, it looked like he was pretty convinced from the get-go that they were just run-of-the-mill teenage suicides, nothing more. That was the kind of sloppy work that could end up letting a killer go free.

Lisa glanced back at the grave and sniffled, then looked at Morgan, "I don't know what I can tell you that we haven't already told the police. We let Maisie drive herself back and forth to her riding lessons. She had been riding three days a week, getting ready for the winter show circuit. At first, I didn't think anything of it when she was supposed to come home and didn't make it, at least, not until late. It wasn't even a night that she was supposed to be at the barn. She texted me after school and told me that she was gonna go meet some friends to study and that she'd be home after dinner. She didn't come home after that. You probably already know, but they found her the next morning in one of the stalls. How she got there, I'm still not sure."

Morgan frowned, "So, she wasn't even supposed to be riding that night? Did you happen to ask the barn manager or her instructor if they'd seen her?"

Lisa nodded, "Of course. That was one of the first questions my husband and I asked. She wasn't on the schedule to ride, didn't have a lesson, and they didn't even see her. Best we can figure it, she must have driven out there after her study group to check on one of the horses. Why, I'm still not sure. Usually, after the last lessons end at about seven or eight o'clock at night, there aren't many people left in the barn. The barn manager told me they check the horses' water at about six, making sure that all of them have enough for the night, and then the staff is gone until the next morning." She stared at the ground for a second and then looked straight at Morgan, her eyes watering, "That's when they found her. It was the next morning when they came in to feed the horses. The stall door was open and they saw her lying there..." Lisa choked back a sob.

Thoughts were racing through Morgan's head. The notes in the file had said nothing about Maisie supposedly attending a study group between school and when she'd ultimately be found at the stable the next morning. "I hate to ask you this, but was Maisie having any issues you can think of? Did she seem depressed or anxious? Did you and your husband notice any change in her behavior?"

Lisa shook her head, "It's okay. Don't feel bad about it. Pretty much everyone has asked me the same question. And the answer is no. Maisie was a quiet girl, but she had a joy about her. Everything was going well. She seemed to have a lot of friends and was doing well in school. There was no change in her grades or anything, if that's what you're asking."

"That helps."

Morgan followed as the women started walking back to their vans, "Dorothy, how about you?"

"Unfortunately, my story is about the same. Sarah loved to swim and was on the swim team at the high school. It's about the same story. My husband and I have gone over it a million times. There is just no real reason that she would kill herself, none that we can find. We have no idea how she ended up at the beach. The only thing we can think of is that she was meeting someone there and something happened to upset her. Believe me, we've ripped her room apart, even pulled up the carpet to see if she'd hidden anything underneath, torn apart her bed and pulled every single drawer out of her dresser and closet. We've scoured every single piece of paper we could find in her room. There is no indication, even in her journal, that she was feeling upset. The thing she was most worried about recently was the upcoming swim season, but that was normal." Dorothy stopped as they reached the two vans and stared at Morgan, "That's the thing — none of this makes any sense. Lisa and I have compared notes on both of our girls. While they had different interests, they were both in the same head space. Sure, they were both a little anxious about their future, but nothing out of the ordinary and nothing that would raise an alarm that they were going to end their life."

Morgan stared at the ground for a second, "This might seem like an unrelated question, but were your two girls' friends? I mean, did they know each other or hang out together? Did either of them have a relationship with Katrina DeLuca?"

Lisa shook her head no, "If they did, we didn't know. The school said they had some classes together, but that's it. Palm Coast is a huge high school. You said your son is there?"

"Yeah, he's a senior."

"So you know, it's impossible for all the kids to get to know each other. I mean, this year's graduating class will have probably around seven hundred fifty kids in it. There are a lot of high schools that don't have that number of kids in their entire enrollment."

"And Katrina DeLuca? Either of your girls ever talk about a new friend they had with her name?" Morgan held her breath for a second. There had to be a common denominator between these girls. Maybe Katrina was it.

"No. Honestly, I didn't even hear about Katrina until you called just a little while ago," Dorothy said.

"Is there anything else the girls had in common? Maybe they saw the same doctor or worked out at the same gym? Is there anything else you can think of?"

Dorothy looked at the ground and then back at Morgan, "The only thing we've been able to think of, other than a class or two they shared, is that they both saw the same therapist. His name is Dr. Solis."

Morgan knew exactly who they were talking about. Dr. Greg Solis was an adolescent psychologist. Danny had been seeing him since they got back into town to help him readjust to being back in Florida, re-assuming his original identity after leaving Dominic Franklin behind, and working through the trauma and grief he'd experienced. It was something Morgan had insisted on when they came back. He'd been through too much to try to keep it squared away in his head on his own. Morgan stared at the ground for a second. Part of her felt like she should tell them that her son was seeing the same therapist as their daughters, but part of it felt like a betrayal to Danny. It could lead to a much longer story, one that wasn't focused on Sarah and Maisie. If she spoke now, they would get off track.

Morgan felt like she hit a brick wall. There was something there tying the girls together, but there was nothing tangible, nothing she could lean on, except for the fact that they were seeing the same therapist. But Morgan had no idea if Katrina was. Even if she was, what did that mean? Was someone targeting girls that were seeing the therapist? Could Dr. Solis be behind what was going on? Morgan chewed her lip. While anything was possible, Morgan had met Dr. Solis on several occasions. He certainly didn't seem the type to stalk his patients, but then she'd been surprised before. Questions started to race through her mind.

None of them said anything for a minute. Finally, Lisa looked at Morgan and said, "Is there any other information we can give you? I'm running late for my appointment."

"No. I appreciate your time."

As Morgan started to walk to her truck, thinking about what the women had told her, Dorothy called out to her, "Morgan, hold on for a second." She waved as Lisa pulled away from the curb and walked over to the truck, "Listen, I need to ask you something, mother-to-mother."

The way Dorothy said it, Morgan knew it was serious, "Sure."

"As far as I know, these cases are closed. So, I have to ask myself, why are you here? I know that you're friends with the DeLuca's, but..."

Morgan pressed her lips together and held her breath. She looked at Dorothy, "But?"

Dorothy narrowed her eyes and leveled her gaze at Morgan. "You think there's something more to these cases, don't you?"

9

Morgan sat in her truck, watching Dorothy's minivan pull away from the curb. Although she hadn't learned anything that pointed to a suspect, motive, or means, at least the moms both had the same thought that she did — that these so-called suicides weren't that at all.

She stared at her phone. She hadn't heard from Paul since she'd seen him at the hospital. She sent him a quick text, "How's Katrina?" She expected the news wouldn't be good based on what Danny said. A minute later, just as she was getting ready to pull away, Paul replied, "Bad. Docs are talking about taking her off life support. Soon. We need a miracle, Morgan."

Morgan's heart skipped a beat. Yes, we do.

The idea of having to take Katrina off life support, watching the machines beep and then flatline sent a wave of nausea over her. She couldn't do that to Danny. How Katrina's parents could survive that, she wasn't sure. She knew she couldn't. They needed answers. The clock was ticking and they were running out of time.

Dr. Greg Solis's office was a few miles from the cemetery. Morgan drove respectfully past the mourners who were still standing at the tent, not wanting to speed by them. Somehow, that seemed wrong. But as soon as she got to the main road, she hit the gas, sending the truck out into a line of traffic, nearly missing a delivery truck that wasn't making a lot of progress.

Turning the wheel on the truck, her hand slipped. Her palms were sweaty. She couldn't get the thought of Katrina laying flat on her back in the PICU out of her mind, Paul by her side, grim doctors and nurses coming in to disconnect the machines that were keeping her alive. She swallowed, hard.

Dr. Solis's office was located on the second floor of the three-story office building on the corner of Gulf Shores Parkway and 45th Avenue. It was a square building, covered with gray stucco, the first floor open for parking underneath, the entire building on stilts. Even by Florida standards, it was a strange building. As Morgan pulled her truck in, choosing one of the spots outside of the building's first story lot, she glanced at it. She'd only been at the building one other time — that was for Danny's intake meeting with Dr. Solis a few months back. Morgan paused for a second frowning. She realized she'd only met him once and only talked to him on the phone one other time. Whatever else went on between him and Danny, she wasn't sure.

There was a small elevator in the center of the parking area, but Morgan ignored it. The space was too small. She jogged to the stairway and took the steps two at a time. Checking the time, she trotted down the hallway. If Dr. Solis was on schedule, he'd have clients leaving just about now. Their hour-long sessions were really fifty minutes, to allow the psychologist to make notes between patients. Part of her wondered if he was just trying to cram more patients into a day. She pushed the thought out of her mind. There was no reason to be overly suspicious of him. Danny was doing fine. He seemed to be thriving at school, even though his life had been ripped away from him not once, but twice between their moves and their time in witness protection.

Morgan walked down the hallway as fast as she could without running. The walls were painted the same gray as the exterior of the building. "This building needs a facelift," she mumbled, reaching for the knob on Dr. Solis's office door.

As she stood in the waiting room, she glanced around her. There was a mom sitting with a young boy huddled in the corner. The mom was staring at the entry door to Dr. Solis's office as if she was willing it to open, her face pale, dark shadows underneath both of her eyes. The boy was staring down at his cell phone, his thumbs moving silently across the screen. Morgan guessed he was playing some sort of a game. Morgan felt tension in her chest. At this point, the only thing any of the kids who'd died had in common was seeing Dr. Solis. While all the victims she knew of had been girls, what if the same thing happened to Danny? What if Danny was now a target because of his connection with Dr. Solis?

Questions pounded through Morgan's head. She stood, her fists stuffed into her pockets. She watched the door, not taking her eyes off of it. A second later, she saw the knob turn, a young girl with swollen red eyes and a mane of blonde hair opening the door. She glanced at Morgan for a second and then stared at the ground as if she was ashamed to be seen with her face red and blotchy. Dr. Solis stepped into the space right behind the girl, ushering her out. He glanced at the corner of the room, waving forward the mom and her boy. Morgan stepped in front of them.

"I need a minute of your time, Doctor," Morgan said.

"I'm sorry, you have to make an appointment. Wait, I know you, don't I?" Dr. Solis squinted.

"Yes, you do," Morgan pushed Dr. Solis back inside of the office with a hand on his chest and pulled the door closed behind her, leaving the mom and the little boy in the waiting room. She knew from experience the door locked. They wouldn't be interrupting her anytime soon.

Dr. Solis took a couple of steps back and then stared at Morgan, facing her. "You're Danny Foster's mom, aren't you?"

"That's right."

Morgan stared at Dr. Solis for a second. He was wearing a pair of khaki pants and tennis shoes with a blue polo shirt. His brown hair was cut tight to his head, a short beard darkening his jaw. Square glasses sat on his nose. Behind them were brown eyes. "Mrs. Foster, I have another patient. I can't do this right now."

Morgan gritted her teeth, "You're going to have to make time for me. Now. Lives are on the line."

Dr. Solis pressed his lips together, "What do you mean?" He turned and walked inside his office going toward the desk. She wondered if he had a panic button installed near it. Would he call the police? Try to kick her out of the office? Morgan glanced around her for a second. There was a wall of windows that stared out over Gulf Shores Parkway, the hum of the traffic buzzing by faint in the background. The office was simple — a large desk in the corner, with a couple of upholstered chairs, a couch, and a coffee table taking up the rest of the space. A box of tissues was on the table along with an open file. Dr. Solis walked to the table and closed the file, carrying it back to his desk.

"I just met with Dorothy Poole and Lisa Hill."

Dr. Solis stopped in his tracks, turning to face her. "Sarah and Maisie's moms? What about them?"

"I'm assuming you know they committed suicide?"

He cocked his head to the side. "I do."

"Did you also know Katrina DeLuca is in the hospital?"

As soon as the words came out of her mouth, Morgan could tell that no one had bothered to tell Dr. Solis about Katrina's status. "I didn't. She doesn't have an appointment coming up until a few weeks from now, I think." He shook his head, "They all kind of run together. I see so many kids."

"Including my son."

"Yes, but what do you want from me? Why are you here? I have other patients waiting."

By the tone of his voice, Morgan could tell he was losing patience. "Were Sarah Poole or Maisie Hill suicidal?"

Dr. Solis walked behind his desk shaking his head, "Morgan, you know as well as I do, I can't talk about them. They are patients."

"Were."

Dr. Solis shrugged, "Were patients, yes. That's correct. But that doesn't mean —"

"They're dead, Greg. They aren't coming back and now I've got Katrina DeLuca, the granddaughter of a good friend of mine, lying flat on her back on a ventilator. Based on what I've seen it looks awfully similar to what happened to these other two girls. The doctors are talking about pulling the plug on her. I need answers and I need them now," Morgan pounded her fists on his desk, sending the cup of pencils and pens rattling.

"I can't talk about Katrina..." Dr. Solis said, holding his hands up like he was surrendering. "You know that."

"But there's no reason you can't tell me about Sarah and Maisie. They're dead. I just saw Maisie Hill's grave in that cemetery. Those two moms are broken into pieces. If something else happened to those two girls, I have to know. So, I'm gonna ask you again, were they suicidal?"

Morgan stood her ground for a second. Technically, Dr. Solis was right, he didn't have to tell her anything. Doctor-client privilege was something sacred and protected by the law, but there was no reason he couldn't tell her if he wanted to.

Morgan began to calculate. If he didn't want to, she'd have to call Amber and see if they could get a subpoena for his records, but that would be wasting time; time she was afraid they didn't have. "Come on, Doc. They're dead. I can call the department and get a court order over here in an hour. That's gonna cause a lot of paperwork for a lot of people, including you. Just tell me what I want to know and you can go out and deal with whatever the problem is with that mom and her little boy."

Dr. Solis glanced at the door to his office and didn't say anything. A moment later, he twisted on his desk chair toward his laptop and sat down, opening the lid. The only sound in the room was the clicking of his fingers on the keyboard. He glanced at Morgan, "All right. If you want me to testify to any of this in a court case, you're gonna have to bring back a subpoena for the information."

"Understood." Morgan held her breath.

"There was nothing incredibly remarkable about what was going on with either Sarah or Maisie. Both of them had relatively stable home lives. I diagnosed each of them with an adjustment disorder — that means they're just finding navigating their current season in life a little difficult." He closed the lid to the laptop, "It's nothing like what Danny has faced, I can tell you that. These girls were more flustered by the social issues at school, their friends, and trying to figure out how to grow up and be independent. General teenage angst."

Morgan stared at him, "Nothing that would indicate they were suicidal?"

He stood up from behind his desk, shaking his head, "From a clinical perspective? No, far from it. Both Maisie and Sarah were making good progress. Their moms had both reported to me they were calmer about things at school and at home and not so reactive. If either of them was suicidal, they must have hidden it well. I had no idea and I'm usually a pretty good judge of that. It's something I see a lot, unfortunately." Greg rubbed his beard as if he was recalling his sessions with them.

Morgan stared at him, crossing her arms, "And Katrina Deluca? What about her?" Morgan wasn't sure he'd tell her about Katrina, but she had to try. Maybe if she pushed a little...

"Morgan, I'm not sure I feel comfortable —"

"Don't waste my time!" Morgan shouted, leaning toward him. "She's on life support for God's sakes!"

Greg paused, not reacting to her outburst. "No. No, she wasn't suicidal. Her family is very intense. I think she was just struggling with trying to figure out who she was since they are all so intertwined. It's a common issue in ethnic families."

Morgan remembered all of the family dinners Paul had referred to. She'd never thought that would be stifling to a kid. "But from a psychological perspective, there's nothing in your mind that would have caused Katrina DeLuca to try to kill herself?"

"Correct." He stared at her. "That said, I will deny I told you any of this unless you come back here with a subpoena." His stare turned into a mask of confusion, "I thought Danny said you weren't with the department anymore?"

Morgan was halfway across the room by the time Dr. Solis got the question out of his mouth. She didn't bother to answer. She opened the door to the waiting room. As she did, the mom waiting to see Dr. Solis was standing just in front of it, a frown on her face as if she was going to try to barge in. She took a step back when she saw Morgan. "Sorry for the interruption," Morgan said, pushing past her.

Morgan ran down the hallway and back down the steps to her truck. She sat for a second with the engine running, trying to process the information Dr. Solis had given her. He was right, he didn't owe her anything, but she was grateful he'd told her as much as he had. As she put the truck in gear, she glanced in the rearview mirror. Her blonde hair had grown wavy in the humidity. She looked down at her jeans and T-shirt. He was right, she wasn't with the police department anymore. There was a heavy weight on her chest as she pulled out of the parking lot. She wondered if the girls Dr. Solis was treating were the only ones that were going through an identity crisis.

10

——————

By the time Morgan got home, Danny's car was in the driveway. It'd only been a few hours, but it felt like she'd been gone all day, between meeting with Dorothy and Lisa at the cemetery and tracking down Dr. Solis for their heart-to-heart conversation, even if it was forced.

Danny met her at the door, "Did you hear anything else about Katrina?" he said, the muscles of his face looking tight and pinched.

"No, nothing more. Any news from Brantley?"

"Yeah, I was just about to text you. He's on his way over. He's bringing Katrina's laptop back."

"Did he find anything?"

"I think so. I'm not sure. He was pretty vague when he let me know he was coming over." Danny shrugged, "He's that way."

"A little awkward?"

"Yeah," Danny nodded, "I like him though. He's funny."

Before Morgan had a chance to ask any more questions, she heard a knock at the door. Bo charged, growling and barking. Morgan watched him for a second. Some people might say she should train that behavior out of him, but after what she'd been through, that growling and barking may give her just the amount of time she needed to protect her and Danny if she needed to.

"Hey, Mrs. Foster," Brantley said, walking into the kitchen and throwing his backpack down on one of the kitchen chairs. "I brought Katrina's computer back."

"Thanks. Did you find anything?"

Brantley sat down in the chair, opening up the laptop, "Yeah, I think I did." He opened up the applications Morgan found when Paul gave it to her. Brantley pointed at the screen, "This one," he said, pointing to the purple screen that had nothing but a login, "I was able to break into the platform. Like I thought, it's an encrypted messaging app called GenChat. Here's the thing that's strange about it, though. You have to be invited to use it. I checked in the back end and they have millions of users, but they're all linked."

"Linked? What does that mean?" Morgan said, sitting down in a chair across from him, leaning her arms on the table.

"Well, normally, anybody could use a piece of software, I mean, other than proprietary sites, like companies and stuff. But for software like this, it's usually open to everyone. You might have to pay a fee, or whatever, but there's no reason you couldn't; if you know what I mean. But this one, it's different. I've never seen anything like it. I think what happens is that once someone invites you, then you can invite other people."

He turned the screen toward Morgan. She could see lists of people that were organized in what looked like a hierarchy. She'd only seen lists like that in one other place -- genealogical records. She frowned but didn't say anything, not wanting to interrupt Brantley.

Brantley's low voice continued, "What that's given the developers are pods of people that know each other in real life. Most of the time there's a certain amount of randomness to how software rolls out — you know, you might pick up a few users here and then you might pick up a few users in Canada and then a few in Russia and it kinda goes from there. That's not how this software works, though. It's actually kinda creepy."

"What do you mean?" Morgan frowned.

Brantley took off his glasses and rubbed his eyes. "The way I figure it is that because you have to be personally invited by someone, then the developers can go back through and reconstruct your social contacts in real life. They pretty much know who you hang out with. They may not know why, but once they know who, that gives them valuable background information on you. Think about it this way -- say I'm a member and I invite Danny. Well, then they know that Danny and I probably live pretty close together, or we're related, or we lived near each other at some other time. And then let's say Danny invites you. Then, they have a second-degree relationship radiating from me. I know Danny, Danny knows you. They can start to construct these networks of people. I've just never seen this done before."

Morgan got up and started pacing, "Why would that be important?"

Brantley shrugged, "I can't expect to be able to explain what's in the mind of the developers, but on a simple level, it gives them a great deal of geographical information about their members. Combine that with demographic, financial, and profile data that's easily accessible now because of social networking, and you can start to construct people's lives from the inside out. The only thing is, they don't know any of the people, but they can certainly track them and learn about them without their permission. That's what I meant when I said it was creepy."

Morgan stopped pacing for a second and looked at Brantley, "And you think Katrina was in this network?"

"Yeah, she was a user for sure. I tried to see who she was connected to, but it's all screen names. There are like ten generations before her and a bunch after. There are some other connections, too, like she knows someone else in the network because she's messaged them, but wasn't invited by them." He scowled, "It would take a lot more work for me to try to break in to see people's real identities. The firewall they have on this thing is pretty massive, something like the NSA would use."

Morgan stopped for a second, leaning her hands on the back of the chair, wondering why there was such high-end security for a messaging app. Brantley was right. If they were tracking people, that was creepy. She pushed the thought aside for a minute. "What about the other website we found?"

"Oh, yeah, the one with the pink screen and the hearts? That's a dating app."

Morgan raised her eyebrows, "A dating app?"

Danny blinked as he looked at his mom, "You know what a dating app is, Mom."

"Yeah, I do, but why do high school kids need one?"

Danny shrugged, "Just because we do, I guess."

Morgan narrowed her eyes. No high schooler needed a dating app, but Morgan wasn't interested in arguing with Danny about it at the moment. "So, Katrina was on the dating app as well? Was she active?"

Brantley nodded, spinning the laptop towards Morgan, "She was. Not a ton, but I found her profile pretty easily. It looks like she's made a couple of connections with guys from some of the local high schools, but I'm not sure that it went any further than that."

Morgan shook her head and started pacing again. The dating app sounded like a dead end. As far as she knew, Katrina wasn't dating anyone, or at least Paul hadn't said anything. A breakup didn't seem like a likely reason for her to try to kill herself. She stopped for a second, closing her eyes. Nothing made sense. Tension filled her chest. She felt like over and over again she was just beating her head against a wall. An encrypted messaging app, a dating site, no psychological reason for her to want to kill herself, a devoted family — nothing made sense. Why was Katrina in the hospital? What was really wrong with her?

Morgan was so angry that she nearly punched a hole in the wall. Instead, she walked out into the backyard, not saying anything else to the boys. The last thing she wanted to do was lose her temper in front of them. Angry flare-ups were something new she noticed about herself since they moved back. Her temper was worse than ever, along with her claustrophobia. It had to be from everything she'd been through. Life was finally kind of stable so maybe things were just working themselves out somewhere in the back of her mind. She slammed the door behind her, nearly catching Bo in the doorway. "Sorry about that, boy," she mumbled as he looked up at her with his big brown eyes.

Outside, the afternoon had cooled off slightly. It did nothing for the fact that her heart was pounding in her chest. The sun was sliding down behind the fence at the back of her yard as it got late in the day. She watched as Bo trotted off, finding a tug rope he'd left in the yard, giving it a shake, and then laying down in the thick tufts of grass to chew on it. Morgan sat down in one of the lawn chairs. The people she'd purchased the house from when they returned to Tampa had left them behind along with a few other pieces of furniture. They weren't exactly what Morgan would've wanted for the house, but it was a good place to start. She glanced around her. Maybe once she figured out what was going on with Katrina and the other cases, she'd start buying a few more things for the house. Peter had left her more than enough money for her to do that. She swallowed, glancing at the ground.

Peter.

She knew that moving back to Florida had been the right move. She couldn't hide in witness protection forever, but somehow, trouble seemed to find her. Here she was when she should have been concentrating on putting her life back together caught up in a case, a case where she didn't have much power to do anything at all, given the fact she wasn't a real cop anymore. She wondered what Peter would think about that. She stared up at the sky, seeing a single cloud floating overhead. The humidity had lowered enough that the sky was bright blue. She rolled her neck left and right, her eyes settling on Bo again. He was laying calmly in the grass, completely forgetting that just a few minutes before he'd been ready to attack whoever was ready to walk in the door. She wished she could be that way, to forget what was behind her and move forward. But she wasn't tuned up that way. She knew only time would push her past far enough from her so she could breathe again.

Morgan was just about to get up out of her chair when her phone rang. "I was gonna call you in a little while," she said.

"You were?" Amber said. "I hope it's good news."

"It is and it isn't."

"What you got?"

Morgan reviewed the information she'd found, starting with her visit with Dorothy and Lisa at the cemetery. She filled Amber in on the information she'd gotten from Dr. Solis too. "It was all pretty vague. I don't have anything in writing, but he didn't seem to think that any of the girls were suicidal, or at least they hadn't presented that way in his office."

"Well, that's good and bad news."

Morgan nodded. "Yeah, what it means is we've got a couple of girls who may or may not have committed suicide and one in the hospital. By the way, Paul DeLuca texted me. Katrina's not doing well. The doctors are suggesting they turn off life support. From the way he was talking, it might be soon."

There was a pause before Amber responded. When she did,

her voice sounded hard, "Then we've got to figure this out before they do."

"Yeah, I know."

"Anything on the computer?"

"Not much." Morgan relayed the information that Brantley had fed her about the encrypted messaging software and the dating site.

"The dating site sounds pretty harmless. I've heard about that kind of stuff before. But that messaging program she has on her computer? What's that about?"

"Honestly, I'm not sure. I don't even have any idea if it's tied to the case. Anyway, you called me. What's going on? Maybe you're just acting like my new supervisor?"

Amber laughed, "I wouldn't touch that job with a thirty-foot pole."

"Very funny."

"I had a little bit of free time today so I pulled some more information. It looks like there have been some other suicides that we didn't connect right away. Happened last year. It was one guy and one girl, one of them from Palm Coast High School like the others and another one from a private Catholic school just up the road. The radius is tight, like within three miles."

"And you think these are connected?"

"I have no idea, but when you and Sylvia started talking about a suicide cluster, I thought I'd better do a little bit more digging just to make sure we weren't missing something."

"Can you email me the files?"

"I can do better than that. Look up."

Just as Amber said the words, Bo took off running towards the fence gate. Amber was standing there, holding the files in her hand, dangling them over. "Easy, killer," she said, opening the latch.

Morgan got up, pulling Bo back in and closing the gate

behind her. Amber handed the files to Morgan, shoving her phone in her pocket. She was wearing a dress with leggings underneath and short boots. "What's with the leggings under your dress?" Morgan frowned, taking the files from her hands.

"It's in case I have to tackle somebody. You know, that way if my dress flips up, no one gets to see my business." She giggled, "It's like the adult solution to the shorts I'd wear under my skirt as a kid."

Morgan closed her eyes and shook her head. Only Amber would be the kind of person who could make being a detective fun. It was probably the only option if they wanted to survive the job.

"Want a beer?"

Amber eased herself down into one of the lawn chairs, taking off her boots, "I thought you'd never ask. Might as well bring me two since I've been doing all of your research for you."

Morgan nodded and opened the back door, grabbing three beers out of the refrigerator, the glass bottles clinking against each other. Danny frowned at her for a second, his face questioning all the beers she had in her hand. "Amber's here."

Danny nodded. He and Brantley were leaning over Danny's computer. "Okay, we're working on the messaging app some more."

Morgan watched them for a second, wondering what they were up to exactly, but decided to let it go. "Sounds good. We'll be outside if you need us."

By the time Morgan got back outside, Amber had taken off her jacket and pulled her leggings up to her knees. Her toes were polished in a deep crimson. As Morgan set the beers down between them, Amber leaned to the side, pulling her gun out of her holster and setting it on the table, too. Morgan heard the rip of Velcro coming apart a second later, the thigh holster Amber was wearing coming off as well. She sighed, "That feels much better."

Morgan smiled, taking a sip of the beer. It was cold and bitter as it ran down her throat. She could smell the alcohol as she held the bottle near her face, ready to take another sip. "Yeah, that was always a good feeling taking the gear off at the end of the day."

"It still is."

Morgan sighed. The two of them sat in silence for a few minutes. Bo trotted out to the back corner of the yard, retrieving his tug rope and bringing it back to them, laying in the grass as close to them as possible, chewing on it and staring at them every few seconds.

Amber was the first one to speak. She set her bottle down on the table. Morgan noticed it was half gone already. "Listen, just between you and me and the lamppost, I need you to keep going on this, okay?"

Morgan raised her eyebrows, glancing at Amber. "It wasn't like I was going to stop anyway."

"Yeah, I know, but this is the real deal, Morgan. If these other cases are connected, then we have a lot more going on here than we originally thought. I stopped in the captain's office today and checked the case board."

"You guys still keep that on the wall? I thought by now all that would be in some digital format in the cloud or something."

"Naw. The captain likes to have it out in the open. Thinks it pushes everybody to get their cases finished. You know, he likes to make a big deal of getting out his eraser and removing a closed case in front of everyone. It kinda guilts the other detectives into getting their work done, if you know what I mean."

"Like Ben Acosta?"

"Exactly," she nodded.

"He's still not doing anything with this case? Did you ask him about it?"

"I tried to, but he blew me off," Amber picked up her beer

and took another sip, holding it between her knees. "When I checked the board today, he's got a couple of home invasion cases he's working now. That seems to be the priority for him. As I told you before, he thinks these are closed."

Morgan narrowed her eyes, "Do you?"

Amber looked surprised, "No. If I did why would I bring you these other files?"

"True."

"Anyway, all that to say, I need you to keep going. I can't really dig into these cases without it taking time from the other work they've already assigned me, not to mention the office politics."

Morgan nodded and licked her lips. There were definitely office politics. Detectives could get very territorial over their cases. Some of the guys didn't like it when other detectives were double-checking their work. It was like they thought they were being questioned. Most of the time, it wasn't that at all. New evidence would emerge or a new lead would come up and someone else would take an interest in the case. Morgan knew how things were.

Amber looked at her, lowering her chin, her face serious, "If we have any hope in solving this, Morgan, you're it."

11

T he slamming of the locker doors and the chatter of the students between classes were deafening. Palm Coast High School was bursting at the seams. Justin tried to ignore the noise, standing in front of his open locker staring inside of it. There wasn't much there — a backpack he never used and almost always forgot to take home, a couple of books for some of the classes he was in, and a single spiral notebook with a yellow cover. He'd gotten a hard time from his teachers for not taking notes until they saw how well he did on their poor excuses for quizzes and exams. Looking over his shoulder, he saw a cluster of girls standing at Courtney Reese's locker about twenty feet away from him. There were four of them standing in a small group, leaning in, whispering to each other, their long, shiny hair cascading forward as they shared their secrets. One of the girls, someone he didn't recognize, looked over her shoulder at him. He saw one of the other girls staring at him at the same time. He looked away. They were probably talking about him. Again.

It wasn't as if he overheard people talking about him all the time. It was mostly in class when his teacher made a big deal about him getting all the questions right on their latest test. The rest of the kids couldn't keep up. That wasn't his fault. He wasn't slowing down for anyone, especially the morons he was forced to go to school with.

Justin pulled out the literature textbook from his locker and took the notebook with him. At least while his teacher was droning on about Shakespeare, he could work on a few more of his formulas.

Slamming the metal door to the locker, he started walking down the hallway in the opposite direction from where the girls were still clustered. He fought the urge to look back at them. He could feel their eyes on his back. Pretty much all the students at Palm Coast high school treated him exactly the same way — like some sort of leper. He was an outcast and he knew it. He wasn't athletic enough to be in with the guys who played sports. He had no interest in wasting his time with music or art, and the students that were into technology couldn't care less about science.

He was alone.

Walking down the hallway, he paused for a second outside the classroom he was supposed to be in. He pulled his cell phone out of his back pocket. Two more hours till he could escape his confinement and get to the lab. The lab was the only reason he hadn't taken his mother up on the option to go away to boarding school. He looked down at the floor for a second. The worst part of every class was walking into the room. Most of the teachers let them sit where they wanted to. They were seniors now, after all. They were supposed to be responsible. But the stares from the other kids as he walked by made his skin crawl. Justin looked down, gritting his teeth. He had months and months of this ahead of him before he got a stupid piece of paper that would allow him to go to college. Sucking a breath in, he let it out and forced his body to walk forward.

Justin crossed the threshold of the classroom just as the bell rang. The teacher, a young woman named Ms. Hardisty stared at him but didn't say anything. She was just another teacher that didn't like him. That's her problem, Justin thought. Even though she was an adult, she wasn't much better at understanding him than any of the other girls he knew. He walked to the back of the classroom, shuffling his feet, and slid into his desk, cracking his book open. He knew where she would be teaching from today. He knew it every single day. Ms. Hardisty, just like the rest of the teachers in the building, was nothing but utterly predictable.

Justin stared around the room. The classroom was about half girls and half guys. Justin silently went through the names of the students in the room, at least the ones he knew. The ones he didn't, didn't matter. He stared at the pages in his notebook and got to work. From where Ms. Hardisty was standing, she'd have no idea if he was taking notes on her teaching or if he was writing down the Constitution from memory.

Just as he was leaving class, he heard a couple of girls talking. They were leaning close together. A guy was with them. He had on a letter jacket, although it was way too warm outside to wear it. He was surprised the guy wasn't sweating. "I heard Katrina's not doing very well," one of the girls, a redhead, whispered. "I know people are saying she tried to commit suicide, but I just don't believe it. She's not that way."

Justin's stomach clenched. How could they not believe it was a suicide? No one had any idea he'd tried his drug on her. They couldn't. He'd been too careful. And look where she was. Last he heard, she was stuck in the intensive care unit over at St. Anne's on a ventilator. Even if she did wake up, she'd have no idea what happened to her. He stared at the ground as he walked into the hallway, trying not to smile. His formula would work. He knew it. It just needed a little bit more tweaking. But if people were starting to talk, that meant time was running out.

He needed to figure out the formula and get the problem solved before it was too late.

THE LAST COUPLE of hours of school were excruciating. Justin was already on his feet when the bell rang ending his chemistry class. He didn't bother stopping at his locker. He shot straight out of the closest exit and walked around the side of the building to his car, getting in. There was work to be done at the lab. Pressing work.

By the time he got to the lab, the rest of the team was huddled in Dr. McCall's office in a meeting. Justin slid in the back of the room, taking the last chair available. Dr. McCall gave him a nod, continuing to lead the meeting. On the wall was a giant whiteboard. On it were chemical formulations that Dr. McCall was adjusting in front of the team. "What we're seeing is that the newest batch is degrading too fast. We need the formula for AnoVest to last for at least two to three hours before the patients wake up. We also need the option to be able to re-dose them without overdosing them and risking them going into a coma."

A couple of the other project managers started chiming in with ideas on how they could accomplish that. Justin stared at the board for a second and then looked down. He had other things on his mind. "Justin, what do you think?" Dr. McCall said, interrupting his thoughts.

Justin looked up and blinked, clearing his throat, "I think I would take a look at the delivery system," he said quietly. "Maybe there is a molecular binder we can use that would slow the entry of the drug into the bloodstream. Like a time-release capsule, but in molecular form."

Dr. McCall nodded and wrote Justin's idea on the whiteboard in big blue letters. Justin stared at it. At least here, in the lab, people knew who he was and why he was there. They showed him respect. It was very different than being at school.

After discussing a few other options, the meeting broke up, everyone leaving with their assignments as the team struggled to get AnoVest to work. Justin started walking out of Dr. McCall's office, watching as two of the project managers sat and copied down the notes from the meeting. All of their ideas would be stored in a secured cloud that tracked the development of the project. No notes were ever left on the whiteboard where they could be seen. It was one of the first things he learned as an intern at BioNova. Corporate espionage was real. Other pharmaceutical companies would love to know what AnoVest could do so they could immediately develop a competing drug and beat them to market.

"Justin, I like your comments on the direction for development. Good thinking." Dr. McCall said, sitting down behind his desk. He looked at Justin, "While I have you, I just sent you another run of the data to take a look at. If you have any other suggestions you can offer..."

Justin's mind drifted, although he managed to nod and keep eye contact with Dr. McCall. In his mind, the formula for AnoVest should have been done three months ago. Andrew could ask for his help looking at data, but it was a waste of his time. They should be looking at designs for a clinical trial by now. After all, they had an entire team working on it. On his own, he'd come up with a competing formula, one that would probably work better in just a couple of months. But he needed time, something that seemed to be running out. If the girls at school were talking about Katrina... Justin glanced over his shoulder.

"Justin?"

"Sorry. I got distracted for a minute."

Dr. McCall furrowed his eyebrows, "Everything okay? You don't seem yourself."

"Yeah, I'm fine. You know, just school stuff going on."

"Are you sure you're okay? Because if you need to take the day and get caught up on homework or something, I'm fine with that. You spend more than your fair share of hours here at the lab. Which I appreciate, by the way. You're doing great work."

Justin shook his head. The last thing he wanted to do was cause Dr. McCall to be suspicious. "No, Dr. McCall. I'm fine. I'll take a look at that data and have it back to you before I leave tonight."

"I appreciate that. Listen, one piece of advice... You are one of the most talented interns I have ever had. You come up with intuitive solutions to things that many of my employees who are halfway through their PhD programs can't manage to think of. Just don't burn out. Science needs good people like you to come up with solutions. Pace yourself. A research career lasts for a long time."

Justin nodded. Part of him wanted to be excited about the feedback he got from Dr. McCall, but part of him already knew it was the truth. He was more talented than most of the people he'd met. The one thing that he couldn't seem to overcome was trying to connect with girls. Hopefully, his experiments would help with that. If he could get his version of the drug to work better, then maybe he'd have a chance. They would see him as romantic and dedicated, not just brilliant. His imagination flickered. He'd find one of the prettiest girls at school, one that maybe liked science as much as he did, give her his version of the drug, and then take her to a remote location for a romantic date. When she found out all of the hard work he'd put into developing the drug so he could steal her away, he was sure she would be blown away by his effort. He'd tried with Sarah and Maisie, but things didn't work out the way he'd hoped.

Justin blinked, getting lost in his thoughts again. He looked at Dr. McCall, who was staring at him. "I'm sorry. I'm gonna go get to work now. I'll be at my station if you need anything."

"Thanks, Justin. I appreciate it."

Just as Justin was walking out of the office, one of the project managers stared at him as he wiped the whiteboard clean. The guy had heard the entire conversation. Justin could tell by the look on his face that the project manager knew Justin was a threat. Sure, he was just an intern for the moment, but within a couple of years, the project manager knew Justin would be coming for his job and probably take it from him.

Walking out into the lab, a half-smile on his face, Justin imagined firing the project manager when he ran the lab. Justin went to his workstation at the back, logging into one of the BioNova dedicated research terminals. No one, except for the senior researchers, was allowed to bring their laptops into the research building. The security measures BioNova took were extensive. They had to protect their investment. Justin entered his password and ran his fingerprint across the reader, the system coming to life. He found the email Dr. McCall had sent with a link to another batch of data. Justin clicked on it, waiting for it to open.

Looking around the lab, his eyes caught on the bank of refrigerated supply cases in the back of the room, just off to his left. One of the other researchers was kneeling in front of it, reaching into the back looking for something. Her black hair was tied into a short bun at the back of her neck, her white lab coat draping the floor behind her. As she reached in, she pulled out the bottle of glycerin Justin had stashed in the back. Frowning, she stood up and tossed it in the trash. Justin stared back at the computer, swallowing. The woman had no idea what she'd done.

A second later, Justin watched as she closed the refrigerator doors and walked to the other side of the lab, disappearing behind a bank of equipment. Justin checked over his shoulders.

No one was watching. He walked over to the trash and pulled the glycerin out, putting it back in the refrigerator in a different spot where hopefully she wouldn't find it. People had no respect, he thought, sitting back down at the computer.

Three hours later, the last people finally left the lab. Justin had finished working on the data an hour before but hadn't sent the report to Dr. McCall. He felt a tap on his shoulder, "How's the data coming?" Dr. McCall asked. He had a backpack slung over one shoulder, his lab coat draped over his arm.

"I'm almost there."

"Okay, but don't stay too late. Remember what I said about burning out?"

Justin nodded. "Yeah. I promise. I won't stay too late."

"Good. I don't want your mom mad at me," he chuckled and walked away, giving Justin's shoulder a squeeze as he did.

As soon as Dr. McCall left, the last couple of people in the lab filed out after him. It was as if they were waiting for him to leave before they could go home. Justin heard the click of the door closing echo off of the stainless-steel tables and the tile floor. He shot up from the stool, his heart starting to beat faster in his chest, assembling more compounds for his next version. He stood at the table for a second, thinking about the woman who had so rudely tossed his glycerin in the trash. People were careless. Lining up the cyclohexanone, etomidate, and metho-hexital on the table, he stared at them. If people were going to interrupt his work, then he might just have to do it at home. But not tonight. He had another sample ready, but he wanted to test one other version. He mixed up the newest proportions, poured it into a plastic vial, closed the lid, and shoved it into his pocket. Although it was tempting to take the materials he'd need home and mix them on his own, that might be too big of a red flag for the lab.

Finishing his work, Justin checked the time. It was getting late. He didn't have time to test his newest formula on the mice, at least not without raising suspicion. He shook his head, feeling tightness in his chest. Most interns seemed to leave as soon as their shift was over, or at least the rest of the ones in Dr. McCall's lab did. He logged out of his computer and put the supplies away, carefully cleaning up the bench and stashing the glycerin behind a rack of test tubes that were growing cultures in a different refrigerator.

Justin stood for a second, leaning his hands on the work-table, drumming his fingers underneath the edge. He sat down on his stool again, thinking. He'd seen Courtney Reece looking at him earlier that day, judging him. It was like she knew that there was something different about him. He'd sent her an invitation to join him on the GenChat messaging app.

He pulled his phone out of his pocket and opened up the app. He'd heard about it from some other kids. Not directly, of course. It was more accurate to say he'd overheard them. He stuck his head in, asking to be invited. The guy he'd asked, a soccer player, nodded and sent him an invitation without even asking a single question. Justin didn't even know the guy. But after doing some digging, Justin discovered he could learn a lot about who was who at the high school if he could figure out their screen names. He checked on the invitation he'd sent to Courtney as soon as the application loaded on his phone.

He held his breath. The other girls he'd found to talk to — Sarah Poole, Maisie Hill, and Katrina DeLuca — they'd all accepted his invitation. It was like they secretly wanted to get to know him, but they were too shy to admit it publicly. That was a hurdle he would have to overcome later. But maybe once he got his drug perfected, that would help move things along in his favor.

Staring at the screen, he realized Courtney hadn't accepted his invitation. They were in the same chemistry class. Why she hadn't, he didn't know. His picture was right there for her to see.

He felt heat build in his chest, the blood filling his face. It was a slap in the face.

Justin stared at the screen. He sent the invitation again. She had no right to ignore him. He waited, staring at his phone. Nothing happened. He scrolled through the network to see if she was connected to other people. He realized he wouldn't be able to discover that until after she accepted. His heart skipped a beat. What if she didn't accept his invitation? What would he do then? Justin shoved his phone back in his pocket, logged out of his computer, and took off his lab coat, carrying it over his arm the same way Dr. McCall had. The last thing he wanted to do was have security ask him what was in his pocket on the way out the door. They did that from time to time. Justin had seen one guy stopped at security because he had a prescription bottle in his pocket. He shook his head. Nothing but a hassle. Justin unclipped his badge from the pocket of his lab coat and held it in his hand as he walked out of the lab, shutting off the lights.

As he went down in the elevator, the only thing that he could think of was Courtney. She wasn't like the other girls. Sarah and Maisie had been nice. Sarah was in his Spanish class and Maisie was in his Literature class. They looked eerily similar, like they could be sisters, both with blonde hair. He'd lured them out by offering to help them study for tests he was sure they would fail otherwise. But the reality was that he'd done his research on them. People had no idea what could be found on social media and how they were sacrificing their personal privacy for a couple of laughs and likes. The students at Palm Coast High School posted practically everything they did. They gave him a lot of information. Sarah had tons of pictures on her profile at the beach. Maisie had pictures of her showing a horse. It hadn't been hard to figure out what they liked to do, especially once they were on the GenChat app as part of his group. He'd practically memorized their profiles and who they were linked to, but only one connection mattered – to him.

Justin blinked as the elevator doors slid open. There was no one in the lobby except for the night security guard, who was half watching the video monitors in front of him, glancing down every few seconds at his phone. As Justin ran his key card through the scanner to leave the lab, he glanced at the guard. He had a football game streaming on his phone, the volume turned down low, the cheering of the crowd barely audible. Justin didn't say anything, just holding his lab coat over the bump in his jeans pocket, holding his breath, and looking straight ahead. The guards they hired weren't exactly top-notch. If he was able to get the formula for his drug to work, that would be something he would have to speak to his mother about. She needed to increase the funding for security, especially if he was going to take over the research for BioNova someday. The things he would design would become the focused targets for other companies, he was sure.

Out in his car, Justin checked his phone again. He smiled. Courtney had just accepted his request to join the app. He leaned back in his seat, sending her a message, "Hey Courtney! Need any help studying? I know we have that chemistry test tomorrow." He'd seen the grade she'd gotten on the last test. It wasn't good. She needed all the help she could get.

He saw dots pulsating on the screen. She must've been writing something as soon as he messaged her. That was a good sign. He could feel the excitement building in his chest. He waited, watching, as the dots disappeared. Frustration filled him as he stared at the screen. He pounded his fist on the steering wheel and then started the engine, staring down at the phone again. The dots had started again, a new message finally emerging. "Justin? Oh my gosh, yes. I'm so confused about what will be on the test. Is it too late for you to help me?"

Justin frowned. Was she asking if it was him? She couldn't

be. She had to know who she could rely on. It was him. "No, of course not. I'm starved, though. How about if I meet you at Jolly Burgers?"

"That would be great. I'm on my way!"

Justin touched the vial in his pocket. This would be the perfect time to test it on Courtney. He could help her with her homework and then see where things went. Before leaving the parking lot, he sent a quick text to his mom, "I'm going to a study group tonight. Home late. Don't wait up."

His mom didn't respond. He didn't expect her to. She was probably buried in her computer or taking a long bath. She might even be online with their suppliers in Southeast Asia and Australia with the time difference. It seemed like the only time he got her attention was first thing in the morning right before she went to work, just long enough for her to try to boss him around. Other than that, they were nothing but roommates.

The drive to Jolly Burgers didn't take very long. It was a knockoff of every other fast-food chain in the area, with the same small, dry burgers and french fries. By the time Justin pulled in, Courtney was already sitting inside. He could see her through one of the windows, her back to him. He stared at her for a second. She'd pulled her dark hair off her face with a clip. Her books were piled neatly on the edge of the table. He liked that about her. It was good that she was orderly.

Shutting off the car, he went into the restaurant and walked over to her, "Hey. You beat me here."

"Oh, I've only been here for a minute." She glanced back at the menu posted on the wall, "I'm starving, too. Is it okay if we get some food first?"

Justin nodded. "Sure."

He followed her over to the counter where they both ordered burgers and fries. Courtney got a strawberry milkshake to go with hers. Justin asked for a vanilla. Courtney was fumbling in her wallet for her debit card when Justin held his hand up, "I've got this."

A wash of concern ran across Courtney's face, "I didn't mean for you to buy me food like this is a date or something," she said, dropping her arms to her side.

Justin felt the sting of heat on his cheeks. He mumbled, "It's not a big deal. I get paid at my internship."

Courtney shrugged.

Back at the table, Justin watched her as she ate her fries, flipping through the chemistry book in front of her. Justin watched her, taking a sip of his milkshake. "I'm glad you accepted the invitation to the messaging app," he said, slowly. "I wasn't sure you would."

Courtney looked up at him. It felt like her brown eyes were staring right through him, "I've never heard of it before. Why do you use it? Why not just text?" she squinted.

"I like technology. That one is pretty cool because it connects people in real life. You'll see. As you invite people, a spiderweb forms on the screen. You can see who knows someone else. When you have a minute, you can play on it."

"Oh, that's interesting. I didn't know. I'll have to look at it later." She glanced down at her phone, a smile pulling at her face. "Hold on, it's my mom. She worries too much. I just gotta text her back."

Justin watched for a second as Courtney sent a reply, wondering why she just couldn't ignore her family. She was with him. "Okay, so what questions do you have about the chemistry test for tomorrow?" His words came out short and direct.

"Yeah, about that," Courtney blinked, opening her book. She pointed to one of the formulas they were supposed to memorize.

Justin spent the next couple of minutes trying to explain to her the formulas and how they worked, but he just wasn't getting through to her. Frustration built in his chest. He was barely able to have a conversation with her. He felt tension crawl across his shoulders, every muscle in his back tightening. Staring at her, he watched her mouth move. What she was saying made no sense. She was going to fail the test. She was pretty, but clearly had no idea who he was. The questions she was asking were so basic that it was hard for him to even explain to her what was going on.

He stared at her and then drew a sharp breath in, "Listen, I think I have something that might help you. I have my notes out in my car. Why don't I just give you all of them. You can keep them overnight and just return them to me at school tomorrow." He waited, a tingle running down his spine. If he could just get her out to his car...

Courtney sighed, putting her elbows on the table, "You know it would! I just learn so much better when I can read something. I don't know what it is about me. I'm just that way I guess." She scooped up her books and stuffed them back in her bag, shoving her phone in her pocket.

As she slid out of the booth, Justin watched her. He followed her out of the restaurant, a lump forming in his throat. There might not be any notes in the car, but he had something far better...

12

Outside, Justin had Courtney follow him to his car. "Hey, that bag looks heavy. Why don't you sit inside? I'll turn the heat on. My notes are in the trunk. I'll get them out and walk you through them and then I'll drive you over to your car so you can head home. How's that for a plan?" He tried to make it sound as natural as possible, though the lump in his throat made it difficult to get the words out.

"That would be great. The temperature really dropped tonight. I'm getting cold just standing out here," Courtney said, shivering.

Justin nodded and opened the car door, hitting the button on the key fob so the car would turn on. The temperature had dropped maybe five degrees. It wasn't as if they were living in Alaska. He raised his eyebrows as he closed the door behind her. Courtney wasn't that durable, apparently.

Justin walked to the trunk, pressing another button on the key fob so it would pop open. He pretended to be rustling around for his notes. He did have a notebook in the back, but it was the one that had his formulas, the one he carried around at school, pretending to pay attention to the teachers. In the glow of the small light of the trunk, he pulled a black case toward him. Inside was an emergency road care kit, one that his mother insisted he take with him everywhere he went. It had things like flares and a can of instant tire fix in it. In the corner of the black bag, Justin had put pairs of gloves. They were the same kind doctors used during surgery, except for the fact that they were skin-colored, nearly impossible to see.

Pulling them out of the bag, Justin glanced around the side of the car, his heart beating fast. He could see the back of Courtney's head through the rear window, her face turned slightly to the side. She seemed to be staring at her phone. From the inside of his pocket, Justin pulled out the vial he'd just mixed at the lab, giving it a quick shake. In the darkness, it was almost impossible to see that he had a glove on. He stared at his hand and realized he'd made a good decision. Initially, he'd almost ordered the same kind he used at the lab — gloves that were bright blue — but then found the ones that were skin-colored. Opening the lid to the vial, Justin poured a few drops in the palm of his right hand.

Carefully capping the vial, he shoved it back in his pocket, picking up the notebook he'd found. He stared at his palm for a second. He could see the sheen of the drug glistening in the lights from the parking lot. All he needed to do was touch her.

Justin closed the trunk lid with his elbow and walked to the driver's side. He didn't want anything about handing her the notebook to seem unnatural. Getting in, he glanced at her. She had on a pair of jeans and a thin, white T-shirt. As long as he laid his hand on her arm or touched her hand, it should be enough to transfer the drug to her system through her skin. His lips felt dry. He licked them as he slid in. He extended the notebook to her, "Here you go, I think these notes will help you."

He watched her for a second and as she opened the notebook. She stared at it and then frowned, glancing back at him,

"These don't look like any of the formulas we are supposed to study for class. Are you sure this is the right information?"

He nodded, easing his hand closer to her, trying to keep eye contact so she wouldn't notice what he was doing. It felt like everything was moving in slow motion. He pointed, "Yeah, let me show you," he said, leaning forward, laying his hand on her arm, leaving it there for just a moment, giving it a gentle squeeze...

"Sleep well, sweet girl," Justin said, staring at her. Maisie and Sarah hadn't moaned the way she did. He made a mental note to try to figure out why as he carefully peeled the gloves off of his hands and tossed them on the floor of his car. The gloves would have to go. He'd stuff them into the pocket of his lab coat the next time he went to BioNova and throw them in the incinerator. No one would care. Tons of stuff went into the incinerator. He'd even seen one of the project managers throw a bag of potato chips in there the week before.

Justin glanced at Courtney as he started the car, slowly pulling out of Jolly Burger. It was dark out, so the only way he could see her was under the passing streetlights. "You shouldn't have waited for so long to accept my invitation," he said, looking at her while he drove. "It's not nice. I would expect your mother taught you better manners. I know mine did."

The very mention of his mother made his skin crawl. Sure, she had raised him, fed him, and housed him, but that was it. He always felt like just another task to her, something she had to get done. Even when he was little, he spent more time with his nannies and his teachers than his mom.

He shook the thought from his head. His mother was the last thing he wanted to think about. This was a beautiful moment, seeing his experiment come to life. He checked his watch. He dosed Courtney at about eight o'clock. If his calculations were correct, she should start waking up between ten and eleven, just in time for him to drive her back to her car and send her home. If her family was mad she was a little late, that was okay. Her mom knew she was out studying anyways. A knot formed in Justin's throat. Hopefully, Courtney hadn't told her mom with who.

Justin drove to a park near the high school to wait out the effects of the drug. He pulled in, stopping the car near the basketball courts. There were a couple of guys outside playing, their shirts off, their skin pale and glistening with sweat against the bright overhead light. He left the car running. Even with the windows closed, Justin could hear the smacking of the basketball against the asphalt of the court. He leaned his seat back in his car for a second. He was tired. As he closed his eyes, he shook his head, worried. There was no way he could have gotten any of the compound on his skin, could he? He'd been too careful. Besides the fact, it would've taken effect much sooner. No, this was just garden-variety exhaustion. He'd been working a lot of hours, especially on his compound. He knew the lab team was getting close. He needed to beat them to the punch, to show Dr. McCall that he had answers no one else did.

He laid back on the seat for a few minutes until he heard a thud on the front of his car. His eyes flipped open, startled by the noise. As he sat up in his seat, he saw one of the basketball players looking at him, waving. Their ball had gotten loose and hit Justin's sedan.

Justin waved the guy off and looked at Courtney. There was a bright red mark on her arm where the medication had gone into her body. It looked like a burn. There were red, fluid-filled blisters all over the patch. He swallowed. That was a new side effect, one he wasn't expecting. His mouth felt dry. From the color of her skin, it looked like she was still alive, but from his angle, he couldn't tell if her chest was rising and falling or not. Panic surged through his body. What if the compound hadn't worked again? He couldn't afford to keep doing these tests without one of them working. He swallowed, panic rising in his throat.

Justin wrapped his sweaty palms around the steering wheel. He put the car into reverse and carefully backed it up, pulling it out of the park. Turning back on Gulf Shores Parkway, he glanced at Courtney, "It's time for you to wake up," he whispered, as if he could will her to open her eyes. The words rang hollow in the car. Justin checked the time. It was nearing ten o'clock. She should be regaining consciousness any time now. Frowning, Justin put his hand on her shoulder. Her skin felt warm. He gave her a little shove. Her body drooped to the side, her head resting against the passenger side window. She was still out cold.

Trying to keep his eye on the road, Justin reached over and put his fingers on her neck, checking for a pulse. He pressed his fingers deeper and deeper, trying to feel for the steady bump of her heart. He didn't feel anything. Justin drew his hand back and licked his lips, staring through the windshield, straight ahead. He felt paralyzed. Why wasn't she waking up? He glanced down at Courtney's arm, the angry red blisters staring back at him. Neither of the other girls had that reaction. Had he gotten the dosage wrong or was she allergic to something in the new cocktail he had worked up? Justin glanced at the floor where he'd dropped the used gloves. He'd reworked the calculations carefully. There couldn't be anything wrong with them.

Panic filled his chest. Justin slammed on the brakes and did a U-turn in the middle of the road, heading back toward the high school. With the other girls, he'd had a plan. He'd taken them someplace they loved, but Courtney had avoided his invitation for so long that he didn't feel like she deserved something special. He knew she loved school. It was as good a place as any to leave her.

As the thoughts surged through his mind, he glanced over at her. None of this would have happened if she had responded when she was supposed to. He would have given her the other sample he'd made the day before. That one was probably better. Maybe he messed up something in the mixing. He was moving awfully fast with all the pressure from Dr. McCall. It was her fault. If she'd responded, she would've gotten the correct sample.

Sitting up straighter in his car, Justin pulled into the high school, the complex of buildings dark and shadowy with nightfall. There were only a few lights on in the parking lot. Justin drove around the back of the building, where the entrances to the locker rooms were. He passed them by looking for a good place to leave her.

Between the tennis courts and the entrance for the locker rooms, there was a line of trailers, mobile classrooms the school was using. The high school was packed with so many students who'd moved in from out of state that there'd been no time to figure out where to house everyone. The best the Board of Education could do was to bring in five converted trailers to house the extra students.

Pulling up in front of the first one, Justin put the car into park. He felt for Courtney's pulse again. There was nothing there. He put his hand in front of her nose and mouth, thinking that maybe he just couldn't feel her breathing. She was as still as a stone.

Justin slumped back in his seat for a second, shaking his head. He almost couldn't look at her he was so angry. She failed him. He sat there for a second, staring straight ahead at the darkness at the converted trailers, gritting his teeth. Getting out of the car, he circled around, pulling the door open with a yank. One last time, he put his fingers up to her neck, feeling for a pulse. Still nothing. He felt a surge of anger run through him. Part of him just wanted to drag her body out of the car and leave it on the ground. Some part of him knew that wasn't right. At least she'd been a good test subject.

Justin leaned in and pulled at her arms and legs, dragging her out of the car. He wrapped his arms under her and dragged her towards one of the trailers, barely making it up the four wooden steps to the door. Dropping her on the landing, he straightened her body up, leaning her back against the door, her head falling to the side and resting on one of the handrails. Justin walked back to the car, getting her bag and setting it next to her, putting it underneath her arm, avoiding touching the spot where he'd put the compound.

He stared at her for a second, pressing his lips together, looking again at the blisters. Walking back to the car, he opened the glove compartment, fishing for the stolen bottle of pills he'd stashed. He'd taken the oxy from his mother's medicine cabinet a few weeks before. She'd had them for a back injury, but had never taken them. Picking at the label, he pulled it off, pouring a handful of the pills into his hand and throwing them into the bushes nearby so it would look like Courtney took them. Walking back to the building, he tossed the bottle inside of Courtney's bag, giving her one last look. "See ya later, Courtney," he sneered.

At least it was one less person to ignore him at school, he thought, walking away.

13

The shrill ring of Morgan's phone startled her out of a deep sleep. She rolled over, blinking. Bo groaned. It was still dark out, the long summer hours having evaporated into the shorter fall days. Pulling her arm out from underneath the blanket, Morgan reached without looking, feeling for her phone on the nightstand. She glared at it. "This better be good," she mumbled, closing her eyes again.

"Another body just arrived at the hospital. Thought you'd want to know," Amber said, her voice low and serious.

Morgan swung her legs down over the side of the bed trying to shake the cobwebs out of her head. "Are you kidding me? What happened?"

"I'm just getting the details now. The captain sent out a broadcast to all of the detectives. I guess a girl from the high school named Courtney Reese was found slumped over in front of one of the auxiliary classrooms outside the high school a little while ago."

"She okay?"

"I have no idea. One of our officers went with her, but he hasn't reported back with any additional information."

Morgan blinked. Another girl? She stood up, crossing one of her arms across her chest, using the other to hold her phone up to her ear. "Did you let Sylvia know yet?"

"She's my next call."

As Morgan hung up with Amber, she walked into the bathroom, brushing her teeth and putting on a fresh coat of deodorant. She glanced at the time. It was just after five o'clock in the morning. Danny wouldn't be up for another hour. She sent him a text, knowing that his phone was on vibrate. "Have to go to the hospital to see someone. I'll have my phone with me if you need me for anything." She skipped telling him about the part that another body had been found. There was no need to upset him until she knew something more definitive.

Grabbing her wallet from the counter, she stuffed it in her pocket and headed out the door. As she drove to St. Anne's, her headlights cut through the darkness, the trees simply silhouettes against the barely glowing sky with daybreak coming. Out on Gulf Shores Parkway, Morgan squinted at the oncoming headlights. There wasn't a lot of traffic, the majority of the stores and businesses along the road were still closed, too early for them to be open for business yet. Morgan put her elbow on the edge of the door, leaning her head into it as she drove. Her mind was numb. How could there be another body? She took a deep breath as she tried to think through the possibilities. Either this was a coincidence or it wasn't. The more bodies that dropped, the less she was convinced it was a suicide cluster. A shiver ran down her spine. Her mind drifted to Dorothy Poole and Lisa Hill, wondering what they were doing as they faced another long day of grieving their daughters. Morgan swallowed, a knot in her stomach.

Pulling into St. Anne's Medical Center, Morgan found a spot in the outdoor lot, slamming the truck door behind her as she got out of the truck. She ran to the emergency room entrance, going to the window. "I'm here about a young girl that was just brought in — Courtney Reese?"

The nurse sitting at the window barely looked up. She just nodded and hit a buzzer. The door popped open and Morgan strode through, scanning the emergency room.

The way the emergency room had been designed looked exactly like the intensive care unit, all white with heavily waxed tile, the smell of latex gloves in the air. Morgan's stomach clenched. Halfway down the hallway, she saw a police officer standing against the wall, leaning against it, staring at his phone. She walked towards him and then stopped. "Are you here with Courtney Reese?"

He furrowed his eyebrows, "I am. And you are?"

"I'm Morgan Foster. Amber D'Amico sent me."

"Detective D'Amico? How do you know her?"

Morgan raised her eyebrows. She assumed most of the people in the department knew who she was, but apparently, some of the new faces hadn't heard her story. "We used to work together. You can call her if you like."

The officer shook his head. Morgan noticed from his uniform that his last name was Gonzales. "No, that won't be necessary. If she sent you then it's all right by me."

"What happened?" Morgan changed the subject before Gonzales asked her any other questions about why she was there. She didn't have the time or patience for that.

"We got a call about an hour ago about a girl that OD'd at the high school. Palm Coast. You know that one?"

Morgan nodded.

"By the time we got there, she was almost gone. The docs are working on her now. I think they took her upstairs for some sort of testing."

"Are the parents here yet?"

"Yeah. They rolled in about ten minutes ago. One of the

nurses took them upstairs to see Courtney. The mom was freaking out."

Morgan didn't say anything. What did Gonzales think was going to happen -- that Courtney's parents would be calm and cool? That just didn't happen. He was clearly new to the job.

Gonzales tilted his head to the side and looked at Morgan, "Wait, I think I've heard about you. You used to be a detective, didn't you?"

"Yeah."

"Why did Amber ask you to come? I mean, you don't work for the department anymore, do you?"

All of Gonzales's questions were reasonable, but Morgan didn't feel like answering them, at least not with the level of detail she was sure he was looking for. "She just asked me for a little help. That's all."

"Okay. What she says goes. I'm not gonna tangle with her," Gonzales said, holding up his hands. "I'll stay here until they bring her back down. I've seen a lot of these cases where they give the kid a bunch of Narcan, let them rest for a little while, and then send them home."

Morgan nodded. Gonzales was right. She'd seen the same thing happen dozens of times, but if this was what she thought it was, Courtney wouldn't be going anywhere at all. Maybe never. Morgan licked her lips, suddenly feeling thirsty. "Listen, did you find anything on her, anything out of the ordinary?"

Gonzales shook his head, "Not really. She had a bag with her. It was under her arm. I gave it a quick search and found a bottle of pills. I handed those off to the paramedics."

Morgan narrowed her eyes, thinking, "Was there any label on it or did you happen to see how full it was?"

"No label. It was about half full. I figured that's probably what she took. At least if the docs have it, they can track the drug. Maybe that'll help." He shook his head a little bit, staring at the floor for a second, "It's a shame. These kids, they've got their whole life ahead of them. Then they get mixed up in drugs and here we are."

Morgan leaned against the wall for a second, staring at the other bays in the emergency room. There was a guy in his forties with a bald head, his leg in a splint, propped up on a few pillows. Down the hallway was an older woman with oxygen over her nose, a man and a younger woman sitting nearby. It had to be the husband and the daughter, Morgan thought. Sighing, Morgan realized she would never be cut out for work in the medical field. Too much sickness and death. She swallowed. She'd seen enough of that in her life already.

Pushing herself off the wall, Morgan looked at Gonzales, "I'll be back. I'm gonna go get a coffee. Want anything?"

"No, thanks. I'm good."

The truth was Morgan was restless. Standing in the emergency room waiting for something to happen was like watching paint dry. There was always the hubbub of people arriving at the hospital in some sort of crisis, the doctors and nurses scurrying around. Once they were settled it seemed like everything slowed down dramatically, the doctors and nurses taking their time figuring out what was wrong with people, not in any hurry at all. Scanning the emergency room one more time, she noticed neither of the other beds that were occupied seemed to be all that interesting. She wondered how long the man with a broken leg and the woman on oxygen had been lying there. Could've been hours, for all she knew.

Turning on her heel, Morgan went out of the emergency department and out into the lobby of the hospital. Unlike her last visit, there was no one at the reception desk. Morgan walked down the hallway, finding a set of steps that led to the lower level where the cafeteria was. At the bottom of the steps, she could smell food cooking, a mixture of eggs and bacon. She wrinkled her nose at the smell, a wave of nausea running over her. It was too early to eat. Near the cash registers, she found coffee pots that had already been filled with the first brew of the day. She poured herself a cup and attached a lid, standing in line behind a woman and a man wearing scrubs as they paid for their breakfast. When it was her turn to pay, Morgan handed the woman at the register cash for her coffee, walking away before the woman was done ringing her up. "You don't want the coins, honey?"

Morgan shook her head, "Leave the money for someone else."

Walking the steps to the first floor again, Morgan slumped down in one of the chairs in the lobby, setting her coffee on a nearby table. She pulled out her phone and texted Amber, "I'm here. No news yet. Gonzales said they took Courtney up for testing."

Her phone pinged almost immediately, "Gonzales is there?"

"Yeah. I think he's afraid of you."

"He should be. Let me know what else you find out, okay?"

Morgan snorted. Amber had an interesting effect on some of the officers, especially the male ones. Why that was, Morgan wasn't sure. She leaned back against the upholstery, reaching for her coffee. Taking a sip, the bitter roast filled her mouth. It wasn't a bad cup of coffee, but it wasn't all that good either.

By the time Morgan finished her coffee, it was nearly six o'clock. The new shift was straggling into the building with their backpacks, the noise of conversation and footfalls filling the lobby. She got up, walking back into the emergency room. Gonzales was still leaning on the wall in the same spot she'd left him in.

"Any news?"

"Nothing yet."

Just as the words came out of his mouth, a nurse walked

towards them, her white tennis shoes squeaking on the floor. "You were waiting for information on Courtney Reese?"

Morgan sized up the nurse. They were roughly the same height, but the woman had dark hair pulled in a ponytail behind her head, the glint of some sort of tinted lip gloss on her lips. Other than that, her face was bare. Morgan couldn't imagine that anyone would be all that interested in putting on makeup if they were working the overnight shift at the hospital. She knew when she worked third shift at the department, that's the way she felt. "We are. Do you know anything?"

The nurse nodded, "They just called down from upstairs. I don't know the specifics of her condition, but I can tell you she's being moved to the PICU. You know where that is?"

Before the woman had gotten the rest of the sentence out, Morgan turned and headed that way. Pushing her way through the emergency room doors, she went back to the lobby, finding the same set of elevators she'd been in to go visit Paul. It'd only been a couple of days but it felt like a lifetime ago. She checked her phone as she waited for the elevator to arrive. She stared at the doors for a second, holding her breath. The ride was just up a couple of floors. It would take less than a minute. As the doors opened, Morgan paused and then she heard Gonzalez over her shoulder, "Is this the way to the intensive care unit the nurse mentioned?"

Morgan let out a breath and stepped inside the elevator, "Yeah. This way." At least she had someone else in the elevator with her. It was better than being alone.

As soon as the elevator doors opened, Morgan walked down the hallway, pressing the buzzer for the PICU. The nurse inside must have seen Gonzales's uniform because the door opened without any questions.

The PICU looked pretty much the same as it had the last time Morgan had been there. The lights were bright at the nurses' station, the screens still reading out the heartbeats and blood pressures of the patients under their care, the bays where the children were dark and quiet. "Who are you looking for?" the nurse at the desk said, leaning over.

"Courtney Reese," Gonzales said. "I just need to get some information for my report."

The nurse stared down the hallway for a second and then looked back at him. "They're getting ready to bring her in, but she's not here yet." She pointed to a couple of chairs. "You can have a seat over there. As soon as they bring her up and get her situated, then I'm sure the parents will be available to talk to you. Could be a little while, though, in case you want to come back."

Gonzales frowned, staring at his phone. Morgan could see the shadow of a beard growing on his chin. He must have been on nights. "Since they aren't ready with her yet, I'm gonna head back to the department and EOS. I'll let somebody else finish the statement in a few hours. That's probably better for the family anyway." Morgan couldn't blame him for wanting to head out. Working the overnight shift was brutal, especially in a department that was understaffed.

Morgan nodded. She remembered when she was on the road, she'd always count down the minutes until she could call and end her service for that day, the simple acronym, "EOS," freeing her from her responsibilities. "That's fine. I'll hang out here for a while. I'll text Amber if anything happens."

As Gonzales walked away, Morgan sat down in the chairs the nurse had pointed to. They were gray plastic, the kind that was contoured to be comfortable, but weren't. She shifted in her seat for a second and then got up, walking down the hallway. Most of the patients had someone in the room with them, parents that looked like they hadn't gone home in weeks, curled up on pull-out chairs, using hospital blankets and pillows to try to get comfortable while their child healed. Glancing in a few of the rooms, Morgan saw some of the patients were sleeping and a few were awake already. Morgan passed a little girl. She was sitting up in the corner of her crib, her hair sticking out every which way, hugging a tattered teddy bear, a frown on her face. A man was curled up right next to her crib, his fingers wrapped around one of the bars. It had to be her dad. Morgan swallowed, looking away.

Morgan heard clattering to her left, a set of two double doors she hadn't noticed before swinging open automatically. A long body, by PICU standards, was laying on the bed, tubes and wires coming out of what seemed to be every inch of the girl. She was clearly a teenager, just young enough for the PICU even though she looked like she had an adult body. Morgan stood back as the bed passed. A nurse walked along purposefully next to Courtney's head, squeezing the bag hovering over her mouth in rhythmic fashion, forcing air into the girl's lungs. Morgan's eyes settled on Courtney as she passed by. The girl had long dark hair, her skin pale, her body limp. A man and a woman trailed behind the bed as it was rolled down the hallway.

Morgan stopped as she watched the orderlies spin the bed around and slide it into one of the bays, the nurse motioning for the parents to remain outside with a grim look on her face. Morgan stayed back. She couldn't take her eyes off them. As the bed pulled away from Courtney's mom, she extended her hand as if she was trying to touch her daughter one last time, a deep wail escaping from her lungs as she doubled over, putting her hands on her knees. Her husband stood next to her, silent, his hand on her back, shifting his eyes between his daughter, lifeless in the bed, and his terrified wife.

Morgan's heart pounded in her chest, her stomach tying itself into a tiny knot. Her eyes darted back and forth between the nurses and doctors at the center station, the hustle and bustle of the staff settling Courtney into her room, and her distraught parents. Morgan's eyes were drawn down the hallway, to the dark room where she knew Katrina DeLuca was still lying unconscious. The hallway started to spin and close around her. Her hands felt suddenly cold, the same cold she'd felt when she was locked in the dark trailer for what felt like days on end. The breath caught in her chest. Morgan stood still, trying to get air into the bottom of her lungs. It wouldn't go. It felt like someone or something was sitting on her chest.

Morgan ran to the door, pounding on the button that would open it, desperately trying to get out of the locked specialty unit. As soon as the door slid open a fraction, she pushed her way out of it, running blindly down the hall past the elevators. The only noise she heard was her tennis shoes on the floor. She darted to the stairwell, not thinking about where she was going. She ran down the three flights of steps and emerged into the lobby. She didn't stop or slow down, shoving her way past a group of medical students in their scrubs.

Outside, she ran for her truck as fast as her legs would carry her, fighting for every single breath. Her mind kept veering back and forth between the girls upstairs and the threats she lived through at the hands of Leo McDaniel. It didn't seem to matter that he was dead and couldn't hurt her anymore. He still had a grip on her. His leering smile emerged in her mind as a shiver ran down her spine. Getting to the truck, she ran to the back, putting her hands on the edge of the bed and bending over. A wave of nausea crashed over her. She stumbled to the grass, her hands on her knees and threw up; a combination of coffee and bile spewing out of her mouth. She stood hunched over for a couple of minutes until she was sure the last of what was in her stomach had come up. Collapsing into the grass, Morgan sat a few feet from where she'd thrown up, her head between her knees, waiting for the dizziness to subside. She hadn't been that claustrophobic in a long time.

The whooshing of the blood in her ears finally starting to diminish, she heard the sounds of the morning around her —

the blare of a car horn out on the street, the wail of sirens as they approached the hospital, and the sound of the breeze in the trees behind her. There was a faint smell of grass clippings in the area as if someone was mowing the lawn nearby. She listened but didn't hear any landscapers working.

Morgan pulled her knees up into her chest, hugging her arms around them. The images in her mind had settled into a dull roar rather than the screams she'd experienced upstairs. The girls in the hospital weren't much different than Danny. They were just teenagers trying to figure out where they fit and struggling to get through each day. None of them deserved what happened to them, especially if it wasn't a suicide attempt. Even if it was, Morgan couldn't imagine the terror that the parents were feeling for their kids right now.

Or maybe she could...

The memory of seeing Leo McDaniel with a knife to Danny's throat right before she killed him rose in her mind. At that moment she would have done anything — including sacrifice herself — to save her child.

But Katrina and Courtney's parents didn't have that option.

Unlike what happened to Danny, all Katrina and Courtney's parents could do was sit and wait. It reminded her of when her grandmother had died, the little family they had gathering around her Nana's bedside, waiting for her to take her last breath. The difference was, Morgan thought, picking at some of the grass underneath her fingers, that all Courtney and Katrina's parents wanted for their children was for them to wake up and for things to go back to normal, nagging their kids about their homework and what time they would be home, cheering them on their activities, and holding their hand and hugging them when someone at school wasn't as nice as maybe they could be. Morgan knew that feeling.

Morgan pulled her cell phone out of her pocket and sent a quick text to Danny, "Are you on your way to school?"

"Yeah. I'm just about to leave. How's Katrina?"

"The same," Morgan wrote back. Something in her wasn't ready to tell Danny about Courtney yet. The reality was she had no idea how Katrina was doing that morning. All she knew was that every moment got closer to them turning off the life support. She swallowed. Just thinking about it made her head spin again. Morgan closed her eyes for a second, putting her palms flat down on the grass, wrapping her fingers in the broad blades, taking a deep breath. She couldn't have another attack. She'd be no good to anyone if she did.

Shifting on the grass, she realized she needed to go back upstairs to see what was going on with both Katrina and Courtney. She lifted her chin, staring ahead of her. She'd run so fast out of the hospital she hadn't paid much attention to exactly what was around her other than the fact her truck was nearby. A few more cars had started to pull into the lots, the hum of their tires on the pavement. From where she sat, she had a view into the emergency room doors. A car had just pulled up front, a man helping his very pregnant wife into a wheelchair.

Morgan shook her head staring at the ground. She'd seen too much. She knew there was no way to protect people from the evil of the world, and when it came, sometimes it took brute force to protect the ones you loved. That was... if they could be protected. She hadn't been able to protect Peter or AJ. How could she think she'd be able to protect anyone else?

She stared at the ground again, wondering if she had any strength left to keep fighting. She glanced at her license plate on the truck. Feeling for the keys in her pocket, she realized she could just get up, slide into the truck and go home. She and Bo could go to the park or go for a walk. She could go grocery shopping, or try a few new recipes and have them ready before Danny came home from school.

But that didn't solve the questions of what had happened to Sarah, Maisie, Katrina, and now Courtney.

Struggling to her feet, Morgan reached for the tailgate on her truck, holding onto it, pushing off the last bit of dizziness swirling in her head. Her stomach lurched, as though she was going to throw up again, but she swallowed, managing to chase the nausea back down where it came from. Using the side of the truck for support, she walked to the driver's side door, opening it up, reaching in for her bottle of water. She leaned against the seat, uncapping the bottle and taking a sip. The water felt heavy in her mouth and in her stomach, but she took another drink, hoping that it would clear the nausea out of her system.

Slamming the truck door behind her, she started walking back towards the hospital, her head down, staring at the ground, focusing on taking one step at a time, putting one foot in front of the other. By the time she got to the main doors of the hospital and walked into the lobby, hearing the whoosh of the doors open and close around her as she passed through, she felt like her breath had finally settled back in her chest again. She stopped for a second and stared around her, blinking. Marianne, the older woman who had greeted her the other day was settling herself in at her computer, her name badge pinned to her chest. She looked at Morgan and gave her a little wave. Morgan lifted her hand in response. Morgan turned away, not wanting to get into a conversation with her.

As she walked towards the stairwell — there was no way she was ready to try the elevator again — she saw a bathroom. She darted in, walking to the sink, setting her bottle of water on the ledge in front of her. Turning on the cold water, she splashed her face a few times and then dried it off with a paper towel. Looking in the mirror, she could see red rings around her eyes from throwing up, her skin pale and drawn, the waves of her blonde hair wild around her head. To anyone else, she probably looked like someone who needed help. Maybe that was true.

But however she looked, she knew she had to get it together. Lives were on the line and the clock was ticking. There were only two possible answers for why there were now two girls from Palm Coast High School lying upstairs. It was either a suicide cluster or someone was behind it -- a deliberate act. Paul and Amber had asked for her help. So had Danny. She couldn't let them down.

Morgan ran the icy water one again and splashed more on her face, staring at herself in the mirror. The color had started to come back in her cheeks. She would be okay. She had to be okay.

Tossing the paper towel in the trash, she walked down the hallway, taking another sip of her water. Moving deliberately, she found the stairwell and opened the door, starting up the first flight. As she moved, she felt the blood start to circulate through her body again, her breathing slow and controlled. She turned past the second floor and then got to the third floor, pushing the door out into the lobby area just outside the PICU open. She stood frozen in front of the door, waiting. Did she have the strength to go inside the locked unit again?

"Morgan?" a gravelly voice said from behind her.

She whirled around, looking in the direction the sound came from. "Paul? I didn't expect to see you here so early."

A half-smile formed on his face, "Can't say I expected to see you here this early either." He furrowed his eyebrows, "Do you have news about Katrina's computer? You could have just called me."

Morgan motioned for the two of them to go sit in the lobby area by the windows where they'd sat a couple of days before. Slumping down into the couch, Morgan rested her full weight on it, closing her eyes for a second, fighting off another wave of nausea. When she opened them up, Paul was staring at her, a concerned look on his face. "What is it, Morgan?"

"Yes, I have a little information about Katrina's computer," she started, then glanced at the ground, "but the reason I'm here is that another girl like Katrina was brought into the PICU a few minutes ago."

Paul leaned back in his seat, cradling the cup of coffee he must've just gotten from the cafeteria in his hands, his eyes staring off into nowhere. He looked back at Morgan, "Another girl? You're sure?"

She nodded. "Yeah, I'm sure. I got a call from a friend at the police department a couple of hours ago. Told me they were transporting another girl and then it looked like an OD or suicide."

"But you're not so sure it is, are you?"

Morgan shook her head no. "As far as Katrina's computer goes, a friend of Danny's was able to hack into the two sites we found. One of them is a dating site. Nothing really to report there. She has a profile up, but not any real activity on her account. The other software we found on her computer, though..."

Paul narrowed his eyes, "I can tell by the look on your face there's more of a story with that one."

"Yeah. You could say that. It's an encrypted software messaging application called GenChat. The thing that's interesting about it is that everyone who uses it has to be invited. I didn't understand it at first, but once the boys explained it to me, it made sense. It's like an old-fashioned club where you have to be invited by a current member, but online. What happens is you have to have some sort of a code to register. You get that from someone you know." Morgan spent the next minute or so explaining to Paul how the families were arranged on the GenChat software.

Paul shook his head, a look of confusion spreading over his face. "I'm sorry. Maybe I'm just slow with this technology stuff, but how does that connect to Katrina? And what about the other girl you just mentioned to me? Was she on it, too?"

Morgan sighed, "I don't know, but that's a good question. What I do know is that everybody has a screen name and they know who is who in their group. If I could figure out who invited Katrina then maybe there might be a link to some of the other girls as well. But right now, I'm more concerned about what's going on with Courtney." Morgan licked her lips, "Do you know if Katrina had a friend named Courtney Reese?"

"Maybe?" Paul said. I've met a few of her friends when she's brought them by the house. There was this one girl. Yeah, I think her name might've been Courtney. She have dark hair?"

Morgan nodded.

"Yeah, maybe. They might have been friends then. Or maybe they just studied together? I don't know." Paul shrugged, a look of frustration on his face. "I don't understand how all of this high school stuff works and I certainly don't understand what's going on with my granddaughter right now." He stared at the ground as if there was a heavy weight on his shoulders.

Morgan looked at him, waiting. It could be difficult to understand what was going on with high schoolers. It was such a closed environment. They had their own culture and their own way of doing things, but it seemed like Paul was worried about something else. She tilted her head, "Paul? Is there something you're not telling me?"

He looked up at her, his lips pressed together, his face suddenly going pale, "We found out late last night that Katrina is pregnant."

Morgan's heart skipped a beat, "What? She's pregnant!?"

Paul nodded and then looked at the floor again, "Yeah. It's a very new pregnancy. According to the doctors, it may be a week or ten days old. I guess they were running some blood work and it came up."

Morgan got up and started to pace, pushing her hair away from her face with the palm of her hand. She turned to face Paul, "She doesn't have a boyfriend, does she?"

Paul shook his head no, his face gray.

"So, she got pregnant around the time that she overdosed? Is that what you're telling me?"

"Seems that's the case."

"Do you think she tried to kill herself because she thought she was pregnant?"

Paul shook his head, "There's no way she could have known. When the doctors came in and told us, they said it's some new test they have. She wouldn't have missed her cycle yet."

"There's no way she would have known she was pregnant. None at all."

"That's correct."

Morgan kept pacing, staring at the floor. Katrina was pregnant. Maybe that would buy them a little bit more time. She couldn't imagine that Paul's family would turn off life support on Katrina if they knew another life was involved, but that still didn't explain the timing of the pregnancy. Morgan's brain began to race. Was there some connection between the pregnancy and the overdose?

She stopped, staring at Paul, her chest tightening. "Listen, do you have the clothes that Katrina was wearing when they brought her to the hospital?"

Paul sighed, "Maybe. They might be in her room. I don't think my daughter-in-law took them home to wash them."

Morgan held her breath. She needed those clothes. "How about if we go to her room and take a look?"

Paul nodded. "Okay."

As they walked towards the sealed door to the PICU, Morgan's breath caught in her throat again. She paused for a second, closing her eyes. She forced her mind to think about walking into Katrina's room and retrieving the clothes. That's all she could handle at the moment.

The door whooshed open in front of them, the same cluster

of nurses and doctors working at the central station, the same monitors showing everyone's pulse, respiration, and blood pressure on the screens. Only one of the nurses looked up and waved at Paul as they walked by. The rest of them were huddled behind their computers, entering notes.

Walking down the hallway, the hubbub of Courtney Reese getting situated in her room had died down. The hallways were empty and dark again, a heavy silence hanging over the intensive care unit. Morgan shook her head a little as she followed Paul. It had to be confusing for the kids that were on the floor, with the light so low all the time. They probably had no idea whether it was daytime or nighttime, or why everyone around them seemed so serious and sad. The PICU seemed to exist somehow out of normal time, the shift changes of the doctors and nurses was the only way to mark the time as it progressed. Other than that, everything that happened there seemed to be encapsulated in its own world behind the sealed door.

The sealed door. Morgan drew in a sharp breath. She couldn't think of that now.

Morgan glanced into Courtney Reese's room as she followed Paul down the hallway. The parents were sitting next to Courtney, the mom holding her daughter's hand, the dad sitting stoically next to his wife. Something in Morgan wanted to go to them and to tell them how sorry she was and that she was trying to help, but there was no point. She didn't have anything helpful to tell them. And it wasn't like she was a detective anymore. It would cause confusion and nothing else. She stood and watched for another moment, barely breathing. Just like so many of the victims she'd worked with, there was an urgency in her to get them justice, but justice took time. She swallowed, looking at them. It might be time none of them had.

Realizing Paul had gotten well ahead of her, Morgan jogged a few steps to catch up as he disappeared inside Katrina's room. "Good morning, sunshine," Paul said, setting his coffee down on the table near the end of Katrina's bed. Morgan stood in the doorway, watching him. He walked over to Katrina's face, leaning over and planting a kiss on her forehead. "Grandpa is here. If you need anything at all, you just let me know, okay?" Katrina didn't stir.

Morgan swallowed. Watching him was heartbreaking. He was so composed, so calm. Maybe it was his military training. Maybe it was his age. Whatever it was that kept him together, Morgan didn't know. For a moment, she wished Charles was that genuine with Danny. She took a couple of steps into the room and looked more closely at Katrina. Her blonde hair had been arranged neatly around her face. It looked like someone had combed it for her, the strands silky next to the white pillowcase. Her eyes were closed, the sheen of something that looked like thick moisturizer coating them. Her lips were pink, closed around the ventilator tube. She looked peaceful; like she was just asleep. Morgan glanced at the IV poles. They were still filled with almost a dozen fluids prescribed for her, entering drip by drip. Part of her wanted to know what each of the medicines was supposed to do for her, but she knew it really wasn't any of her business.

Morgan glanced at Paul. He was opening drawers in a nightstand next to Katrina's bed. Out of one, he pulled a plastic bag. He looked at Morgan, "Here. These must be the clothes she was wearing when she came in. Doesn't look like anybody's done anything with them yet." He handed Morgan a clear plastic bag.

Morgan took it from him, looking at it. She didn't open it, not wanting to risk contaminating what was inside. A pair of jeans and a T-shirt, a pair of shoes, and some underwear were visible through the plastic. They were rumpled, not folded, as if someone had hastily shoved them inside while they were working on saving Katrina's life. "Thanks. Is it okay for me to take these to a friend? She might be able to help."

Paul set his jaw before answering, "Yes. Whatever will get us answers." He gave her a short nod as if he had just given her orders for a mission, "I'll leave you to it. Let me know as soon as you find out anything."

"Copy that." Morgan turned on her heel and walked out of the PICU. She knew what she needed to do next.

14

"Meet me at Sylvia's."

Morgan sent the text without any other explanation. Amber would be able to tell by her tone that it was an emergency.

Morgan dropped her cell phone into the cup holder in the truck, tossing the bag of Katrina's clothes on the passenger seat as she started the engine. A steady stream of cars was rolling into the hospital, people coming to visit loved ones or people who had procedures scheduled for that day. Morgan wove her way through traffic, fighting off the urge to lay on her horn. She hated hospitals. Everything in her wanted to leave St. Anne's and never come back. Somehow, she wasn't sure that was going to be in the cards.

Driving to the Medical Examiner's Office, Morgan left the windows down, letting the tropical morning air circulate through the truck, feeling the gathering humidity collecting on her skin. She hoped it would get the smell of the hospital off of her. Taking a deep breath in, she glanced down at her phone. No answer from Amber. Hopefully, she would get the message and meet her there. If not, it didn't matter. She'd talk to Sylvia on her own.

The drive between St. Anne's Medical Center and the County Medical Examiner's Office took about twenty-five minutes. It was time that Morgan was grateful for. Taking a few sips of her water as she drove, she stared ahead, trying hard not to think about anything she'd seen or experienced in the last couple of days. It was one thing to work a case as a detective, she realized. She'd always had the benefit of showing up after things happened. There was no emotionality to it, except for the victim's feelings, which had to be managed, but she'd never gotten caught up in such a raw case before, that was until it became personal with the Sons of Goliath. She swallowed, thinking. She remembered how she'd been able to go to a murder scene, have it processed, and then go home and make dinner for her family like nothing had happened. Where she'd lost that ability to compartmentalize, she wasn't sure. Or maybe she did know. She'd lost it inside that trailer she'd been locked in.

Now everything seemed personal.

About two miles from the Medical Examiner's Office, Morgan passed an elementary school. Class must have just been getting ready to start. There was a stream of yellow buses parked in front of the school, kids flooding into the building, adults holding the doors open and waving the kids inside, their blue and pink and green backpacks dotting the sidewalks like confetti. As she stopped for a red light, she could hear the noise of their chatter and giggles, the occasional sound of a parent or teacher calling to one of the kids. Her heart ached. She longed for that kind of simplicity.

Pulling into the parking lot at Sylvia's office, Morgan looked around for a car that could be Amber's. Her personal car wasn't there, not that Morgan expected her to drive one. She'd likely come in a navy-blue detective unit from the department.

Morgan pulled into a spot, checking her phone again. Still no message from Amber. She shook her head, getting out of the truck and grabbing the bag. Slamming the door behind her, she walked towards the entrance, going inside the front door.

Morgan hadn't been in the Medical Examiner's Office since she'd gone to West Virginia. It looked like they'd updated the sitting area, wide windows inviting the sunshine in, new couches and carpeting looking a little bit more welcoming than the drab beige furniture she remembered. A long hallway extended in front of her. At the end of it, she saw somebody walk by in a white coat. Morgan jogged down the hallway, trying to catch up. "Excuse me?" she said.

It was a young man, wearing jeans and a polo shirt underneath his lab coat. He didn't stop moving, not bothering to look at her. "I'm sorry, if you have an appointment, you'll have to wait out front. Someone will be up to help you in a minute."

Just as Morgan was about to say something, she heard a voice behind her, "Hey, Jake. That's no way to treat my friend."

Morgan spun around. Amber was walking down the hallway, wearing a cognac-colored jacket and pants with a charcoal-colored T-shirt underneath. The slogan on the front of the T-shirt read, "It's all good" in white letters. Amber's hair was up in a high ponytail, the long strands trailing down her back, the kiss of pale pink lip gloss on her lips, a rim of black liner on her eyes. "This is Detective Foster. I don't think you guys have met before."

"Oh," a flash passed over his face. "Sorry about that. It's nice to meet you."

Morgan couldn't tell by his reaction if the "oh" was because he knew her name or because he didn't know she had been a detective. Had been. Why Amber had introduced her that way, she wasn't sure. She felt heat in her cheeks, a nervous smile pulling at her face. She shook off the thought. It didn't matter.

Amber looked at him, "Is Sylvia in her office?"

"Yeah," he nodded, pointing. "She told me she's got some paperwork to do. I think she's hunkered down with her first cup of coffee."

"Thanks," Amber said, starting down the hallway.

Morgan followed. "I wasn't sure you got my text."

Amber glanced over her shoulder, smiling, "I did. I was just in the middle of this," she motioned to her clothes and makeup. "Not all of us are natural beauties like you, Morgan."

Morgan groaned, remembering what she'd looked like in the mirror at the hospital after throwing up in the parking lot. That was a story for another day.

Stopping in front of a closed door, Amber looked back at Morgan. "You didn't say why we're here. I'm guessing that bag you're holding has something to do with that, huh?"

Morgan raised her eyebrows "Wow. You should become a detective."

Amber's laughter filled the hallway as she pushed the door to Sylvia's office open.

Dr. Sylvia Knapp's office was functional and that was it. There was a desk in the center of the room with two plastic chairs, just like the ones she'd sat in at the PICU, a computer on her desk, and a bookshelf pushed against the wall. There weren't any pictures or rugs or anything to make the space feel homier. It was as bare and clinical as the autopsy room. For a second, Morgan wondered if Sylvia's house looked the same.

"I didn't know you guys were coming to visit this morning," Sylvia said, setting down the mug of coffee in front of her.

Morgan could smell the dark roast across the room. Her stomach rumbled. "Sorry about the intrusion. It's on me. I need your help." She set the bag of clothes in front of Sylvia in the middle of her desk.

"What are these?"

"The clothes Katrina DeLuca was wearing when she came into the hospital."

A frown passed over Sylvia's face, "Did she pass?"

Morgan shook her head, "No. They just found out she's pregnant."

"What?" Amber said, leaning her palms on the desk. "When did they find out?"

"Late last night. I bumped into Paul DeLuca at the hospital while I was checking on Courtney Reese this morning. He said the doctors found the pregnancy in a blood test yesterday. I guess they were checking her levels and it just popped up. They don't think she could be more than a week or ten days pregnant at this point. She wouldn't have even missed her cycle yet."

Sylvia raised her eyebrows, "So much for an unwanted pregnancy as the motivation for suicide," she frowned, glancing at the bag. "I'm assuming you want these tested?"

"I do." Morgan looked at the two women, realizing she had no power to ask either of them to do anything. She swallowed, the weight of the fact that she was no longer with the Tampa Police Department hitting her like a ton of bricks. "I mean, I'm requesting it. I realize I -- "

Amber waved her off, "You're one of us, Morgan. Whether you're on the payroll or not, it doesn't matter. You're still one of us."

Morgan looked down at the floor. It was nice that Amber said it, but was it actually true? Did she want it to be?

From inside her desk drawer, Sylvia pulled out a set of gloves and a large plastic bag with red tape at one end. "I'm gonna go ahead and process this like it's evidence just in case we find something."

Morgan and Amber stood silent for a second, watching as Sylvia pushed the plastic bag of clothes inside the larger evidence bag, pulling the red tape and sealing it. Using a pen, both Amber and Sylvia signed it.

Morgan watched them for a second. "How fast can you

figure out if there was some sort of sexual component to what happened to Katrina?"

"Come with me."

Morgan drifted behind Amber and Sylvia as they moved down the hallway. Sylvia had on a matching lab coat to the one Jake was wearing when they arrived, the peek of a set of navy-blue scrubs underneath, heavy black work shoes jutting out from the bottom of the cuffs.

Inside the autopsy room, Sylvia flipped on a set of switches that were near the door, the blinding fluorescent lights filling the space. Morgan stood in the doorway for a second, staring, waiting for her eyes to adjust. She watched as Sylvia and Amber walked over to one of the five stainless steel tables laid out in the line across the width of the room, each of them scrubbed completely clean, the metal shining under the lights.

Morgan pressed her lips together and then walked over to the table. Looking down, she realized her hands were shaking a little. She balled them into fists and shoved them into her pockets. The last time she'd been in the morgue was to see AJ's body after the Sons of Goliath had blown him up. Memories of that day streamed into her mind, the smell of the disinfectant, the white sheet pulled over his body, the way the previous coroner had asked her again and again if she was sure she wanted to see him in that state. A part of her now wished she hadn't. His body had been ripped apart by the pipe bomb the motorcycle gang had left for him, incinerating one of his arms, only shreds of skin dangling from his shoulder and destroying part of his face, brain matter exposed across his forehead. Seeing his body torn up had fueled her obsession to get Leo McDaniel and his cronies, to bring them to justice. Now that Leo was dead, all she was left with was the deep grief she felt at losing AJ and Peter.

Morgan glanced at the floor for a second, trying to steady herself and then looked at Amber and Sylvia. She took two steps closer to the table, resting her hands on the edge of the stainless steel. Sylvia had opened the evidence bag and was laying out the clothes from Katrina's room. Morgan watched as she worked, Sylvia's hands moving deliberately, slowly, laying out the fabric as if there was a body still inside of them, smoothing out the wrinkles as she did. "Gimme a sec," she said, pulling off the gloves and walking to the doorway. She hit a buzzer.

By the time Sylvia walked back to the table and put on a new set of gloves, Jake appeared at the door, "You called, Doc?"

"Yes. I need you to photograph these and start a data file for me in case we need to send them out."

Jake nodded, pulling on a pair of gloves and grabbing a clipboard that had a stack of white forms on it. From a nearby shelf, he reached for an oversized digital camera with a long lens with his other hand. He ambled up to the table, cocking his head to the side, "Who's the victim?"

"Katrina DeLuca. Make sure you mark her as hospitalized. She hasn't passed. We're going to do a quick test here and if we find anything then we'll have to pack this up and send it off to BCI for further testing."

Jake nodded, taking pictures of the clothes that had been artfully arranged on the table. Morgan took a step back, crossing her arms over her chest. There seem to be two speeds in police work — breakneck pace and slower than a snail. Being back in Tampa, the more she remembered how the pace changed from moment to moment. She remembered times when she was driving so fast to get to a scene that it was impossible to think she wouldn't get killed herself, the lights and sirens the only thing preventing her from getting in an accident on the way. On the flip side, once the crisis was over it was as if everything stopped while reports were written and evidence was collected, that was except for the adrenaline surge that seemed to hit every officer differently.

Watching Sylvia and Jake, Morgan remembered that unlike law enforcement, forensic work was snail's pace. Always.

Capturing the pictures took a few more minutes, Sylvia carefully flipping the clothing over so Jake could photograph the back of it, the two of them mumbling to each other as they moved each piece. Amber stepped back and stood next to Morgan, shoving her hands in the pockets of her dress pants. "Miss this?"

Morgan glanced at Amber, licking her lips, "I don't know. Maybe. I miss the people, but the heartbreak? I'm not so sure." She couldn't think too deeply about what Amber was asking her. She wasn't exactly concerned about her career path at the moment. All she wanted was answers for Paul's family.

As Jake finished up the first set of pictures, Sylvia flipped the clothes back over again, as if Katrina's body was lying face-up on the table. "Okay, this is the fun part," she said, waving Morgan and Amber back to the side of the table. "Jake, get the lights?"

"Sure," he said, setting down the camera and walking over to the doorway. The room was plunged into blackness for a second before Sylvia clicked on a single light. A purple glow pointed out of the end of a flashlight. "All right. Now the proof is in the pudding. Let's check these clothes and see if we find anything suspicious."

Morgan stood at the edge of the stainless-steel table, her fingers wrapped around the rim. Sylvia's purple flashlight started moving over the clothing, focusing on her pants and underwear. Flipping the material inside out, she directed the violet UV light on the surface of the interior of Katrina's jeans. Sylvia pointed to the inside of the denim, near the seam that ran under her legs. "See that?"

Morgan and Amber leaned forward. Morgan could see a white stain near the area where Katrina's inner thighs would have been. "Is that...?" Amber frowned.

"I'm guessing it's semen, but let's check her underwear."

Sylvia held up Katrina's jeans under the light as Jake took a few pictures, documenting what they'd found. He gave her a brief nod, putting the camera down. He folded the jeans neatly, leaving Katrina's T-shirt, bra, and underwear on the table. Sylvia flipped Katrina's underwear inside out and pointed the light at the fabric, the purple glow covering it. There was another white stain in the center of the crotch. She held it up for Jake, who took a few more pictures and then gave him a nod, "Lights, please."

Jake stepped away and flipped on the lights, nearly blinding Morgan. She closed her eyes for a second, staring at the ground before glancing back at Sylvia, who was stripping off her gloves. "Well, this changes things. I'm gonna have to bag these up and send them to BCI and see what they can find out."

Morgan's head was reeling, a tightness passing across her chest. She stared at Siliva and Amber, who had grown quiet. "This looks like a sex crime now, not just a suicide," Morgan said. She held her breath for a second, wondering if Sylvia and Amber felt the same way. They had to. They couldn't argue with the results of the UV test, could they? It's what the evidence was saying.

Sylvia's face hardened, as if truth was hitting her square in the chest. "I don't want to get ahead of myself, but there's definitely evidence of some sort of a sexual component. Given the fact that these are the clothes she showed up at the hospital in, I would think we could make the argument that the overdose and the fluid samples left behind happened at the same time."

Morgan shook her head, her face getting hot. "How can we think anything different? I mean, it's right there! Someone took advantage of Katrina, either before or after she got knocked out."

"That's certainly how it appears, but we need more

evidence, Morgan," Sylvia's voice was low, not much above a whisper.

Morgan turned away for a second, feeling like she had just gotten caught stealing a piece of candy. That was the one thing about forensic scientists. It was always the same — evidence, evidence, evidence. They weren't even willing to make a basic jump in logic a lot of the time. She remembered how many times she'd been infuriated when it was clear that a crime was been committed, but the coroner or the DA or someone else said they didn't have enough to move forward on the case. Listening to Sylvia's caution-filled tone was irritating at best. Morgan drew in a deep breath, trying to calm herself down. She had to remember she was a guest in the Medical Examiner's Office, not a detective. Not anymore. She shoved her hands in her pockets and waited, then spoke.

"If this is a sex crime, then what about the other girls? What about Sarah Poole and Maisie Hill? Is it possible those incidents were more than just suicides, just like Katrina?" Morgan held her breath. She knew she was treading on thin ice insinuating that Sylvia might have missed something in her autopsy. The beginning of a good friendship might be over before it started.

Sylvia looked down for a second then at both Amber and Morgan. "The thing is, we didn't do an autopsy on either Sarah Poole or Maisie Hill. If I remember right, both girls were transported to the hospital and the doctors just chalked it up to suicide. I know I never saw them."

"That's correct," Amber said. "Why Ben didn't ask for an autopsy, I have no idea. Seems like a slip if you ask me." She shook her head, "But now that we know Katrina DeLuca has evidence of seminal fluid on her clothes and she's pregnant, what are our options on the forensic side with the other two girls? Can we have her examined now?"

That was the million-dollar question. Morgan was glad Amber asked it before she did.

Sylvia sat down on a stool that was near the head of the stainless-steel table where they'd been standing. Jake moved around them, folding the clothes and putting them back in the evidence bag. He held it out for Sylvia to sign. "Well, the first step is to get this off to BCI. In terms of examining Katrina now, I think it's been too long. Anything that was on her would either have degraded or been compromised. BCI is our best bet."

Morgan knew that BCI, the Bureau of Criminal Investigation, had sophisticated technology that the county labs just didn't have. "What are you hoping they will find on Katrina's clothes?"

"The first thing they'll do is run an acid phosphatase test to make sure what we saw is seminal fluid. After that, they can send a sample to their DNA specialists if there's sperm in the semen."

"And if there isn't?" Amber said, fiddling with her ponytail.

"If there isn't, then there will be no DNA evidence. In locker room jargon, it's called 'shooting blanks,' if you know what I mean." A smile crept across her face. She held up her hand, "Sorry, that's something I learned from my son when he was in high school."

"And if they do find DNA evidence?" Morgan asked.

"Then they'll run it against the database. The thing is, we don't have DNA for every single person in this country. We have access to the DNA databases from the local, state, and federal governments, but that only represents a small portion of the population. You can imagine what a constitutional crisis it would cause if we required everyone to submit their DNA."

Morgan raised her eyebrows. Sylvia was right about that. She knew what it meant to be sensitive to privacy, especially after being in witness protection for a couple of years. Privacy was everything. That wasn't the most important question on her mind. She stared at Sylvia, "But what about the other girls, Sylvia? If you didn't examine them, then what?" Morgan knew the answer to the question, but she wanted to see what Sylvia would say.

"Well, the only way for me to examine them at this point is if we had them exhumed. You know that takes a court order, and we'd have to be relatively sure the cases are linked."

Amber started pacing next to the table, "I think we have a good argument to get the order. We've got at least two other victims from the same high school, kids that are about the same age, that have died within a short amount of time. I mean, wouldn't the CDC want to have firm evidence it was a suicide cluster in the area and not something else?"

"Like a serial killer?" Morgan blurted out.

Quiet descended over the autopsy room for a second. It felt like the three of them had been dancing around the obvious for days. They'd been so focused on the fact that ODs and suicide were prevalent in high school they missed one of the most logical, but devastating, explanations. It was possible someone was targeting the girls and had taken them out, one by one. A shiver ran down Morgan's spine. She'd only been back in Tampa for a couple of months and here she was, in the middle of trying to solve something that was way above her pay grade, especially given she had no pay grade anymore.

Sylvia was the first to speak, shaking her head from side to side, "I think it's enough to get the judge to order the exhumation, but I gotta tell you, this kind of process is really tough on the families."

Morgan pressed her lips together, staring at Sylvia. Didn't she want to get the answers? Morgan spoke, choosing her words carefully. "I get that, but Sylvia, these families want answers. I talked to both of them and these moms are really upset. They don't understand what happened to their daugh-

ters. I even talked to their therapist. Off the record, he told me
he didn't think either of the girls was suicidal."

Amber looked at her, her eyes wide, "You did what?"

Morgan glanced at the ground, "Yeah, sorry. Forgot to tell
you that part. I kind of have a relationship with him. Danny's
been seeing him since we got back into town." She skipped the
part about how she'd barged into his office and demanded
answers. "He said if we wanted anything formal, we'd have to
provide him with a subpoena."

Amber chuckled, "Man, you're not even on the job anymore
and you're making waves!"

Sylvia raised her eyebrows, "Speaking of which, if we go
forward with this, what's the response gonna be from your
department, Amber?"

Amber stopped pacing for a second, staring at the other two
women. She raised her eyebrows, "With Ben Acosta, you
mean?"

Sylvia nodded, "From what you've told me, he thinks these
cases are closed. Is it gonna rattle some cages if you move
forward on this without him?"

Amber pursed her lips and nodded. "Probably. I'll go call
the captain and see what he says."

Morgan's eyes followed Amber as she walked out of the
autopsy room, leaving Morgan alone with Sylvia. Sylvia leaned
behind her and grabbed a bottle of cleaner, spraying the table
down, putting on another pair of blue gloves and wiping the
surface with a paper towel until it was dry. "Thanks for taking a
look at this," Morgan said, hoping to smooth over any feathers
she'd ruffled.

"Yeah, sure." Sylvia glanced at her and then sat back down
on the stool, "One other thing. I got a call from the hospital.
One of the other girls came in with strange blisters on her skin.
Keep an eye out for that, okay? Could be a transdermal delivery
system." Sylvia tossed the towels in the trash, "If Amber can get

this cleared through her department, I'll take care of the paper-work this morning, call the families and get the order from Judge Green. He's got teenage girls. I'm sure he wouldn't want someone out there targeting his daughters."

Morgan frowned, "And then what?"

"Jake and I get to work."

15

It had been one of the longest days of her life and the day had hardly begun, Candace thought, slumping down behind the expansive mahogany desk in her office. She'd been up at four o'clock in the morning, which wasn't unusual, except that she had to deal with production issues from their facilities in the Pacific rim. There was a string of problems with their machinery. A complete shutdown of production. Unlike the States, where repairs moved along at a rapid pace, it looked like at least one of the plants would be down for at least a week, slowing production to a complete halt.

That would not be good news to her Board of Directors.

More than anything, Candace just wanted the problem to go away. But everything she suggested to get the problem fixed didn't seem doable. She stared at her phone, her face hot. There had to be a way to get production up and running again faster than an entire week. That represented millions of dollars in loss, not to mention the delay in the supply chain getting BioNova's medications back to the States for sale. Candace sent a text to the VP of Operations for the Pacific Division, Keith

Reynolds, "Get on a plane. I need you in India to sort out these problems with production now. We are hemorrhaging money."

She was sure he wouldn't want to go, but that was the job. A second later, she got a text back, "No problem. I'll let you know when I land."

Candace closed her eyes for a moment and then opened them, staring out the window. At least one hassle was handled. It wasn't the only one in front of her. She had a Board of Directors meeting coming up in forty-eight hours. They expected to have an update on the expansion on the progress of several of their new drugs, including one that was coming out of the lab where Justin had his internship. She'd hoped, at the time she placed him, that he would keep an eye on the progress of the drug for her, feeding her information even before Dr. McCall provided his reports, but Justin was useless, as usual. She knew he spent a lot of hours there, but trying to get him to talk about it was something else. Drumming her fingers on the desk, she considered buying him a new car to get him to talk, but lately, he'd seemed even more surly than usual, not wanting to have any conversations with her at all and staying in his room most of the time if he wasn't at school or at the lab. In the past, she'd been able to lure him to spend time with her by offering to take him to his favorite restaurants, but no more. He wasn't interested.

Candace had just turned back to her computer, smoothing the black skirt over her knees, when a knock came at her door. "Come!"

The thick wooden door that separated her office from her assistant pushed open. Nate Ambrose poked his head in, his voice quiet, "You have a couple of minutes for me?"

Candace waved him in, her eyes settling back on her email. Nate was one of the few people she let come to her office without an appointment. As the Chief of Security for BioNova, if he had something to say, she needed to hear it. There were always people, agents from other companies, posing at salesmen, consultants, and technicians who were trying to get a look at what their labs were developing. She closed the lid of her laptop, turning towards him as he pushed the door open, folding her hands on the desk. Dr. Andrew McCall followed. Candace furrowed her eyebrows only slightly. She'd gotten good at keeping her facial expressions to a minimum. It was normal to see Nate in her office, but Dr. McCall, not so much. She kept her face still, her gaze steady.

"I didn't expect to see you this morning," Candace sniffed.

"Sorry for the intrusion, but Dr. McCall and I wanted to pass along a few concerns he has to you."

Candace narrowed her eyes. Anytime someone said they had concerns, it set off alarm bells inside of her. The way Nate phrased it, she could tell he was playing along with Andrew, but didn't totally believe what the researcher was thinking. She kept her face steady, not allowing her expression to change. When she became CEO of BioNova, no one told her she needed to have one of the best poker faces in the business, but after a few years in the role, she'd mastered taking all sorts of news — the good and the bad — without flinching. Something in her gut told her Nate was bringing her flinch-worthy information.

"What's on your mind? I have a few minutes to talk, but I'm preparing for a Board meeting, so if we could get to the point, that would be helpful." She motioned to the two leather chairs in front of her desk, giving them permission to sit.

"Well," Nate said, glancing at Dr. McCall, "Andrew came to my office last week with some concerns. He thought maybe he was imagining things and wanted to get my take on it, but it's a sensitive subject. I've spent a considerable amount of time looking into the problem, but we thought it best if we brought it to you and let you handle it directly."

Candace moved her folded hands from her desk onto her

lap where she clenched them into fists. "What kind of information are we talking about?"

Dr. McCall cleared his throat, "As you know, we don't keep extremely tight reins on the number and amounts of chemical agents we use in the lab. As you have said to me many times, if we had to account for every drop of alcohol or hydrogen peroxide, that would slow the work down, which obviously isn't the goal. But I have had my project managers tracking the amounts of certain compounds we keep in the lab for the last six months. Three of them — cyclohexanone, etomidate, and methohexital — have been disappearing a little faster than we would expect. One of my project managers came to me late last week and said he'd noticed there had been a spike in usage. We've definitely been running out of it faster than usual. He'd been walking around the lab watching, to see where the chemicals were going, but hadn't been able to figure it out. Nate had given me access to watch the video feed from inside the lab. I'm sorry to say I think we have someone in the lab who is using the compounds. The problem is it doesn't seem to be for the project that we've been assigned."

Candace frowned. She could tell by the way they were dancing around the subject they were avoiding telling her what was going on. If it was one of the senior project managers, that wasn't a problem, she would just replace them. Even if it was one of the senior researchers, she didn't care. Candace didn't say anything for a second, running through the list of employees she knew about that were working on Dr. McCall's project. She knew some of them, but not all. "That's a serious allegation, but I'm glad that you brought it to me. As you know, I always have an open-door policy for issues like this. Controlling the use of our compounds is critical. Do you have any suspicion that the missing chemicals have left the building?"

Nate cocked his head to the side, "I can't give you a firm answer on that one way or the other. What I can tell you for sure is that we have certain amounts of chemicals that are unaccounted for. When we compare what's been logged in the experiments to the stock on hand, it should match. It doesn't."

Candace gave him a sharp nod. In the first few months after Nate started working as her chief of security, he'd brought her too many theories about security breaches at BioNova, not enough of them laced with actionable facts. She tamped down that bad habit before it got out of hand. Now, when he came to her with a concern, he was clear about where his evidence ended and his suspicions started. "Let's not waste any more time. If you have an idea who is behind the missing chemicals, now's the time to tell me."

Dr. McCall looked down at his lap. "I'm sorry, Candace, but I think it's Justin."

"Justin?" Candace said the word slowly, disbelief running over her. She pressed her lips together. "And you have specific evidence of this, Dr. McCall? You've seen it on video or security has caught him with bottles of chemicals stuffed in his pants on his way out of the building?" Her tone was sarcastic, cutting.

"Not exactly," Andrew stammered, his face becoming pale. "I mean, he's the only one that's left in the lab at night by himself. He's there for hours. Based on the feed, I can see him walking back and forth in the lab."

Candace leaned forward over her desk, "But can you actually see him doing anything wrong?"

Andrew blinked, "No. I just see him moving around the lab like he's doing something at a work table. It's like he's in a blind spot in the lab."

"But you don't have any actual evidence?"

Andrew shook his head. "I'm sorry, I realize Justin is your son, but I thought you should know. I've known everyone else on the team for years. I can't imagine they would —"

Candace interrupted, "Maybe this isn't about missing chemicals in your lab at all, Andrew," she said, her eyes boring into him. "Maybe this is because you know I need that drug finished and you haven't figured it out yet."

"We're on the alpha seven derivative. We're seeing great promise. I'm getting ready to test —"

"You're fired."

As soon as the words came out of Candace's mouth, she looked away. Her exterior might have looked calm, but inside, her blood boiled. How dare Andrew McCall come into her office and accuse her son of doing something wrong when he was the one that was behind on his development schedule. It had been a mistake putting McCall in charge of AnoVest, a mistake that could cost them millions of dollars in development time. The Board would question her about this. It wouldn't go well. They didn't like delays.

"But I didn't do anything wrong! It's your son that's the problem. I know it!"

Without saying anything else, Candace reached over and pressed a button on her phone. Dr. McCall kept stammering, standing up and pacing, waving his hands at her. Candace glanced at Nate, who had uncrossed his legs. He looked like he was ready to jump into action. A knock came at the door. "Come!"

A mountain-sized man with dark hair and matching dark skin appeared in the doorway, wearing a black suit, his jacket buttoned, making the bulge of his pistol at his side only slightly visible. "Reggie, could you please escort Dr. McCall to his lab and help him pack up his items? He's been terminated. Please have him out of the building within the hour."

"Yes ma'am," Reggie nodded. He glanced at Dr. McCall, whose arms had slumped to his side seeing the giant of a man appear in the doorway. "Come on, Dr. McCall. Let's go gather up your stuff and get you to your car." His voice was soothing, even conciliatory. Candace tried not to smile. People always had that response around Reggie. It was as if they knew they lost the fight before there ever was one. He was so big, their only option was to comply. She liked compliance, it made her job easier.

The door clicking closed behind her, Candace turned her gaze to Nate. "Do you believe all of this nonsense he was spewing?"

Nate shrugged, looking at the floor and then back at her. "Not really. I watched the videos he sent me, but I didn't see anything. I can't imagine Justin would be involved in any kind of trouble. He's a real hard worker, just like his mom."

Candace felt her face start to relax a little bit. She smoothed the fabric of her skirt again, staring at her lap for a moment. "Even if Andrew had the suspect wrong, he might be right about the lab. Can you take a look into it and let me know what you find?"

Nate nodded, standing up. "Of course. Let me get to work on it. I'll get you an update as soon as I have something." As he walked to the door, he turned around, his hand resting on the thick wood, "And say hi to Justin for me. I haven't seen him in a while. I'll have to drop by the lab and say hello."

Candace nodded, lifting the lid to her laptop. Now, in addition to preparing for the Board of Directors meeting she had in two days' time, she'd have to find a new head of research for AnoVest. The hits just kept on coming.

16

Sitting in Candace's office always gave Nate exactly the feeling that something was crawling up his spine. He felt like he was trapped in a scene from a movie with aliens, the kind that appeared to be human, but weren't. Candace was otherworldly, that was for sure. No matter what happened, she was calm, eerily so.

Nate lifted his hand and half waved to Candace's assistant of the week on his way out of the office, a young man wearing a perfectly pressed suit jacket and tie with a matching pocket square, his hair clipped short, hunched over his computer. Candace went through assistants faster than he went through socks, it seemed. Nate had given up trying to keep track of their names.

Pushing the door to the waiting room open, he turned right leaving Candace's suite of offices and strode down the hallway to the stairwell. When he'd first started as the Chief of Security, Candace had offered him space in her suite, an office that wasn't quite as large and opulent as hers, but similar. He'd declined, wanting something a little bit more private and out-of-the-way, explaining that it was better for the Chief of Security to be under the radar. Having a prominent place in her suite of offices wouldn't give him the type of invisibility he needed in order to do his job well. She acquiesced, grudgingly, shrugging at his refusal. The assistant at the time had walked him around the building, showing him three other available offices. The last one was the one he chose. It was at the far end of the building, down a long hallway where only half of the offices were occupied. It was the largest of the three they offered, in the corner of the building, with two banks of square windows on either wall. The view wasn't much, just the BioNova parking lot, but in the distance, he could see some trees.

Using his key card to get into his office, he heard the door beep and click open. Pushing it open, he felt a sense of relief when the door closed behind him. Being the Chief of Security for BioNova wasn't all that it was cracked up to be. He felt like he was constantly dealing with a stream of corporate espionage issues, rowdy personnel that was unhappy about their raises, or worse, workplace love affairs that went south.

Dropping into the chair behind his desk, Nate stared at the ceiling. Just the week before, he had a couple, a man that worked in the HR department and a woman from finance who had a bad breakup and decided to get into a near fistfight in the parking lot. He'd called the Tampa Police Department, had them arrested, and promptly fired both of them. Their department heads weren't happy, but Candace had given him the authority to eliminate people that were causing distractions at work without question. They'd both broken the terms of their work contracts by being arrested, worse yet, it was on-site, right in front of him. As the police cars pulled away, carrying the newly former employees, Nate remembered standing with his arms crossed across his chest, looking at Reggie, "If nothing else, it's always interesting, isn't it?"

Reggie nodded, his big head bobbing up and down on his thick neck, "Sure is."

"How about if you go grab somebody from HR and get their offices cleaned out. Have their division heads call them and tell them to come back tomorrow to get their belongings. We'll leave them at the main security desk. I don't want them to come any farther into the building than that."

"Copy that."

"And remember to document everything. You know these people get lawsuit happy."

Sitting at his desk after meeting with Candace, Nate crossed his foot across his ankle, staring outside. From where he sat, the only thing he could see was the sky, a few errant clouds floating past. The day had started off clear, but with the Florida weather, rain could be coming at any minute, driving the humidity up, even in the early fall weather.

Twisting in his chair, Nate opened up his laptop, keying in a PIN and then pressing his thumb across the reader. His mind circled back to the information Dr. McCall had shared. Candace was right. They didn't have anything concrete to go to her with. Nate had told Dr. McCall that, but he'd insisted on telling Candace. Now he'd lost his job. Predictable. Candace didn't like any type of disruption, especially one she didn't start herself.

Nate shook his head, drumming his fingers on the desk. Something in his gut told him that if there was any truth to what Dr. McCall had said, Nate was the only one who could find out. He opened the video access portal on his laptop. From his office, he had direct access to the servers where all of the video was held for the nearly five hundred cameras that were placed around the campus. The only areas of the building that didn't have surveillance were the interior of the bathrooms -- by

law they weren't allowed to invade people's privacy that way --
and Candace's office. She claimed she needed privacy for her
business negotiations. Nate wasn't sure he believed that. His
own office was the final exception, although no one knew. After
working for BioNova for a couple of months, Nate had come in
on a weekend and disabled the surveillance cameras in his
office, as well as the microphones. It was one thing to be the
Chief of Security. It was something else entirely to be the focal
point of that security effort. He'd never told anyone about it
and no one had ever asked. There were so many cameras with
so much information coming to his team on a daily basis that
missing an office here or there wasn't a big deal.

Until it was.

Nate pulled up the video surveillance of Dr. McCall's lab.
The live feed popped up almost immediately on his screen. He
slid the images over to an external monitor that took up most of
his desk. It was big enough to allow him to watch four different
feeds at one time instead of having to squint on his laptop. He
leaned forward, frowning. At that very moment, Dr. McCall was
in his office, filling boxes. Reggie was leaning against the door,
watching him. Nate checked the time on his cell phone. By his
progress, he'd be out of the building well ahead of Candace's
one-hour deadline. Not that she'd know anyways. She was
probably still hunkered down in her office putting out fires or
schmoozing a Board member.

Nate cracked his neck and rolled his shoulders. No matter
how long he worked for BioNova, he still didn't like conflict.
Part of his job was avoiding it at all costs. He slipped off his suit
coat and continued watching the video feed for another
minute. He had on a pale blue button-down shirt. He never
wore a tie. Hated them. As far as he was concerned, it was a
security threat. The last thing he needed was some joker trying
to grab it and hang him up while he was trying to get the

person out of the building. Although his guys wore ties, most of them wore clip-ons. All of the guys working for BioNova security were either former police or former military. They knew better. Nate was too — he'd been a Marine for four years after going to college, part of the University of Alabama's ROTC program. He never saw combat, only spending his time in the Psy-Ops Division, running psychological profiles on terrorists and warlords the Marines were targeting.

Nate glanced back at the feed. As he unbuttoned his cuffs and rolled them up above his forearms, he saw Reggie was escorting Dr. McCall out of the office. Reggie had a stack of two boxes cradled in his thick arms. Dr. McCall had one, his head hanging low. Nate watched them as they walked down the hallway, stood in the elevator, and then emerged on the first floor. The lobby cameras caught Dr. McCall's final exit. Dr. McCall and Reggie stopped at the security station where Andrew surrendered his badge, his posture straight and stiff. Nate watched as Reggie followed Andrew outside into the parking lot, still carrying the boxes. A minute later, the cameras captured Dr. McCall driving off the property, Reggie giving him a wave with his meaty hand as he pulled away.

Shaking his head, Nate leaned back in the chair. It hadn't been his decision to fire Andrew, but part of him wondered if Candace had been right about it. Nate had given a hard look at the video clips Andrew had brought to him — all of their department heads and research team leads had access to the video feeds in their own departments -- but not building-wide like Nate and his team. Andrew had been so insistent that it was Justin that was the problem, that even when Nate suggested that they perhaps should look into it further, he refused. He wanted to go to Candace directly.

And now he was out of a job.

Andrew's fatal mistake was accusing Candace's son of being

the one who'd taken the drugs without any evidence. Heck, at this point, Nate didn't even know if it was actually an issue. The labs went through a lot of chemicals. That was a fact of the job. Nate had told Candace a couple of years before he thought they should do a better job tracking the compounds and chemicals used in the labs, but she was firm on not making it too difficult for the scientists to do their work. "Nate, it's our job to set up an environment where these people can succeed. All of our jobs depend on it. I don't want somebody hamstrung because they have to account for every drop of every compound."

They'd had an ongoing discussion about some of the other substances in the labs, ones that could be sold on the black market or ones that could be combined to create opioids or opioid-class drugs themselves. "It would be a bad look for the company if somebody managed to skim drugs from the building and then someone gets killed because they took them," Nate remembered saying to her.

That Candace agreed with. The labs that had access to those compounds were more regulated, including Dr. McCall's, though still not nearly as tightly as Nate would like. Was that what Dr. McCall suspected?

A pile of paperwork on the edge of Nate's desk caught his attention. He had work that needed to get done, but he couldn't shake the feeling that maybe there was something to what Andrew had said. He flipped open a pad of paper he kept on his desk, finding the place where he'd scrawled the video times and dates that Andrew had told him about. Frowning, he cued up the video and put it on his large monitor, watching it for what felt like the thousandth time. He added three other shots of Dr. McCall's lab to the screen, hoping he could see Justin as he moved in and out of the frames. Leaning forward, Nate saw Justin sitting in the back of the lab, perched on a stool at one of the work tables, using one of the company computers. There couldn't be an issue with that. No one from IT had come to Nate with any type of a breach out of Dr. McCall's lab. And if there was, they would find it. They spent all day long dealing with firewall and intrusion issues that threatened the company.

Inching the video forward, he saw Justin get up and look around the lab. It was as if he was trying to find something. Nate bit his lip, scowling. Something wasn't right. Dr. McCall had said that he'd been suspicious for a week or so, so Nate had only looked at the video feeds of the week Andrew was concerned about, plus the week before and the week after. He figured a three-week span of video review was plenty. But what if it wasn't?

Nate looked back at his laptop and pulled the video feeds from two months before, comparing them based on the time and date stamp when Justin's key card had been active in the building. Their system was sophisticated that way. He could go into the log, see when a particular employee entered the building, click on the link and the feeds from that person's time on the property would be displayed. It was a slick feature the surveillance company had recently added.

Seeing the amount of time Justin had spent on the BioNova campus, Nate would have his work cut out for him looking at months' worth of feeds. For a second, he considered asking one of his security techs to do the work but decided against it. Word might get out they were looking at Candace's son...

TWO HOURS LATER, Nate needed a break. He'd watched clip after clip of Justin working in the lab. A few things were for certain — Justin spent a lot of time going to the refrigerated units in the lab after everyone was gone, and he seemed to know exactly where the surveillance cameras had a blind spot because that's where he was hunkered down doing whatever it was he was doing. To add to the intrigue, Justin spent an awful lot of time walking back and forth to the incinerator chute dumping things inside. Nate shook his head. The kid was up to something, but what?

Taking a drink of water from the bottle on his desk, Nate sighed. Going through hours and hours of video was exhausting. Although he had suspicions about Justin, there was nothing concrete to work from. The kid was clever. If he was doing something he shouldn't be, it was nearly impossible to tell. If he wasn't up to something then it was just dumb luck that he'd managed to find the one spot in the lab that wasn't covered by the cameras.

Nate shook his head. Figuring out what was happening felt like scaling a rock wall covered in ice. Nothing was sticking. When Dr. McCall had come to him the week before, Nate pulled up the files on what his team was working on. With all the scientific jargon, Nate still wasn't sure he understood it. Checking the online log for the number to Dr. McCall's assistant, Nate sent her a message and asked her to report to his office.

Ten minutes later there was a knock on his door. He pressed the buzzer on the side of his desk unlocking it. Tia Barry, a slight young woman with long, frizzy hair and large round glasses walked into his office. "Mr. Ambrose? You wanted to see me?"

"Yeah, Tia. Come on in and have a seat."

He could tell by the way she kept her arms close to her body and her chin tucked that she was nervous. Most people that came to his office behaved the same way. She slid down into one of the chairs in front of his desk, pulling her sweater tight around her body. "I heard about Dr. McCall. Is that why I'm here?"

"Sort of. Listen, let me just start with this. You're not in trouble. I just have some questions about the drugs you guys are developing in your lab. Just trying to get to the bottom of Dr. McCall's allegations."

"But he was fired, wasn't he?" Tia stared at the ground as if she'd said something wrong, "I mean, that's what everyone is saying. Is that true?"

"Yes, I'm sorry to say it is." Nate had learned early in his career that it was better to just tell the truth about people's employment status. The rumor mill would run wild. It might as well run wild with the correct information. "That wasn't my decision, though. That was Mrs. Shaner's decision. I'm sure she has her reasons. It's not my job to know them. But I still do have some questions about what's going on in your lab. I'm hoping you can help me out." Asking for help always seemed to buy him enough goodwill to at least get the conversation started, even if it was a difficult one.

Tia nodded, "Sure. What do you need to know?"

Nate folded his hands on the desk, "Listen, I'm not a scientist. I'm a security guy. Can you tell me a little bit about the drug that you are developing in Dr. McCall's lab?"

"We're actually developing two different ones — AnoVest and

Vikeria. They are both anesthesia drugs. We're just in the alpha stage of testing AnoVest."

"Okay, slow down. Can you do this in English, please? What is the drug supposed to do and what is the alpha stage of testing?" It seemed like every single lab director had their own way of defining their testing levels. There were certain industry benchmarks they all had to hit before clinical trials, but before that, the experimental structure was not exactly random, but not exactly standard either.

Tia held her hands up, "Fair enough. The two drugs we are developing are designed to make anesthesia easier and safer. There are lots and lots of people that have negative effects on anesthesia every single year. There's also the problem of how to perform emergency procedures, or even regular procedures, in areas of the world that don't have access to the high-tech medical equipment that most of our hospitals have here in the United States. Think of it this way, if you're in the middle of the village in Africa and you have to have your leg amputated, wouldn't it be nice if you could sleep through it?"

Nate nodded. Although he'd never been deployed, he knew guys who'd come back who'd wish they could have slept through their injuries. "That makes sense. These drugs, they improve our point of access in the international markets, then?"

"Yeah, from the way I understand it. Small clinics here in the US, too. The goal is that the drugs are so easy to administer that you wouldn't need an anesthesiologist to do it. You'd give someone a pill, or slap a patch on them..."

"A patch? You're talking about a transdermal delivery system?"

Tia nodded, "Yeah. Drugs embedded in patches are easier to ship, they stay viable longer because they're individually sealed, and administration is super easy. Open it up, stick it on someone's arm or thigh and wait for them to fall asleep — at least that's the goal."

"And you mentioned you're in the alpha stage of testing?"

"That's with AnoVest. We have two sets of tests running. Dr. McCall used the names the marketing department already came up with to avoid confusion. AnoVest is in the seventh round, that's why we call it Alpha-seven. Vikeria is in the fifth round."

"I'm guessing that's Victor-five?"

"Correct."

"What does that mean in practical terms? These haven't gone off to a clinical trial yet, have they?" Nate didn't think they had, but sometimes the trials went so fast that he had a hard time keeping up. BioNova was constantly developing new drugs — as many as fifty at a time. Many of them never got out of the developmental phase, but the ones that made it through, the company pushed hard.

"Oh no!" Tia squeaked, "No, neither of these drugs are ready for human consumption. That wouldn't be safe. We're still trying to not kill the mice with them." Her eyes got wide for a second, "Not that I don't value the lives of our mice..."

Nate closed his eyes for a second, trying not to laugh. Tia was a very nervous personality. He knew a quick and dirty psyops profile would reveal she was the kind of person that could be convinced to do things easily if she could get past her fear. He pushed the thought aside. Her mental status wasn't the point of the interview. The drugs were. "No, I didn't take it that way. I know that all of our labs are careful with the animals we use."

Tia's shoulders relaxed, "Yes, that's what I meant to say. The point is, no, none of the drugs are ready for testing on humans. We're starting to get closer to the point we can run more in-depth tests, but we're still trying to get the formula right. Human testing is still probably at least two years off." She shrugged, "You know, these ideas, they're good, but we have to make them work."

There was something in the way that she said it that made Nate think she had questions about the progress of the drugs. He furrowed his eyebrows, "And you're not sure these drugs will?"

Tia shook her head, her hair swinging behind her in a fluffy, frizzy curtain, "I don't know. I know we've put a lot of money into them, but we don't have any results. At least not yet."

Nate nodded. "Before I send you back to work, let me ask you about one of your interns, Justin. How has he been in the lab?"

Tia's eyes got wide. She stammered, "Well, I know he's Mrs. Shaner's son. He seems fine. Kinda keeps to himself."

"So, you don't interact with him much?"

Tia shook her head, "No, but I can tell you he's usually still in the lab when I leave. Stays late all the time."

"Do you have any idea what he's working on?"

"No. Nobody does."

17

M organ was tired of pacing as she waited for news from Amber and Sylvia. It was impossible to concentrate on anything else other than Sarah and Maisie's bodies coming out of the ground. Hopefully, their corpses would give them the answers they needed.

After scrubbing the stove, she'd taken Bo for a second walk, cleaned out the refrigerator, run a load of laundry, and even pulled a few weeds in her yard, all while keeping one eye on her phone. Amber texted mid-morning to let her know that Judge Green had granted the exhumation orders and they were working on it, but that was the last Morgan heard. It took every bit of Morgan's self-discipline to not call Amber and Sylvia every ten minutes, asking for an update.

Going into her bedroom, Morgan pressed her finger on the pad of the gun safe, the door popped open as it read her fingerprint. She pulled out her pistol, dropping the magazine and racking the slide to get the last round to pop out. Walking into the kitchen, she set her pistol down on the table and went into the laundry room to find an old towel she could use. At least while she was waiting on news from Amber and Sylvia, she could take it apart and clean it.

From a shelf in the front closet, she grabbed a plastic storage box that was filled with her cleaning supplies. She laid them out in a row on the towel, the bottles of cleaner and oil along with the metal rod she used to get the white cleaning pads through the barrel. She set the empty pistol in the center of the space. Pulling the slide the entire way back, she flipped the lever that pushed it off the rails, exposing the inside of the barrel, the spring, and the trigger. Working slowly, she took the gun apart, laying out the parts exactly as they were meant to go back in. She glanced at her phone. Still no information from Amber and Sylvia. She sighed. "A watched pot never boils," she muttered to herself as Danny walked in the door.

"Hey buddy, how was school?" she said, as she dabbed gun cleaner on a small white square of lint-free fabric. The smell of the solvent filled her nostrils.

"Good." Danny slumped down in the chair next to her. "Any news?"

"Not too much."

"I heard there was another girl that tried to kill herself. Is that where you were this morning?"

Morgan could feel the weight of his words. There was no point in lying to him. She rested her hands on the edge of the table, "Amber called early this morning, while you were still asleep. She asked if I could run over and take a look."

Danny cocked his head to the side, narrowing his eyes. "Why didn't she just go?"

"I don't know," Morgan started, then stopped. She did know. "The thing is, just like in any business, there are politics in the department. Amber isn't exactly assigned to that case. Another detective is."

"And he wasn't there?"

"Not when I was there. But I'm sure he went later. He was

probably just giving the doctors and the family a chance to figure out what was going on." At least Morgan hoped Ben Acosta showed up at some point. From what she'd heard of him, she wasn't impressed.

"It was Courtney, wasn't it?"

Morgan nodded. "Yeah." She tried to change the subject off the details. "I saw Paul at the hospital. He said Katrina and Courtney were friends? Is that right?" Morgan skipped telling him the part about how Katrina was pregnant. That was the last thing the DeLuca family needed — to have information about their child get out into the school community that way. Even though Morgan trusted Danny with her life, that was the kind of information he might tell someone in confidence. Those kinds of secrets were hard to keep. The person he told might not be so careful with Katrina's reputation.

"Yeah. They were friends. I think they hung out together some."

Morgan picked up an old rag and started wiping the interior of the gun, cleaning the black residue away, and checking Duncan's work. The new trigger was seated correctly in the frame. It was hard to believe it had only been a couple of days since she got her gun back and heard about Katrina. She looked at Danny, "Did you and Brantley come up with anything else on that encrypted app?"

"I got a message from him earlier today, I think," Danny scowled. He pulled his phone out of his pocket, "He said he managed to get himself invited into the group. Now he's trying to figure out who is who. He said the firewall between people's screen names and their actual data is problematic."

Morgan raised her eyebrows, "Problematic?"

Danny shrugged, "That's Brantley speak for he hasn't been able to get through it yet." Danny stood up, picking up his backpack. "I'm going to go do homework." He glanced in the kitchen, "What are we eating?"

Her thoughts elsewhere, Morgan had completely forgotten about dinner. She didn't have much of an appetite anyway. "There are some leftovers in the fridge. Mind having those for dinner?"

Danny shook his head, "That's fine."

As Danny walked away, Morgan swallowed. She'd been so focused on Katrina that she felt like she was losing connection with Danny... again. Was he doing okay in school? Was he excited about his new friends? It was the same way she'd felt when Leo McDaniel was stalking them in West Virginia. She knew she was just trying to protect him, but at some point, they had to go back to being mother and son. Morgan shook her head and focused on her gun again, wiping cleaner over the spring and wiping the inside of the barrel again just to be sure she got all the residue off. Her maternal instinct would have to wait until after they figured out what was going on at the high school. She reassembled the pistol, using a tiny amount of gun oil on the slide and the trigger. Giving it a final last wipe to get any extra oil off, Morgan double-checked the gun was empty and pulled the trigger to make sure it was functioning correctly. She heard a click, retracted the slide once more, and pulled the trigger again. At least her gun was clean. Standing up, she grabbed the magazine and the extra round from the counter where she'd put them and reloaded her gun.

As she was about to put the gun back in its safe, Morgan heard her phone ring. She glanced down at it, grabbing a towel and wiping off her fingers before picking it up. "Sylvia?"

"Morgan, I'm glad I caught you."

"What's going on? I haven't heard from you guys all day long."

"Sorry about that. It's been a little hectic. Judge Green went ahead and signed the exhumation order, so then I had to go to the cemeteries and get the cemetery managers to dig up the bodies for me. I didn't get them back here until about lunchtime. Jake and I have spent all afternoon working on them."

A shiver ran up Morgan's spine. It was one thing to be at a scene when someone had just died. It was something entirely different to be around bodies that had decomposed for a while. Morgan remembered a training she'd gone to where they went to a body farm — a place where forensic scientists put dead bodies that were donated to science out in the elements to see what would happen to them. She felt like she hadn't been able to get the smell out of her clothes or her nose for weeks after that. Even though Sarah and Maisie hadn't been dead that long, she still couldn't imagine what Sylvia and Jake had been doing all day. "Did you find anything?"

There was silence on the other end of the line for a second. "We've finished the work on Sarah, but still have some more testing to do on Maisie. By the way, you were right about the moms. They were at both sites and seemed relieved that we wanted to do further testing. I'll tell you what, it's not always that way. I've had families who have fought me tooth and nail to leave their loved ones in the ground. That was a good call. I hope we can get them some answers."

Morgan wondered if murder would be a better answer than suicide for the families. "Thanks for that. What did you find?"

"I can't speak to toxicology as of yet. I've got samples running here in the lab on both Sarah and Maisie and another set that Jake is taking to BCI as we speak. Nothing has come up yet, but the BCI lab has more sophisticated testing technology than we do. I've asked them to run a full panel — not just the normal standard tests. We'll see what they can come up with. It'll be a good chance for them to stretch their legs on a big question."

"Anything physically?"

"That's why I'm calling. There is evidence that both of the girls were attacked, just like Katrina, although we don't have their original clothes. They were both dressed for their funerals. Jake and I found tearing and abrasions in their vaginas."

Morgan stopped, dead still. If that was the case then three of the girls had been attacked when they were drugged. "So, these are no longer suicides."

Sylvia cleared her throat, "No. As a matter of fact, I have recalled both of their death certificates. They will be amended to homicide. It's a paperwork nightmare, but it can't be avoided."

"And their cause of death?" Morgan thought she knew the answer to the question, but she wanted to hear exactly where Sylvia was on the issue.

"I can't say definitively yet, but given the fact there's no other obvious physical cause of death — no strangulation, gunshot wounds, stab wounds, or the like — I'm guessing it's going to fall under some sort of category of overdose. But as I said, we don't know what the drug combination was yet. I can't speculate further until we have more information back from the lab."

"And the standard tox screens aren't coming back with anything? It's not heroin or fentanyl — anything like that?"

"Nope. That's why I sent the samples off to the lab."

Morgan frowned. If the girls had been embalmed, then there wouldn't be any blood for them to test. "Wait, what kind of samples are you sending to the lab?"

"Tissue. With the embalming process, there's not enough uncontaminated blood in their bodies to figure out what was in their system. But the embalming fluid doesn't necessarily soak into the tissues, so the lab will have an easier time getting a clean sample from that." Sylvia sighed, "I'm glad you pushed Amber and me on this, Morgan. I would never have given this a second look without you. Those families need answers. I'll keep working my end, but you have to figure out who's doing this."

Morgan pressed her lips together. How this case had

become her responsibility, she wasn't sure. Paul, Amber, Sylvia -- they were all putting pressure on her. She stared at the floor for a second, thinking about Courtney and Katrina in the hospital. "I'll do what I can, but there are still a lot of questions left. Let me know when you hear anything else, okay?"

"Will do. Let's just hope there are no more bodies in the meantime."

18

J ustin sat in his car, staring straight ahead. He'd gone to the lab earlier in the day, but left when the entire team had gotten called into a meeting. One of the project managers told him about Dr. McCall. It was just like his mother to try to ruin everything he was working for. He gripped the steering wheel, his knuckles going white. What would happen to the drug trials they were working on now, he wasn't sure. It would be just like his mother to scrap the entire program before he had a chance to solve the problem. He pounded his fist on the steering wheel.

During his brief stay at the lab, he'd managed to mix another sample of his drug cocktail while the rest of the staff was in a meeting with the HR department, stuffing the new vial in his pocket. With Dr. McCall gone, he'd have to finish his work before his mother pulled the funding for the anesthesia project. She'd come home and bragged about doing exactly that on more than one occasion, seemingly proud that she had the opportunity to trash years of research with the swipe of the pen or a few lines in an email.

Justin hadn't been home since he left for school that

morning and he wasn't planning on it anytime soon. Starting his car, he followed a dark green sedan out of the parking lot of the library. He knew who was in the car in front of him. Ava Banks. She was friends with Katrina and Courtney, another one of the girls that didn't want to give him the time of day. He didn't have anything particularly against her except for the fact that he'd heard her whispering a few days before as he walked past. They all thought they were better than him. They weren't.

He shook his head. At the time, he was sure she was talking about him, but now, his brain felt foggy. Was that actually the case? He ignored the thought, setting his jaw. She was part of the group that continually dismissed him, girls who seem to prefer boys who were all as dumb as they were. It was typical, he thought, following Ava's car as she stopped at a gas station. He pulled in behind her at the pump and watched as she got out of her car, heading into the convenience store. He leaned forward, watching for the right moment. Opening the door to his car, Justin slid out, pulling a hunting knife from his back pocket. He walked to the far side of his car, his breath ragged in his chest, opening the blade with a single move and knifing her tire. He heard the satisfying hiss behind him as he walked back to his own car.

Justin flipped open the fuel door on his car and started filling up his tank, using the credit card his mother had given to him. He glanced over his shoulder, watching as Ava's car slowly tilted to the side, now sitting on a completely flat tire. He smiled.

Turning away as soon as he saw Ava come out of the gas station, he swallowed and licked his lips. It was showtime. His heart fluttered in his chest.

He kept his back turned to her as she walked to her car. This wasn't the time to make eye contact, at least not yet. As the pump clicked off, the tank on his car full, he heard Ava shriek, "You've got to be kidding me!"

He turned towards her, a blank look on his face, "Are you okay?"

She was standing with her hands on her narrow hips, her black leggings jutting out from underneath a nearly see-through white crop top. Her stomach was showing between the top of her leggings and the bottom of her shirt. The skin was bronzed, as if she spent a lot of time in the sun. "I've got a flat tire. How am I going to get home now?"

Justin walked over to her, feigning a concerned look on his face, kneeling down next to the wheel, poking at it with his finger. "Yeah, that's a bad flat. You don't want to drive on that. You'll trash the rim. Probably gonna have to have it towed."

As he stood up, Ava cocked her head to the side and narrowed her eyes, "Wait, don't I know you? You go to Palm Coast, don't you?"

"Yeah. I think I've seen you around there, too." He tried to keep his face steady although fury rose in Justin's gut. How could she pretend not to know him? They had two classes together and she was always at Courtney Reese's locker which was just down from his own. She was a liar, a pretender. He wasn't interested in playing her games and unlike the other girls, he wasn't interested in her at all. He gritted his teeth together.

"Isn't your name John, or something? You're the one that's so good at chemistry, right?"

Bile rose in the back of his throat. Ava Banks was a typical mean girl, trying to manipulate the situation. "Justin. You're Ava Banks, aren't you?" The reality was he knew a lot more about her than just her name. He knew she was a swimmer and had just gotten a scholarship to compete in college.

"Oh, that's right, I remember now." She shrugged one shoulder up and looked at him, "I hate to ask, but do you think you can run me home? I live just a couple of miles from here. There's no way I can drive on that flat tire."

"Sure, I guess," Justin said, trying to look bored by the idea. His heart thumped in his chest. Things were going exactly as he planned.

"Great!" she chirped, "Let me just run in and tell the guy at the counter what happened, okay?"

"Sounds good. I'll be here."

Justin watched as Ava ran into the store, a sheet of brown hair cascading behind her. As soon as she was out of sight, Justin went to the trunk of his car, pulling on a pair of skin-colored rubber gloves, adding a few drops of his newest sample to the palm of his right hand. He pulled the sleeves of his shirt down a little lower so she wouldn't be able to see the gloves as easily.

As he slammed the trunk lid, Ava came out, staring at him, "Ready to go?"

"Yep," he said, getting into the sedan.

As Ava got in the passenger side, Justin could smell her body lotion. It was citrusy and filled the car with her scent. He glanced at her, licking his lips as he backed the car carefully out of the line of pumps and turned back out onto Gulf Shores Parkway. "I live right up there," Ava pointed. "You know Coastal Gardens? That's my street."

Justin nodded. She'd been a recent addition to his list, with not enough time to invite her to the messaging app, but he'd figured out where she lived, a two-story cream-colored stucco house with a red tile roof and a two-car garage. He'd only driven by it one time, but it was burned in his memory.

As he drove, Ava chatted away, though he only grunted in response, "Boy, this is a nice car," she said, leaning back into the seats, rubbing her back on the leather upholstery. "You are so lucky. I'm driving the car my brother left behind when he went to college. It's a rattletrap. I'm not surprised I got a flat tire. I've been telling my dad that I need new tires. Actually, I've been telling him that I needed a new car, but my parents are all obsessed with paying for my brother's college right now. Maybe I'll get a new car when I graduate. It probably won't be as nice as this one, though."

Justin grunted. She kept talking.

"I'll bet you're going to college for chemistry, aren't you? You're like the best person to talk to if anybody needs help in chemistry. I bet you spend a lot of time tutoring." She giggled, "I mean, I'm pretty good at other subjects. I really like art. Actually, I may go to school for graphic design. That's what I'm thinking about. Do you have any idea where you want to go to school?"

Justin glanced at her and pointed at her street, ignoring her questions. "Is that where I need to turn?" he said, laying his hand on her arm, pretending he was just interrupting her.

As she nodded, his heart started to pound in his chest. If the new formula worked the way he designed it, she would be out cold almost immediately and then wake up in about three hours with no memory of what had happened.

As he made the turn onto Ava's street, he held his breath, looking at her. He slowed the car down, pulling off to the side of the road. Ava glanced at him, her eyes glazing over, "Hey, why are we stopping? My house is over there." She put her hand up to her forehead. "I don't feel so good," she said, before she slumped over on the seat.

Justin's stomach fluttered. He turned off the headlights and put the car in park. They weren't far from Ava's house now, maybe only a hundred feet or so. He stripped off the gloves, throwing them in the wheel well, staring at her. He waited two minutes, running a single finger over the skin between her shirt and the waistband of her leggings. It was just as soft as he expected it would be.

He drew his hand back, not wanting to get distracted. He'd gotten distracted with a few of the other girls, but he couldn't, not with how close he was to getting the formula right. He checked the time on his cell phone. It had been five minutes since he dosed her, four minutes since she'd fallen asleep. By now, her heart rate and respiration should have stabilized. He lifted his fingers and pressed them on the side of her neck, checking for a pulse. Nothing. He felt his stomach tighten as he felt again, trying the other side of her neck. Maybe it was just the way her head was tilted. Still nothing. He shook his head, gritting his teeth together. Why was this happening? He had rerun the formula nearly one hundred times trying to get it just right. "Ava, you are disappointing me," he said, holding the back of his hand up to her nose. He didn't feel any breath coming out of her.

Frustrated, Justin unclipped his seatbelt and looked around the neighborhood. There was no one anywhere nearby. He scooted up in the seat and leaned over, putting his ear on her chest. He waited for a second, listening. Nothing.

He pushed himself back in the street and pounded the steering wheel again, the whole car rattling, "Come on!" he yelled. "You've got to be kidding me!"

Furious, he started the car, leaving the headlights off. He drove to the end of Ava's street and flipped around, heading back towards her house. The only lights on were upstairs, the entire first floor dark and quiet. Justin pulled his sedan up in front of her yard and got out, running around the back of the car and opening her door. Grabbing her under her arms, he pulled her lifeless body out of the car and tossed it on the grass like a piece of garbage. To him, it was. Not bothering to look back, he jogged back to the driver's side and got in, pulling away from the curb without another thought.

19

———

The next morning, Morgan had just gotten back from walking Bo when she heard a noise at the side door. Startled, she wheeled around as Bo growled. The door opened. It was Danny.

"What are you doing home?"

Danny bent over and scratched Bo behind the ears, "They sent everyone home. Closed the school down. I guess another girl committed suicide last night. They're bringing in grief counselors. Somebody said the phones are ringing off the hook in the office."

Morgan froze. Another girl? How was that possible? Morgan hadn't checked her phone since she had gotten back from walking Bo, thinking it would be a day or two before Sylvia had any results from the toxicology tests on the bodies they'd recovered. Looking at it, she saw a message from Amber that read, "Call me."

Morgan swallowed. "Are you okay? What did they say exactly?"

"I went to homeroom as soon as I got to school and we were getting ready to head off to our first classes but then the teacher decided to hold us there for a minute. He got some sort of a text or something. An announcement came out over the PA system — I can't believe they even use that thing anymore — and the principal said another student had died overnight and that the Board of Education had decided the best path forward was to shut the school down for the rest of the week."

"For the rest of the week?" Morgan raised her eyebrows, resting her hands on the back of one of the kitchen chairs. The school was finally catching up. She wondered what they would do if they knew law enforcement suspected a serial killer was on the loose.

Morgan's mind began to race, imagining the cold body of the killer's next victim. Questions pounded through her mind like a jackhammer — who was the girl? How had the killer gotten to her? Who had found her? Was her naked body laying on the cold metal of Sylvia's examining table, next to the decaying bodies of Sarah and Maisie?

Morgan stared at the ground, saying a silent prayer in the hopes that the girl's parents hadn't found her. Their grief was unimaginable. Morgan couldn't begin to understand what that might feel like as a parent. Her mind flashed to Paul, the way the skin on his face looked tight, the hollows under his eyes, his stare a little more vacant each time she saw him at the hospital. Her stomach clenched.

As Morgan's mind settled on Paul's face, the room began to spin, the walls of the kitchen closing in on her. As she looked up, she didn't see her own home but the walls of the inside of the trailer as Leo closed and locked the door trapping her inside. Her breath caught in her throat as she dropped to her knees, her heart pounding in her chest. All she could think of were the corpses lined up in a row in Sylvia's examining room, their bodies splayed on the sterile metal tables, the killer looking on, laughing...

The room went black.

By the time Morgan opened her eyes, she felt Danny's arms around her, "Mom! Mom! Are you okay? Wake up!"

She tried to say something and then the world went black again.

By the time she came to the second time, she heard noises by her head, the feel of something warm over her mouth and nose. She batted at it with her hand, trying to make sense of the smell near her mouth.

"I think she's coming around," Morgan heard someone say.

Blinking, Morgan opened her eyes, staring at the faces of two people she didn't recognize. She ripped the oxygen mask off her face, rolled to her side, crawling away from them. One of them grabbed her arm, "Morgan, you're safe. I'm a paramedic. I'm here to help. Just lie down, okay?"

The panic that washed over her head started to recede enough that she could bring them into focus. A man and a woman, maybe a few years younger than she was, were sitting on the floor with her, their equipment scattered behind them. Danny stood just behind, tears running down his face. "Mom!" he said, running to her side and kneeling next to her, "Are you okay? What happened?" Morgan heard sniffing near her ear. Bo stuck his nose in her hair, ruffling her blonde waves; as if he was doing his own exam. Satisfied she was okay, he walked away, laying down on his bed, still watching her.

Morgan reached for the oxygen mask again. Holding it up near her mouth, she took a long breath in, feeling her head start to clear. "I don't know. You just told me about the other girl and then everything went black."

"Let's check her blood pressure again and then get her ready to transport," the woman said to the male paramedic.

"Transport?" Morgan stuttered, sitting up. "I'm not going to the hospital!" Morgan spat, the words coming out clipped and short. "No way. I'm fine."

Danny put his hand on her shoulder. She felt the warmth of

his skin through the fabric of her T-shirt. She didn't look at him. She couldn't. Everything in her wanted to lay back down on the ground, but she couldn't. She had to stay strong for him. She reached up, giving his hand a squeeze and then pulled it off of her. She lifted the oxygen mask off her face again. "I have claustrophobia. I just had a bad attack. That's all. I don't need anything other than some food and rest."

As the words came out of her mouth, she felt the tightening of the blood pressure cuff on her arm inflating, the cool of the man's stethoscope on the inside of her elbow. "Her blood pressure is back to normal. Pulse seems steady as well."

The female paramedic scowled and then looked at Morgan, leaning forward, flashing a penlight into each of her eyes. "Ma'am, are you on any medication? Could this have been a reaction to something you took?"

Morgan struggled to her feet. They apparently weren't listening to her. "No, I told you. I just had an attack. It's nothing. And I'm not going to the hospital." She licked her lips. The edges of her vision were becoming fuzzy again. She slid down into one of the kitchen chairs. Her body had never felt so weak, so out of control. There was no way she was going to be able to help figure out what happened to the girls if she didn't get it together. Staring at the ground, she swallowed. "Danny, can you get me some juice, please?" As her eyes met his, there was worry etched over his face. She knew he'd be more comfortable if she agreed to be transported, but there was no way she was going into that hospital, not with what was going on right in their backyard.

"Yeah, sure,"

A second later, Danny handed her a small plastic bottle of orange juice. He'd cracked the top open for her. As she put it up to her lips, she could taste the sweet and sour taste of the fruit juice in the back of her mouth, the acid going down into her stomach. She couldn't remember when she'd eaten last. She looked down for a second and blinked a couple of times, staring at the paramedics. "I'm okay," she said to them. "Really. I'm glad you came. Thank you for checking me out, but I'm not going to the hospital."

The young man shrugged, not seeming to care whether she went or not. He started to gather up the equipment they brought into the house. The woman sat on the floor for another second, her head cocked to the side, "If you don't want to go to the hospital, that's fine, but I do have a form you'll need to sign."

"Sure. Whatever it takes."

As a woman wrapped the blood pressure cuff back onto itself and stuck it in her duffel bag, her partner came back in with a tablet and handed it to Morgan. Morgan scrawled her name on the screen and hit enter. The female paramedic stood up and slung the bag over her shoulder. She glanced back at Morgan one last time, "Are you sure you don't want us to take you in? That was a pretty serious panic attack. I'd hate to have that happen again and you fall and whack your head on something."

Morgan held her hands up as if telling the woman to stop, "No, I'm fine. Thanks for your concern, though."

The woman narrowed her eyes, "I would recommend you check in with your doctor and let them have a look at you. There are lots of drugs on the market now..."

Morgan stood up out of the chair she was sitting in, blood rushing to her face. How dare this woman indicate that she needed medication. She knew nothing about Morgan or what she'd been through, about the losses she'd suffered and the years she'd spent in WITSEC. She didn't need to give the woman details, she just needed the paramedic to get out of her house. Morgan's life was none of the paramedic's business. She tried to keep her tone even as she spoke, but she could feel the muscles pull tight across her face, "Thank you for your concern, but I'm fine."

Morgan sat back down at the kitchen table and took another sip of juice while she watched Danny close and lock the door behind the paramedics, the two of them leaving without another word. Danny walked towards her and sat down in the chair next to her, twisting to face her. "Mom, are you sure you're okay? I can drive you to the doctor. It's not a problem. It's not like I need to be in school or anything."

"I'm fine, honey," she felt her heart skip a beat as she took another sip of the juice. That was the worst attack she'd ever had, but she couldn't let Danny know that. Her head was still swimming a little, the effects of passing out still surging through her system. Morgan stared at the ground, wondering if they'd made a mistake coming back to Tampa. When they'd left witness protection, they could've gone anywhere in the country, but she thought coming back to Florida would be the best for Danny. And it probably was. But after the attack she just had, maybe it wasn't the best fit for her. She looked at the floor, feeling the cool of the bottle on her fingers. But she couldn't think about that now. She had to get herself together.

Morgan struggled to her feet, standing still for a second, the room wobbling just a bit. Maybe the paramedic had been right, she thought. Maybe she should have gone to the hospital and gotten checked out. But what would they tell her? That she'd experienced a bout of claustrophobia that led to a panic attack? She knew that. They'd end up hooking her up to a bunch of monitors and give her a dose of something to calm her down, keep her in bed for a couple of hours and then send her home with a prescription and fifteen follow-up appointments with doctors she had no intention of ever seeing. She shook her head. No. It was better if she just stayed home. She just needed a few minutes to regroup. The news that another girl had died caught her off guard. The mistake had been hers. In her head, she thought they were getting ahead of the killer, making some progress with testing the bodies of Sarah and Maisie, but obviously, the killer was still at work.

Morgan shook her head, not sure what to think. She needed to focus, stay strong. Her mind flipped between concern for Danny and the news that another girl had died. Danny had been under enough stress when they came back to Tampa, but adding the school drama on top of it -- it was too much. "I know you are going to be home for a few days. Let's make the best of it," she said, trying to sound positive although the knot in her gut told her something different. "There are always plenty of chores to get done around the house here. You could help me with those."

Danny nodded, staring at his phone. "Sure, Mom, whatever you want." He glanced at her, "Listen, I just got a message from Brantley. He wants to come over and work on that messaging app in a little while. That okay?"

"Of course. He's welcome to stay as long as he'd like." Maybe the boys would be able to figure out something that she, Amber, and Sylvia hadn't thought of yet.

As Morgan turned on her heel, she felt the energy return to her body as the hair on the back of her neck stood up. Whoever was killing these girls was escalating, and escalating fast. She went back to her bedroom and got out her pistol, clipping the holster to her belt and sliding it in. She covered it with the T-shirt she was wearing. It might seem strange to some people to wear a loaded gun in her own home, but although the killer had only gone after girls so far, there was no telling what his next steps might be. Morgan wanted to be prepared for whatever was next.

By the time mid-morning rolled around, Morgan felt like herself again. Danny hadn't left her side, setting up his computer at the kitchen table and supposedly working on homework, although she saw him watching her as she moved around the house, straightening up. She wasn't exactly sure what else to do. Her mind still felt a little foggy, as if she'd been up all night, but it wasn't that. She knew it was the after-effects of the panic attack. She moved a little more slowly than usual, trying to remind herself to take deep breaths. She made each of them a sandwich, figuring if she ate something, it might help restore her strength.

Setting paper plates in front of each of them, Morgan slid down into her chair, putting a potato chip in her mouth. There were two bottles of water and another bottle of juice in front of her, Danny's contribution to lunch. She took a bite of the sandwich, the salty ham and cheese filling her mouth. She glanced at Danny just as his phone pinged. He glanced up at her, "it's Brantley. He's on his way. Are you sure it's okay? I mean, I know you weren't feeling well a little while ago."

"Of course. I'm fine, Danny. He's welcome to come over any time." She knew Danny was just trying to be sensitive. But she was fine, at least for the minute.

20

Exactly thirty minutes later, there was a knock on the front door. Bo scrambled from his spot on his dog bed between the kitchen and the family room, running toward the door, growling and barking. As Danny opened the door, Bo trotted outside and herded Brantley inside. Morgan watched as Danny locked the door behind him. Morgan picked up her plate, throwing what was left of her sandwich in the trash and running her fingers through her hair.

"Hey, Brantley. How are you?" Morgan tried to sound casual as she leaned against the counter, fighting off a new round of dizziness.

"I'm doing fine, Mrs. Foster." He narrowed his eyes, "Danny said you weren't feeling good this morning. You okay now?"

Danny. Part of Morgan wished he hadn't said anything, but she realized watching her pass out and having to call the paramedics was yet another notch in his trauma belt. The poor kid had seen way too much. "Yes. I'm fine. Just didn't have breakfast. Things have been a little crazy around here."

"I get it. That happens to my mom too. No big deal." Brantley plopped down at the kitchen table and pulled out his laptop. Danny pulled up a chair and sat right next to him, dragging his computer alongside. Morgan stared at them for a second, watching them get settled, "Brantley, what are you working on? Danny said you needed help with something?"

Brantley looked up from his computer through his thick glasses and blinked, "I gotta be honest with you Mrs. Foster, I don't think these are suicides and I think that somehow this GenChat encrypted messaging app is connected to whatever is happening. There are a few things I want to try to see if we can figure out who's involved. Maybe I can get a name or something and I can pass it on to the police. It's just not logical that so many girls would die so fast at the same place." He glanced at Danny and then back at Morgan, "Do you know what the odds are for all these girls dying within a two-month span from the same high school? Like a billion to one. There has to be something more to it."

Morgan licked her lips. If the kids in the high school were figuring out it wasn't a coincidence that the girls were dying, then it wouldn't be long before other people would too. Brantley seemed to be ahead of the curve, but once the community got wind of the fact there was a serial killer roaming around, the people that live there might never be the same. Worse yet, it could spook the killer and their leads could dry up. Katrina's face floated in her mind. She leaned on the counter, staring at it. The clock was ticking, not only for the girls at Palm Coast High School, but for the entire community. They needed answers, and soon.

Morgan looked at the two boys, picking up her keys. "Listen, I'm going up to the high school to see if I can figure out what's going on. If you two find anything, let me know." She looked at them. It struck her how young they were. "And don't snoop into anything that would put your lives in danger, please. If you think you're getting close to something, stop and let me know so we can get some help. Okay?" she said, raising her eyebrows, hoping they understood how critical it was.

They both nodded. Whether they understood or not, Morgan wasn't sure.

IT WAS JUST after lunchtime as Morgan pulled into the parking lot at Palm Coast High School. Outside, there were two police cars and three other blue unmarked units parked nearby. Detectives, Morgan thought, getting out of the car, probably from the city as well as the county. Someone must have decided that the last body was the tipping point. It was finally time to do something.

The front doors of the school were unlocked, the building silent for the most part, the hallways empty. Standing just inside the front doors, Morgan could smell a combination of old textbooks and the hint of body odor mixed with some sort of lemon cleaner. The scent hung in the air like a heavy curtain. She scanned the space around her. Ahead of her, there was a long main hallway, another one off to her right and left. She knew from the tour they'd gotten with the principal a few months before that the high school was built in the shape of a rectangle, the main hallway running the length of the high school, the parallel hallways running along the outside edge, classrooms smashed in between. Looking around her, she couldn't imagine how loud the hallways were between classes with all the hard surfaces, the metal lockers, scuffed linoleum tile, and harsh fluorescent lights. It gave her a headache just thinking about it.

From out of the school offices off to her right, a woman wearing jeans and a Palm Coast High School T-shirt approached her, "Can I help you? The school's closed today."

"Who's in charge?"

"I'm sorry, I don't know what you mean."

Morgan leveled her gaze at the woman, "Kids from this school keep dropping left and right. Who's in charge?" There was an edge to her voice that revealed the impatience she was feeling.

"I, I don't know who you want to talk to? We have grief counselors here in the building and law enforcement is working on our records as we speak," the woman stammered.

The woman was useless. Morgan glanced through the glass windows of the office. She saw at least seven officers in the small space, talking to people Morgan assumed worked for the school. Without saying anything, Morgan pivoted on her heel heading down the hallway where the grief counselors were supposed to be. She wanted to see for herself how many kids were in the building. Walking down the hallway, she could hear the voices of people as she entered the gymnasium. There were tables set up near the door, people with pads of paper and tablets in front of them. Only a few kids were sitting in the seats that had been reserved for them, their bodies huddled, a young girl sniffling behind her. Morgan watched for a second, seeing a woman get up and usher a young boy with gangly arms and legs out of the gym. She led him down the hallway. Morgan turned to watch as she pointed the young boy into a classroom and closed the door behind him. The counselors must have taken up residence in some of the classrooms. From behind her, she heard a voice, "Mrs. Foster?"

She wheeled around. It was Greg Solis. "Dr. Solis. I didn't expect to see you here."

"I could say the same about you. Is Danny okay? Is he here? I can meet with him if you want..."

Morgan didn't give him a chance to answer, "No. He's fine. He's home with his friend Brantley."

"Okay, that's good to hear." He narrowed his eyes at her, "Then why are you here?"

"I'm trying to figure out what's going on." Her voice was low and gravelly. After the excursion to his office, he had to know how serious she was about figuring out what was happening, and not just to Katrina DeLuca.

Greg looked at the line of people sitting at the table and put his hand on Morgan's arm, escorting her out into the hallway. She was ready to shrug his hand off when he dropped it. "I heard about Sarah and Maisie, about how the medical examiner dug up their bodies. I'm assuming you had something to do with that?"

How he figured that out, she wasn't sure, except for the fact that she'd specifically asked about them when she'd been in his office. "You could say that." She studied him for a second. He looked down at the floor, pulling his glasses off his face and rubbing his eyes. She realized how tired he looked, much more so than when she was in his office just a few days before. He was pale, his lips almost white. Morgan stared at him. "What's going on here? You look awful."

Greg looked up, his face cracking into a little smile. He chuckled under his breath as he put his glasses on his face. "Danny said you were blunt. I can see what he means." He stared at the floor and then looked back at her, catching her eyes. "It's exhausting. I've been dealing with this at work for the last couple of weeks. Now it's all over the high school and they've called out the crisis team. I've already sent two kids to the hospital this morning. They're so distraught and scared they're not even making sense anymore." He sighed, his shoulders slumped. "I have to be honest. It's a lot even for somebody who's trained. I can't imagine what these families are going through."

Morgan furrowed her eyebrows, watching him. Part of her felt bad for him, but part of her knew that he'd signed up for this kind of work, just like she'd signed up for the risk inherent to being a police officer. It was what was to be expected. "What are people saying? Have you talked to anyone from law enforcement? Have they even been around?"

Greg nodded, "Yeah, they've been around, but they're not saying anything."

Their silence wasn't much of a surprise given the fact they were in the middle of an ongoing investigation. Morgan looked over her shoulder. Was Ben Acosta in the building? She was sure he wouldn't be happy to see her. Morgan didn't care. Other than Amber and Sylvia, they were moving way too slow in her opinion. Kids were dead and now that there was a trail of bodies law enforcement was showing up? Morgan glanced down the hallway and then back at him. "Do you have a theory about what's going on here?"

"I think I have one." Greg looked at the floor as if he was trying to collect his thoughts.

"Care to share?" Morgan leaned all her weight on one of her legs. She took a deep breath, reminding herself to stay calm. The last thing she needed was to have another episode, especially in front of Greg. She would earn herself a one-way trip to the hospital if she lost control like she did earlier that day. She sighed, trying to stay calm, hoping he was unable, or too distracted, to notice her breathing slowly.

"I know a lot of people are saying this is a suicide cluster. We've already talked about Sarah, Maisie, and Katrina. The two newest victims, Courtney and Ava..."

"Ava? That's the name of the latest victim?"

"Yeah, Ava Banks. They haven't released it to the school body yet, but I'm sure the news is spreading like wildfire."

"What happened?"

"I don't have a lot of information, just what the principal has told us so far. I guess Ava was out last night at the library studying with a couple of friends. She texted her parents and told them she got a flat tire at the gas station. Her dad told her to stay with the car, but by the time he got there, she was gone."

"Did the car actually have a flat tire?"

"Yeah. From what the principal said, it looked like someone had knifed it."

"Knifed it?" Morgan's thoughts started to spin. If the killer had knifed the tire, that represented an escalation. That was an active method of getting access to a victim by eliminating her ability to travel. "Then what happened?"

Greg cocked his head to the side, "That's where things get hazy. From what the principal said, the dad arranged for a tow truck and kept trying to call Ava, but she didn't answer. He figured that her phone just ran out of battery and she must've gotten a ride home with a friend. He had the car towed to a local auto body shop, but it took a couple of hours by the time he got back. When he pulled in the driveway, he found her. Her body had been dropped in the front yard near the street."

Morgan felt the breath catch in her throat. The killer had targeted Ava, done something to her to knock her out, and then dumped her body at her house. Possibilities roamed through her head. If two hours had gone by between the call and when Ava's dad arrived at home, there was no telling at which point the killer had dropped off the body. Had he done to her the things he had done to the earlier girls? The fact that he dumped the body at her house told Morgan one of two things -- either the killer knew who she was before she was abducted, or he rifled through her bag and figured it out. Either way, it was a bold move, one that said he no longer cared about what anyone thought. Morgan stared at the floor and swallowed, then looked at Greg again, "What about video surveillance? Has anybody said anything about that? Most gas stations have cameras."

"They weren't working. I guess after the last big storm knocked them out, the owner hadn't gotten around to having them fixed yet."

Everything in Morgan wanted to punch the closest locker, driving her fist right through the metal, but she held back. She had to control her temper and her emotions. They just couldn't catch a break with this case. The killer was one step ahead of them, again. She shook her head, searching Greg's face, "So are you still thinking this is a suicide cluster?"

He pressed his lips together, "Up until this morning I did. Now I'm not so sure…"

Morgan nodded. At least he was finally on the same page she was. That could be helpful. "All right. Help me understand — what kind of person would do this?"

Greg narrowed his eyes, "Wait. You're not in law enforcement anymore."

"I told you before that I have a friend who's asked me for some help. She's a detective with the department. That's really all you need to know." Morgan set her jaw, hoping the answer would satisfy him enough that he would help. She held her breath, waiting to see what he would do. His eyes narrowed for a second and then relaxed. That was a good sign.

"Okay. If what we are looking at is a series of murders and not suicides, then I'd guess the offender is likely male."

Morgan listened, making note of the fact that he called what was likely a serial killer just an offender. She chewed the inside of her lip, trying to avoid saying something snarky about not facing the truth. She needed to get information out of him, not rile him up. "Okay, male. How old do you think?"

Greg rubbed his hand through his hair, "Well, we have to figure the person is able to drive, so at least sixteen, probably older than that, though. But it could also be someone from the community, someone who has a thing for young girls and has targeted the school. If that's the case, then your target demographic is anywhere from someone who just got their license up to about mid-forties."

The breath caught in Morgan's throat. That was a pretty wide demographic to look at. "Any idea what motivates somebody like this?"

Greg started to pace, staring at the floor, "Honestly, it could be a whole host of things. I've done some work on cases like this through the juvenile justice system. We see all kinds. It could be somebody who has delusions from drug use, it could be someone who's selling drugs and these girls are involved and not paying him. If that's the case, it could be retribution. It could be somebody with social issues or sexual fantasies." He stopped and stared at Morgan for a second, "Men work out their issues in a lot of different ways. What I can tell you is this is someone who clearly has sociopathic and psychopathic tendencies. They may not even see the girls as human. They may just see them as objects. It could also be a combination of social and family history, past trauma, or even a man who has a hard time relating to women and can't figure out how to have a normal relationship with them."

"You mean like Incels?" Morgan had read about men who called themselves that, claiming they weren't celibate by choice and then went after women.

Greg nodded. "Yeah, that's certainly one possibility. There's a lot of communities on the Internet for men who are not celibate by choice, but because they feel the women around them reject them. They generally have problems socially and just don't know how to connect. They can get aggressive" He stopped, looking at Morgan for a second, lowering his voice, "The thing that really concerns me is the long-term impact of this. If we are looking at a series of murders and not a series of suicides, we have to figure out how these kids are ever going to feel safe in this building again." He shook his head, "I gotta tell you, that's going to be nearly impossible, especially if we find out that the perpetrator happens to be somebody within those walls."

Morgan's heart skipped a beat. Would Danny be one of those kids that didn't feel safe? She blinked, trying to clear her mind. "What are you thinking? Like a teacher or a coach?"

Greg looked over his shoulder in both directions before speaking, leaning closer to Morgan, "Could be. It could also be a student or a former student, someone who feels wronged by the school or the people here."

Morgan took a half step back staring at the bank of lockers just over Greg's shoulder. The idea that a teenager from within the building could be hunting girls was unthinkable, but he was right. If the perpetrator was from within the building, it would be years before the kids felt safe again. It wouldn't matter what steps the school took to help them feel better — increased security, more counseling, more training for the teachers. If it happened between the walls of the building, restoring that trust among the students would be nearly impossible.

Greg's voice interrupted her thoughts, "And what's worse is the police officer we spoke to this morning said that whatever is going on is happening more frequently. You know what that means, don't you?"

"It means we're running out of time."

21

N ate Ambrose checked his watch. He'd spent the majority of the day going over the video surveillance that captured Justin Shaner. By the time late afternoon rolled around, Nate had tossed his sport coat off to the side, wrinkles crisscrossing the sleeves of his pressed shirt where he'd rolled up the fabric. He rubbed his eyes. They were dry from staring at the screen.

What had become completely obvious after hours of watching and rewatching the video was that Justin spent a lot of time going back and forth between the supply refrigerators and the worktable in the lab. Nate shook his head. Whether that was accidental or by design, Nate still didn't know.

Reaching into his desk drawer, Nate pulled out a bottle of eyedrops, squeezing a little in each one of his eyes. He waited for the scratchiness to subside. It felt like he'd been caught in a sandstorm. He blinked a couple of times and then tapped his keyboard again, restarting the video. The section of surveillance Nate was working through showed Justin walking back to the corner of the lab where the lab mice were kept, cleaning their cages and taking a single cage with a single mouse back to his worktable in the blind spot.

Nate shook his head. Part of him wanted to go down to the lab and adjust the cameras so he could see exactly what was going on, but another part of him knew there were blind spots all over the building. No surveillance was one hundred percent foolproof, and by what he'd seen, the cameras at BioNova weren't either. But moving the camera now would look like he was trying to deliberately frame Justin to Candace. That wouldn't work. Nate chewed the inside of his lip. Once he got through the mess with Justin and his mother, he made a note to call the surveillance company and have them come out to remedy the situation. For the time being, he would just have to live with it and make the assumptions based on what he saw.

And what he saw wasn't good.

Nate stared at his monitor and enlarged a single view. The video frame took up the entire screen. He'd spliced sections of surveillance together so he could watch them all at one time, trying to piece together what was going on with Justin. Staring at the screen, waiting for the footage to load, his mind wandered. He thought about when Dr. McCall came into his office to tell him he thought Justin was up to something. At first, the idea was almost impossible to believe. But now, watching what was actually going on in the lab, Nate had formed his own suspicions. He knew going to Candace with only his suspicions would end his career at BioNova the same way it ended Dr. McCall's. He'd be out on his ear. Even if he did find something, it was a treacherous situation. It was bad enough that he was accusing someone of stealing from the lab. Worse, it was the CEO's son.

Nate sighed again, rolling his shoulders and stretching his neck from side to side. Once he'd gotten a few of the kinks out, he leaned forward, starting the video he'd pieced together. He leaned back in his chair, intertwining his fingers, watching.

The video surveillance Nate had managed to splice together encompassed activity just from the last week, though he had gone back as far as three months. That's when Justin's frequent trips to the refrigerators had started. But that's not what Nate was most interested in. It seemed that over the last several weeks, Justin's trips to the refrigerator had increased in frequency. As Nate watched the video, leaning back in his chair, he could see a pattern. Justin would come into the lab for his shift, clocking in at a little bit before two o'clock in the afternoon. According to his HR file, that was the time he was due to arrive. He was also due to leave the building no later than five o'clock, working three hours a day, five days a week for an internship total of fifteen hours per week. The thing was, Justin never left the lab at five o'clock. He was always there after hours.

After watching the spliced video, Nate was hoping he could figure out why.

Justin was prompt every single day. He saw the boy scan his key card in at the security desk, giving a nod to whoever was working the desk at that time, barely making eye contact. He always went straight to the elevators. Once he got to the lab, Justin would put on his white lab coat, go to the workstation at the rear of the lab, log in and check his emails. Nate heard a chime on his laptop. He glanced over, seeing a report come back from the IT department on Justin's usage. Finally.

A few hours before, he'd called the head of IT, a woman not much older than Justin who'd managed to graduate with her Bachelor's and Master's degrees in computer science by the time she was twenty. Nate had asked for a report on Justin's usage. She seemed suspicious. "There's nothing going on, Megan," Nate said. "Justin's internship is up for review and I'm just doing a standard security check."

"I don't remember us doing this for current employees in the past unless we have a problem with them. Is there a problem I should know about?" Nate could hear the edge in her voice.

"No," Nate lied, "This is a new thing. It's a brand-new policy Mrs. Shaner wants us to implement. You know, corporate espionage. They can get to anyone. We've seen some new research that other companies will tempt junior employees and interns with bonuses and cash in order to get access. We've just got to stay on top of it, if you know what I mean."

"And you think Candace's son is a potential problem? That seems like a stretch."

"No, not at all," Nate lied. "Like I said, it's just standard."

"Okay. I can probably get that to you later on this week. I'm buried in budget paperwork."

Nate cleared his throat, "Listen, I hate to bother you with this, but I need it in the next couple of hours. Sorry, that's on me for not being prepared. I'll do better in the future. I guess he's having his review sooner than later since Dr. McCall got let go."

Megan sighed, "Yeah, okay. I can get it running for you now. Might be a little rough when you get it, though."

"Doesn't matter. Whatever you've got is fine."

LEANING FORWARD in his desk chair, Nate clicked on the report, opening it up. He scanned it to see if there were any areas of concern for Justin on the tech side. Based on what Megan had been able to find, his usage was normal. There were no emails from outside sources, he hadn't sent any emails to anyone except for Dr. McCall and the project manager, and there had been no uploading of software from the workstation where he had been logged in. He'd only used one workstation at the lab and that one was clean.

Nate frowned, leaning back in his chair. He lifted his hands and interlaced them behind his head, staring at the ceiling. If there was a problem, then the problem with Justin was within the lab itself. He wasn't misusing BioNova's tech. Nate raised his eyebrows and cocked his head to the side. Even if his email and workstation were clean, that still left questions about the video surveillance Nate had found.

He started watching the pieced-together video again, studying Justin as he walked back and forth to the refrigerators several times during each shift. Every single time, he seemed to check over his shoulder. Nate frowned, checking the other views on the screen. By the time Justin started going to the refrigerators, the lab was empty. It was always after five when he did it. Every single time. Nate furrowed his eyebrows, referring back to the description of his internship and Dr. McCall's weekly notes on Justin. Whether Candace liked Dr. McCall or not, he was a fastidious notetaker and kept great records. Through the terms of his contract, he was required to have those available to not only the head of the research division but Candace and Nate as well. Opening them up, Nate scanned them. There was no mention of any need for Justin to do lab work. About halfway through the description for Justin's internship, Nate's eyes caught on a sentence, "This internship is focused on learning the art of collaboration and data analysis in a research lab setting. This is not a research process position, per se, but has been designed to be the step before that, to familiarize a talented high school student with the processes of professional research in a large pharmaceutical company such as BioNova."

Justin's job wasn't to do anything with the drugs. According to Dr. McCall's own words, Justin was there to look at data and go to meetings. That was about it.

"What are you doing in those refrigerators every day, Justin?" Nate mumbled, staring at the computer as the feed ran in front of him, Justin happened to look back at the camera just as the words came out of Nate's mouth. The hair stood up on the back of his neck. Nate stopped the feed and stared at him for a second. Justin was up to something, but what?

The one thing Nate had learned in the military was that patience nearly always paid off. There was one other thing he could try.

Nate stood up from his desk, opening a secured locker in the back corner of his office. From inside, he pulled out a small silver case with a built-in handle, closing the locker doors as soon as he was done. He rolled his wrinkled sleeves down and re-buttoned them, shrugging on his sport coat and straightening the collar, making sure the flaps covered the pistol at his side. Reggie wasn't the only one in the building that was armed. Most of the security team was. Nate required them to carry while they were on duty. Candace didn't care as long as her buildings were secure.

Leaving his office, Nate gave the door a firm pull to close it behind him, hearing the lock pop into place as he left. He took the elevator up to the fourth floor where Dr. McCall's lab was, or had been before he'd been let go. The elevator doors beeped quietly as they slid open. Nate stepped out on the floor, glancing up and down the hallway. There was no one around. With Dr. McCall terminated, the rest of the team had been sent home for at least the remainder of the day, if not longer, until they determined who would lead the project. BioNova had a requirement that a research scientist was assigned to each project. No one had been reassigned to the anesthesia project Dr. McCall was working on, at least not yet, so work couldn't continue. If Nate had to guess, Candace was waiting until the Board of Directors meeting to decide what to do about the project. There was no point in putting more man-hours into something the Board might want to throw in the trash. From what Nate had been able to glean from Dr. McCall's notes, Candace had been right — Dr. McCall hadn't made a lot of progress on solving the problem that had been put in front of him. That wasn't to say Dr. McCall wasn't able to do it. What it did say is the problem might not be as easily solvable as Candace had hoped.

Nate used his key card and fingerprint to access the secured lab. The muscles in his back tightened, his breath shallow. There was no one around. The only noise in the room was the quiet humming of the ventilation systems and a single light buzzing overhead. Nate walked to the back, looking left and right. He knew where Justin had been sitting and which computer he'd accessed through the surveillance video, but seeing it in person was something completely different. The lab was more packed with equipment than it appeared on the surveillance cameras. Nate dodged a line of work tables and some enormous testing equipment he couldn't identify as he walked to the back of the lab. He stood in front of the stainless-steel table and stool where Justin had taken up residence, looking up and over his shoulder, trying to see where the closest surveillance camera was. It was a few feet away, bolted to the ceiling. Based on what Nate saw in the lab, the surveillance company must have focused more tightly on the millions of dollars of equipment on the other side of the lab, not in the direction of where Justin and the mice were. In reality, they were right. From a surveillance perspective, Nate would always want to know what was going on with the equipment rather than some mice and a single worktable... except in this case.

Pulling a pair of rubber gloves out of his pocket, Nate tugged them on, setting the silver case down on the work-table. He hadn't used the fingerprint kit before. It was a sample that had been sent to him by a security company with a new way of gathering prints. Instead of having to use powder and a brush and then pull them using acetate tape, all he needed to do was spray their reagent on the services and then scan them using an app he'd already loaded on his phone. Whether it would work or not, Nate wasn't sure, but it was worth a try.

Based on the video he'd seen of Justin, Nate knew Justin was primarily going into the second and fifth door on the bank of refrigerators. The camera angle was so bad that anytime someone went to the refrigerator all Nate could see was the fact that they were in it, not what they were getting out of it. And that's what he needed to know.

Nate opened up the software on his phone, importing Justin's fingerprints from his human resources file into the new fingerprinting system. They were accepted and displayed at the top of the screen. So far, so good. Nate walked over to the refrigerator door, staring at it. He opened it up, noticing that everything on each shelf was in a tray. At least that would make his life a little bit easier. He pulled the first tray out, walking it to the closest workbench. Pulling the bottle of reagent from the case, he took the cap off the small bottle and sprayed a fine mist over the bottles and canisters that were lined up in the tray. The instructions from the company said he needed to wait for fifteen seconds for the reagent to collect any fingerprints before scanning. He walked back to the refrigerator and pulled the second tray, spraying it as well. At least the first tray would be ready for scanning by the time the second tray was on the table. He felt a flutter in his stomach, hoping the new system would work.

Opening the camera application on his phone, he used it in combination with the software he loaded from the fingerprint company to scan the first tray, guiding his phone over the areas he'd sprayed the liquid. He waited to see if anything would happen. His chest tightened a little bit. He needed to know exactly what Justin was accessing in the refrigerators. If the fingerprint kit didn't work, he'd have to go back to his office and get an old-fashioned one. That could take hours, hours he might not have, especially if Candace got wind of the fact that he was in the lab looking into her son. He stared at his phone, waiting for something to happen. A second later, a red banner appeared across the screen. No matches. He looked at the screen again. Justin's fingerprints were still at the top. He scanned the second tray and waited again. Still no matches.

Trying to fight off feelings of frustration, Nate replaced the two trays exactly as they had been and pulled the third and fourth trays out of the refrigerator. The bottles on these trays were larger. Nate hoped that they would be easier for the fingerprint program to identify who had been touching them.

Following the same procedure he'd completed with the first two trays, Nate misted the third and fourth trays from the refrigerator and scanned them into the program. He waited, fighting off the urge to pace. A second later, a green banner popped up on his screen. There was a match. Frowning, Nate tapped on the screen and the program highlighted where the target fingerprints had been found. It was on a small bottle from the back. Nate enlarged the image and saw it was cyclo-hexanone. He leaned forward, staring at the tray, using the camera on his phone to take a picture of it. He never heard of it before, but then he specialized in security, not pharmacology.

Nate replaced the last two trays in the refrigerator that Justin seemed to frequent and then went to the fifth door, repeating the process. He got several more hits. In total, it seemed that Justin was touching bottles of the same drugs over and over again, based on the trail of fingerprints from the program. Checking the report that was generated, some of the bottles had layers of the same fingerprints all over them. Justin must have picked up the bottles multiple times, over weeks or months. Nate stopped to think. Was it possible that Justin was the only one that was using some of the lab supplies? He sighed, realizing anything was possible at BioNova. Maybe the designs for the drugs that Dr. McCall had been hired to create didn't take full advantage of every item in the lab. That made sense. It followed human behavior. Nate realized it was much like the clothes in a person's closet — everyone had favorites. There were always items that were fine and functional but never got any use. He wondered if the same thing applied to creating new drugs. It would make sense that the researchers would lean on compounds they knew would behave a certain way rather than testing everything they had access to.

As he'd learned in the military, basic human psychology always won.

Staring at his phone, Nate sent a copy of the results to the private server at his house, just like he did with every investigation. No one knew that he kept copies of sensitive reports off-site. It was just one of the secrets he had in play to protect himself. If somehow this Justin Shaner business blew up on him, he wanted to have evidence that couldn't be contaminated or manipulated by Candace.

Working quickly, Nate stuck the remainder of the trays back in the refrigerator and packed up the fingerprint kit. He stood for a second, listening. He heard the lab mice behind him scurrying around their cages. Someone from the husbandry team should be coming in shortly to take care of the mice since the lab was closed. Nate stared at them for a second. The poor creatures had no idea what was going on around them. At that moment, Nate felt like one of those white mice. He wasn't sure he had any idea what was going on around him either, but it was time to find out.

22

———————

C andace had gotten a call from Justin earlier that morning saying that school had been canceled because of a cluster of suicides. She gave the whole mess about thirty seconds of her attention then promptly told Justin to work on his college applications and that she'd be home later.

Except it was later and she was still at the office.

Part of her wanted to go home and try to spend time with Justin, but she knew it was a futile pursuit. He wasn't all that interested in spending time with her, that he had made abundantly clear. Even if she did show up at home with his favorite food tucked in a carryout bag, she wasn't sure he'd emerge from his room any longer than to collect it and walk away, turning his back on her again.

The other part of her knew that she needed to stay in the office as long as she could tolerate it. The Board of Directors meeting was coming up, and coming up fast. With the firing of Dr. McCall, she would have some explaining to do, not only to justify getting rid of him but also her plans for the project itself now that he was gone. The company had sunk millions of dollars into the research and into hiring Dr. McCall from a competitor. The Board would want answers, and she wasn't sure she had any.

Getting up from her desk, she started to pace, walking in front of the windows that flanked her office. The sun had already gone down. By the looks of the parking lot, she imagined most of the people that worked for BioNova were home with their families, eating dinner, laughing, and sharing details about their day.

She was not.

Buzzing her assistant, she asked him to come into the office. The door cracked open a second later, the young man looking as neat and well-groomed as he had at eight o'clock that morning when he brought her a cup of coffee. "Could you please order dinner for me and have it dropped off at the security desk? One of the security guys will bring it up here once it arrives. Once you get the order placed, you're free to go for the evening."

Her assistant nodded, "Charge this to the company account, ma'am?"

"Yes. Use my company charge. Thank you."

The young man turned on his heel and closed the door without saying anything else. He hadn't worked for her for very long, but so far, she liked him. He didn't say much, was neatly dressed and did what she asked unless he had a pertinent question. He didn't waste her time. That was good. She didn't have time to waste.

Slumping down in the leather furniture on the other side of her desk, Candace tugged a crystal tumbler closer to her. She poured herself a single finger of Scotch and sipped on it, leaning back against the leather upholstery. She normally saved the Scotch for a celebration, but tonight, she just needed to relax enough in order to finish her work. She felt the warm liquid flow down the back of her throat. She probably should have waited until she ate dinner to have any, but firing Dr. McCall hadn't been part of the plan. That put a wrench in the works, a significant one that could tank her own career if she wasn't careful. She'd spent time that afternoon, distracted from the work she should've been doing, looking into his progress on the AnoVest project. From what she could see, it was clear he hadn't made any. That was a problem. In a way, she thought, pressing the cool crystal up to her lips, he may have done her a favor by charging into her office with his unfounded claims against Justin. He was due for a review shortly and he would likely have been terminated or demoted based on his lack of progress anyway. The cycle just happened faster than she anticipated. Even so, she didn't like surprises.

Taking another sip of the amber liquid, the warmth filling her mouth before she swallowed, she realized the only part of it that was problematic was his accusations towards Justin. She felt heat gather in her cheeks. The fact that he'd been brazen enough to accuse her son of stealing told her everything she needed to know about Dr. Andrew McCall. He was a man with not nearly as much talent as she thought and clearly less common sense than that. It took a certain level of chutzpah, or flat-out stupidity, to walk into your CEO's office and accuse her son of stealing. Which one it was, Candace didn't know, she thought, draining what was left of the Scotch in the glass. She stared at the carafe, the lights in her office glinting off of the cut crystal. She lifted off the stopper and poured herself one more finger. Given the day she'd had, she'd allow herself exactly that. Taking another small sip, she made a mental note to have a car and driver pick her up and take her home when she was done working. There was no reason for her to take any chances and get her name splashed across the news for drinking and driving.

Twenty-seven minutes later, there was a knock at her door. "Come!"

A uniformed security guard came into her office, carrying a brown paper bag by the handles. "Mrs. Shaner, this was a drop off at that main security desk. I checked it. Looks like you ordered yourself a lovely dinner." It might seem strange to others to have their food checked, but their competitors had been known to slip listening devices into bags delivered into BioNova before.

"Thank you. You can leave it right there." She pointed to the coffee table where the empty glass of Scotch was still sitting. She watched the security guard for a second to see if he would react. He didn't. At least some people in her office had sense, she decided, watching him as he walked away and closed the door behind her.

Candace looked at the bag with her dinner in it for a second, but there was something other than hunger nagging at her stomach. She pulled up the surveillance feed that Dr. McCall had provided to Nate. She ran it, watching it again. It was roughly edited, clearly by someone without much experience in splicing video. Trying the best she could to be even and dispassionate even though she was Justin's mother, she watched it three more times. All she could see was Justin working at his computer, getting up, going to the refrigerator and then going somewhere else. There were a couple of shots of his back as he walked through the lobby, but nothing more than that. Candace scowled. Certainly Dr. McCall couldn't have expected her to take action on something this vague? A few random shots of her son didn't prove anything.

Feeling the issue was settled, she got up and went to the coffee table, taking her phone with her. As she opened the bag and pulled out the carefully presented salad she'd ordered, she checked her phone to see who was left in the building. Most of the names she didn't recognize, but she did see that Nate Ambrose was still lurking around. Good. That was his job. She reflected on the meeting they'd had with Dr. McCall. He hadn't said much, which wasn't like him. He usually came in, presented his case, and left. But with Dr. McCall, Nate was silent the entire time. He just stood back and let the man hang himself. Candace wondered about that for a second, a half-smile pulling at her cheek as she put the first piece of poached salmon in her mouth, the briny taste from the fish and the dressing dotted with capers filling her mouth. Nate had been a good employee so far. A much better hire than Dr. McCall was, that was for sure.

Candace's phone beeped. It was a text from Justin. For a second, her heart skipped a beat, excited that her son was initiating contact with her. For once, she wasn't chasing him. "Are you still at the office?"

"I'll be home soon!" Candace tried to make her text sound chipper and waited for a response.

None came.

———————

23

"Gotcha," Nate hissed, staring at the screen.

He'd been back in his office for an hour after gathering the fingerprint samples from the lab. Doing a little research, he realized the bottles Justin touched were powerful anesthetics and opioids -- cyclohexanone, etomidate, and methohexital. He shook his head. Candace didn't want to hamstring the researchers into monitoring what they were using, but the fact that there were powerful drugs laying around in the lab unsecured was unacceptable. Sure, the door to the lab was locked and only verified employees could get in the room, but it wasn't enough. He would write a memo about that in the morning, recommending that at a minimum they were kept in a locked refrigerator unit, preferably tracked the same way that hospitals did, the amounts automatically doled out and logged based on barcodes assigned to each of the researchers. BioNova was exposing themselves to an awful lot of liability out of convenience. That had to stop.

But that wasn't what was exciting to him.

Frustrated by the lack of visual evidence to substantiate Dr. McCall's claims, Nate had accessed a whole different set of cameras and gone back to compare the views with the ones that Dr. McCall had shared with him earlier that day. He'd found two shots that told the entire story. All of it.

There was a camera just outside of what had been Dr. McCall's office before he'd been fired. On the face of it, it looked like the view was too far away to catch Justin doing anything, but Nate enlarged it as far as it would go, zooming in on the portion of the screen where he could see Justin moving. The resolution was grainy at best, but even after watching it just once or twice, he could see Justin had vials and bottles set up at his workbench. According to his internship description, that was a no-no. And, there were no notes in Dr. McCall's logbooks to indicate he'd asked Justin to do anything with the drugs, especially after the rest of the lab team had left. Nate marked the spots on the videotape, clipping them into a new montage, using bright yellow circles to point out the bottles of opioids and anesthetics on the workbench. Nate squinted, feeling his breath quicken, watching the rest of the feed from just a few days before. He saw Justin look over his left shoulder, sticking something in his pocket. Nate clipped that section of video as well, putting bright yellow circles around it.

But it wasn't enough.

Nate knew Candace would argue that Justin may have put something in his pocket but didn't take it out of the building. In actuality, she was right. It only became a crime as far as the company was concerned if Justin took whatever he had poured into that vial off BioNova property. Until then, it was considered research material and was part of the proprietary process they used to develop drugs. The question was, had Justin done that?

Squinting at the screen, Nate adjusted the view on the surveillance footage to see the entrance by the security desk. Nate paused, checking the security logs, making sure that Justin had never used another checkpoint. Satisfied that Justin's habit was to come in the main research entrance and exit the same way, Nate resumed looking at the feed. The first angle he looked at only showed Justin from the back as he exited the elevators and walked to the kiosk where he swiped his badge to leave the building. Nate checked several days' worth of Justin's exits but didn't find anything. A knot formed in Nate's stomach. He just couldn't see well enough. That was the problem. He tried two other camera angles but had the same problem. The overhead camera only captured the movements of the people in the lobby and their relative positions within the building. The other camera angle was focused on the space between the elevators to the front doors, looking at everyone from the back who was leaving.

Nate made a note to go through every single camera angle in the building with the surveillance company. He'd trusted them to do the work they needed to do, but now that he was seeing what was going on, it was clear they hadn't managed to capture all of the angles necessary. He felt his stomach sink. He was disappointed in himself for trusting the contractors – he knew better.

Based on the logs, there was one more camera angle he could check. He clicked on the icon displayed on the floor plan. Although the camera angles weren't as helpful as he'd hoped, at least the software was easy to use. The company had provided him with a floor plan layout of where all of the cameras were. All he had to do was click on it to see what that camera had captured.

The last camera that covered the main research entrance was posted just inside the doors. Unlike the other ones, it faced into the building, toward the elevators. Nate felt butterflies in his stomach. Even from watching the first few frames of people leaving the building, he could see it was a better angle. He fast-forwarded to the spot in the video where Justin was exiting the building a few days before, the same day Nate had found Justin working with the anesthesia drugs on his bench. He'd seen a vial that Justin was filling on the worktable. The question was, where had it gone from there? Nate closed his eyes for a second, thinking, running through what he'd seen in his mind. Justin hadn't gone back to the incinerator door after working on whatever project he was doing. Whatever he'd made, he must have taken with him.

Nate felt the muscles in his jaw tighten as he leaned forward, enlarging the view. He watched as Justin got off the elevator, holding his lab coat over his left arm. Nate scowled. That was strange. Justin always left his lab coat upstairs. He ran the video forward again, watching as Justin paused for a second, switching the coat to cover his right arm, but not before reaching into the pocket of his jeans, as if he were touching something inside. Nate stared at the screen. Justin shifted the lab coat to his right arm, the fabric draping down over his pant leg, holding the key card to his left hand.

Nate stopped the video and stared at the ceiling. Why all the switching? Nate closed his eyes for a second and realized that Justin was likely right-handed. In every video he'd watched of the intern, he'd seen him use his right hand for the majority of the activity. And now he was going to swipe out with his left hand, having to cross his body to access the kiosk? No, something wasn't right.

Stopping the video, Nate froze it on the frame showing Justin coming out of the elevator. He stared at the screen, enlarging the view as much as possible. Although he had to blow it up, the resolution was much better than the camera in the lab. That was another thing he needed to ask the company about. When they'd been hired, Nate insisted they use 4K cameras, but the resolution of the feed left him with questions. If they hadn't, then they were in breach of contract. Nate scrawled a note on the pad of paper on his desk. He didn't have time to deal with that at the moment. He had to get this business with Justin Shaner resolved one way or another.

Blinking, Nate stared at the screen again, inching it forward, frame by frame. He watched as Justin got off of the elevator and then stopped for a second. There were no other people in the lobby at that time. It was late, by the timestamp, after seven o'clock. Justin stopped by a planter that flanked the security desk, out of sight of the security guy. Nate cocked his head to the side studying Justin's movements. There was something he hadn't seen before – a new behavior. Justin turned slightly, sticking his hand in his right front pocket and then pulling it out, glancing down and then shoving his hand back in his pocket. What was he looking at? Nate zoomed in even further on the image.

It was a vial.

Nate's heart started to pound in his chest. Dr. McCall had been right. Justin was up to something. Nate tapped the screen and marked the video so he could come back to that spot to add to his montage. He let the rest of the video run, watching as Justin used his lab coat to cover the lump in his pocket, swiped his key card and walked out the door as if he was doing nothing wrong.

While it was clear Justin had exited the building with a vial, the last piece of information Nate needed was to see if he left the property. BioNova employed sophisticated license plate readers to document every vehicle that entered and exited the property. Pulling up Justin's parking permit information, he saw that he drove a sleek silver sedan, a nicer car than Nate even drove. Nate shook his head. Candace wasn't doing Justin any favors. If it'd been his son, he would have enlisted him in the military and sent him off to get a taste of the real world. That would straighten him out. Coddling him didn't seem to be teaching him anything, especially if he was playing with the drugs from the lab like it was some sort of game.

Setting up the search parameters for the plate reader, Nate double-checked to see if Justin's vehicle had left. Within a few seconds, the software had come up with a report, logging the times Justin entered and left the property. Sure enough, the information was right in front of his face. Justin had left the property with the vial and whatever it contained.

Nate shook his head, staring at the screen. He knew Justin was brilliant. How could a smart kid be so stupid?

Getting up from his desk, Nate started pacing, interlacing his fingers behind his head and staring at the ground as he walked. Questions raced through his head. Did he have enough to go to Candace with? His stomach started to flutter. He hadn't felt that way since he was deployed. He knew his gut was telling him he was in danger. Whether personally or professionally, he wasn't sure.

Nate spun his desk chair towards him and sat down. Moving as fast as his fingers would allow, Nate pieced the video together, highlighting the sections where Justin had been working on something in the lab, tracking the vial from the time he left the lab to the security checkpoint and then adding in the information about when Justin left the building. From inside of his desk drawer, Nate pulled out two flash drives, making identical copies of the montage and attaching another one to an email he sent to his personal account, then logging into the private server he had at his house and directly uploading it. Maybe he was being paranoid. Maybe he wasn't. He sat back in his chair for a second. His chest felt heavy. He knew he had a responsibility to expose what was going on in the building, but he wasn't sure how Candace would take it.

Standing up and putting his sport coat on, he shoved the two flash drives in his pocket, his heart skipping a beat. He'd worked hard to become the Chief of Security for BioNova. Exposing the CEO's son wouldn't be a popular move, but it was the right thing to do.

Or was it?

24

Candace had just closed her laptop and shoved it in her briefcase when she heard a knock at her door. "Come!" she yelled. The thick wooden door made it difficult for people to hear her respond. It was becoming annoying to have to holler every single time someone wanted to come into her office. She made a mental note to speak to her assistant in the morning about a better process. He seemed organized. Perhaps he would have a better solution.

Nate stepped into her office, leaving the door open. "I'm glad I caught you before you left," he said, standing in front of her desk with his hands stuffed in his pockets.

"I was just about to. Can this wait till the morning?" she said, noticing the takeout containers from her dinner sitting on the coffee table along with the crystal tumbler from her two fingers of scotch earlier. The cleaning people would have to take care of it. She didn't have the energy.

"I don't think so."

Candace glanced at him. Nate looked tired, his five o'clock shadow darkening the edges of his jaw. There was something about his demeanor that seemed stiff, strained; like someone had jammed a rod up his back. "Okay. What's this about?"

"I think Dr. McCall was right."

Candace narrowed her eyes. "I'm sorry?"

Nate cleared his throat, "I think Dr. McCall was right about Justin. Something's going on."

"Other than the fact that he is a brilliant teenager stuck in high school?" Candace stared down at her desk and chuckled. Dr. McCall wasn't the first person to misunderstand Justin. She was sure he wouldn't be the last. She gathered up her cell phone and stuffed it into her purse. There was a car coming for her in five minutes. Nate better make this quick.

"Yes, Candace. More than that."

She felt the heat rise to her face, "Spit it out Nate! What exactly are you saying?"

"What I'm saying is that I think Justin has been playing around with some of the more potent chemicals in Dr. McCall's lab and taking them off-site."

The words landed like a ton of bricks on her chest. This was the second time her staff had gone after her son. Was this a vendetta? Had someone on the Board set them up to try to get rid of her? Candace glanced down at the floor for a second, holding her breath, counting to three in her head. She couldn't afford to lose her temper. If she was being set up, then how she responded would get back to the person who was coming after her, she was sure of it.

She lowered her voice. "I hope that unlike Dr. McCall, you aren't coming to my office with unfounded accusations. I'm assuming you have evidence?"

Nate gave her a sharp nod, pulling a flash drive out of his pocket, "I do."

Candace pressed her lips together, barely breathing. What had Nate found on Justin? Was this the explanation for why Justin had been so distant? Had he done something wrong at the lab and was afraid to tell her? Her mind raced as she pulled her laptop out of her bag and opened it up, sliding the flash drive into one of the ports on the side.

Nate moved behind her desk. She could feel his eyes on the back of her neck, the heat of his body behind her. As she cued up the video, she knew she would watch it politely, tell him she would talk to Justin, and then send Nate home. That was it. That was exactly what was going to happen in the next few minutes. Enough of the nonsense already.

Candace checked the time in the corner of her computer as the video loaded. The car taking her home would be downstairs in three minutes. She had every intention of being there when it arrived.

Clicking on the video, she glanced up at Nate, trying her best to sound calm and patient. "What am I looking at?"

Nate pointed to the screen as the first images started to run. "I pulled video surveillance from this week, from Dr. McCall's lab and of Justin traveling in and out of the building. As you can see, in this first clip, he has a bunch of bottles on his work table and he's mixing something."

Candace frowned, stopping the video. If this was the evidence Nate had, it was laughable. "So? He's an intern in a research lab. What did you think would happen?"

Nate raised his eyebrows, looking surprised, "Candace, that's not part of his internship. If you go back and read the description, he's supposed to be basically attending meetings and helping with data analysis. He's not been given access to any of the compounds in the lab."

Candace felt her body tense, "That's ridiculous. Where does it say that?"

"Right in the description Dr. McCall wrote for his internship. It's in black and white in the HR documents. He's not supposed to have any access to the materials at the lab."

Candace wrapped her fingers around the edge of her desk,

gripping it tightly. "You know how brilliant he is, Nate. I'm sure he was just messing around with some of the materials they have in the lab. I'm sure it's nothing."

Nate cocked his head to the side and pointed to the screen again, "Keep watching. You'll see him. He makes some sort of a mixture and then pours it into a vial. The thing is, Candace he's not playing with inert compounds. The stuff on his work table — that's the very stuff I have been telling you we need to lock up."

"Like the opioids and protocol derivatives? Is that what you're talking about? There's no way he'd use those materials!" she said, throwing her hands up in the air. "Why on earth would he do that? You don't even know that!"

"Actually, I do. I have his fingerprints on the bottles for cyclohexanone, etomidate, and methohexital. They are all over them."

Candace shrugged, "Maybe he was just playing around. You know how kids are."

She caught Nate's eye. He was staring at her, his eyebrows raised as if he couldn't believe the words that were coming out of her mouth. "This isn't that big of a deal. He probably is running his own experiment. You don't know how he is. I do."

Nate lowered his voice, "Candace, he took the drugs off-campus. Keep watching the video. You'll see."

Candace swallowed, hard. Whoever was framing Justin to get at her had done a good job. The hair on the back of her neck stood up, her mind racing. Was it Nate? Had he been gunning to get rid of her this whole time? Even if it was, it wasn't as if he was going to become CEO, though. He was just an overpaid security guard with a lot of fancy toys. She pressed her lips together. It had to be someone on the Board, someone who had something on Nate.

Glancing at the screen, she watched Justin as he exited the elevators. Nate interrupted her thoughts, "See there?" he pointed, "The video clearly shows he has a vial in his hand which he shoves into his pocket. He uses his lab coat to hide the bulge in his jeans pocket. Our guys know to look for this kind of thing, but Justin covered it up."

Candace sniffed, "You mean like him?" She pointed at the screen, the video showing the security guard as Justin passed by, "He looks like he's busier messing with his phone than watching my evil son walk out of the building. Looks like you should fire him. Or maybe I should."

Nate walked around her desk without saying anything. He stood in front of her, his hands shoved deep in his pockets again. For a second, she wondered if she should call one of the other security guys and have Nate removed, or maybe the police. She decided against it. Nate ran the whole security division after all. They were loyal to him.

"No one is saying Justin is evil," Nate said, his voice barely above a whisper. "But I have to tell you, this is incriminating, very incriminating. I mean, what is he doing with those drugs off-campus? It's bad enough that he's messing around with them in the building, but where is he taking them? Candace, does he have a drug problem you haven't told me about?"

The insinuation that Justin might have a drug problem knocked the wind out of Candace's lungs. She felt the blood rush to her face as she stared at Nate, her mouth open. Would she even know if Justin did? Her own son barely spoke to her. "No! Of course not! And I know you think you have proof that he's been using the drugs we have in the lab, but what do you really have? Just a little bit of video and a few fingerprints. Maybe he was cleaning up after the researchers and got his fingerprints on them when he put them away. You don't know what you're talking about!" Candace slammed the lid of the laptop closed, ripping the flash drive out of the port and throwing it at Nate. "How dare you come into my office and accuse my son of doing something like this. Who do you think you are?"

"I'm your Chief of Security. It's my job to bring these threats to you."

"Threats?! Are you kidding me? He's a kid!"

"A kid that has access to dangerous drugs that he is now taking off of our property. Do you understand the amount of liability this represents for this company? For you?" Nate said, leaning toward her.

Candace had heard enough. She stormed around the desk, standing face-to-face with Nate. "You son of a..." she yelled. "Someone has put you up to this! Someone wants to destroy me and they're going after Justin to do it. I know your games. You might think I can't see what's happening here, but I see it all too clearly."

Nate took half a step back, staring at her, his eyes never leaving her face. "That is not what is happening here, Candace," he said calmly. "You know it and I know it."

The fact that Nate was staying so calm was the final straw. She reached down and picked up the carafe with the Scotch and hurled it with everything she had, barely missing Nate's head. It crashed against the wall and shattered, the smell of the alcohol hanging in the air. "If you breathe a word of this to anyone," she hissed, "I will kill you. You can't threaten me! I own you! Now get out!"

25

N ate stood his ground for a second, staring at Candace. Her face was blotchy and red, her lips pulled tight across her face, exposing perfectly straight, white teeth. He'd never seen her like this before. He glanced over his shoulder staring at the shards of crystal scattered on the tile floor. What was left of what he was sure was very expensive Scotch was running down the wall and pooling by the mahogany floorboards.

He didn't expect her to take the news well, but he also didn't expect her to go completely nuts.

Without saying anything, he turned and walked out of her office. If he'd had eyes in the back of his head, he would've used them, thinking she might hurl something else at him as he left.

Nate took short clipped steps down the hallway, covering as much ground as he could without running. He scanned his key card at the front desk, keeping his face calm. "Have a good night," he said to Rodney, the guard on duty for the overnight shift.

"See you later."

Pushing his way out the doors of the building and heading

to his car, Rodney's words echoing in his ears, he wondered if he would. Candace was so irate it was impossible to tell what her next step would be. Getting into his car, he started it, pulling out of the parking lot. Thoughts were lining up in his head, not in a way that was overwhelming, but in a way that posed more questions than answers. It was strange that Candace had assumed that someone on the Board of Directors was trying to frame her. He knew that being the female CEO of a major pharmaceuticals firm painted a target on her back, but she couldn't certainly believe that her own Board of Directors wanted to take her out and would use her son to do it, could she?

But the bigger question was what to do next. Justin was up to something. What that was, Nate wasn't sure. He didn't really know anything about Justin other than he was Candace's son and in high school. The only other fact he had in his arsenal was that he'd pretty much been given the internship by his mother. She was a force of nature. No one, including Dr. McCall, would say no to her, not if they wanted to keep their job and work in the industry ever again. Was he willing to risk his own career to find out?

That was the one notable fact about his meeting with Candace, Nate thought, stopping at a red light. She hadn't fired him on the spot. When she hurled the carafe at him, he expected that might be the next set of words out of her mouth, but they didn't come.

Interesting.

It didn't take long for Nate to get home. Although he was paid well by BioNova, he preferred to keep his money in investments and cash. He pulled in the driveway of the small house he owned. It was a three-bedroom, two-bath house on a canal that he'd gotten in a short sale for just over one hundred thousand dollars. With the booming Florida real estate market, it was worth more than triple of that now that he'd owned it for a few years. Walking in the door, he tossed his keys down and pulled the gun off his hip, laying it on the counter, shrugging out of his sport coat. He stopped for a second, leaning his weight on his hands, using the kitchen counter for support. The same question kept rattling through his mind -- what was Justin planning on doing with the mixture of chemicals he'd stolen from the lab?

Part of the problem with Justin was his own fault, Nate realized, going to the refrigerator and pulling it open. There was a box of Chinese food from the day before. He pulled it out and flipped the lid open, picking at it with his fingers. He'd told Candace they needed to secure all of the powerful drugs and compounds in the labs, but he hadn't insisted. He'd crumbled like a two-dollar suit when she pushed back. At the time, he'd only been on the job for a couple of weeks. He realized at that moment that he'd been more afraid to lose his job than to do the right thing.

But now things had changed. Justin had clearly taken drugs off the property, drugs that could potentially kill someone. The kid might be brilliant, but he was clearly lacking common sense. Nate shook his head. Justin should know better. Hadn't Candace taught him anything?

Grabbing a fork from the drawer, Nate took the cold Chinese food over to a stool at the counter and shoved a few bites in his mouth, not bothering to warm it up. He hadn't eaten all day, but he wasn't really that hungry. Chewing, he leaned over to where he'd tossed his sport coat, retrieving the second flash drive from the pocket. He set it next to the container of Chinese food as he ate. Staring at it, he felt like it was burning a hole in his gut.

The memory of one of his commanding officers surfaced in his mind, "Ambrose, at the end of the day, you have to decide if you can lay your head on the pillow with a good conscience or not. My advice? Sleep is easier if you do the right thing, no matter how hard it is." The man's gruff voice rattled through Nate's mind. As much as he wanted to give Candace a chance to do the right thing, her reaction told him everything he needed to know. She might not need to sleep at night, but he did.

From the back pocket of his pants, he pulled out his cell phone, dialing the non-emergency number for the Tampa Police Department. It felt like he was moving to Defcon One as he dialed. There would be no turning back if he completed the call. Once Candace got wind of the fact that he got the police involved, he would almost certainly lose his job. Knowing her, she would smear his name all over the city. He'd be lucky if he could get a job as a trash collector after that, although, given how the day had gone, collecting trash didn't sound too bad.

"Tampa Police. How can I direct your call?"

"I need to speak to one of your detectives about a theft, please?"

There was a pause on the other end of the line. Nate thought for a second they might tell him to call 9-1-1 or that he'd need to file a report in-person first. It didn't happen, "Hold one moment, please."

"Detective D'Amico."

"Detective, my name is Nate Ambrose. I'm the Chief of Security for BioNova Pharmaceuticals. Is this a bad time?"

"Nope. That's the thing about the police department, we're always open. How can I help?"

"I have reason to believe that we have an employee who has been removing drugs from the property. I wanted to see if I could meet with someone and pass along the evidence I've found so you guys could follow up?"

"What kind of drugs are we talking about, sir?"

"It's a mix of opioids and compounds that are used in the drugs manufactured by the company. I'm just concerned if they get into the wrong hands, you might see an uptick in drug deaths. Honestly, I'm not sure what's going on. That's why I'm calling."

"The pharmaceutical company has access to opioids?" She sounded surprised.

Nate stood up from the stool, starting to pace, "Yes. BioNova has a federal drug license that allows us to buy compounds so that we can create new drugs. It's part of our research. The drugs that are missing are ones that are typically used for anesthesia. They can knock somebody out cold in no time at all. If you want, this can wait until the morning. I'd be happy to stop by your office if that's easier?"

"No," Detective D'Amico blurted out. "No, in fact, I would like to meet with you right now. You said you have evidence?"

Nate furrowed his eyebrows. Something didn't seem right. He was surprised the detective would seem so interested in what he had to offer. "Yes. I have video surveillance and fingerprints to turn over to you."

"Where do you live?" The words came out short and clipped as if the detective couldn't speak fast enough.

"Bayshore."

"Okay. I have to make a stop, but can you meet me at the South Shore Beach in thirty minutes?"

Nate nodded but didn't answer. It seemed strange that the detective didn't want to come to his house or have him come into the station, but if she had to make a stop... "Sure. I know where that is."

"Great. Let me get your number just in case."

Nate gave detective D'Amico his full name, address, and telephone number over the phone and promised to meet her in a half-hour. Hanging up, he sat back down on the kitchen stool, taking a few more bites of the cold Chinese food. He picked up the flash drive in his left hand, tapping it gently on the counter. Had he done the right thing? His stomach growled. Apparently, the truth was sitting with him better than he thought.

26

Morgan was just finishing the dinner dishes that had been soaking in the sink when someone pounded on the door. Bo jumped up, charging and barking. Morgan felt her heart skip a beat. She lifted the hem of her T-shirt, exposing the butt of her gun, resting her right hand on it as she walked to the door. Glancing through the side window, she saw it was Amber. She took her hand off it as she opened the door, "You startled me. What's going on?"

Amber stepped just inside the house. "Can you take a drive with me?"

Morgan blinked, "I guess. Where are we going?"

"I just got a call from the chief of security at a lab here in town. He has some information about drugs that have gotten out on the street."

"And your thinking...?"

Amber started to pace. "I don't know. He said it's one of their employees. I just think the timing is, well, suspicious."

Morgan glanced back towards the kitchen. Brantley and Danny had been glued to their computers all day long. Brantley kept saying they were getting close, but she wasn't sure what they were close to. It had something to do with the messaging app. Brantley had managed to get himself invited in and they were close to identifying who the people were that were involved.

"I guess I can go," Morgan said, walking into the kitchen. Amber followed her, the thick heels of her boots clunking on the tile floor.

The boys still hadn't moved. The two of them were sitting stock still as they stared at their computers. It was as if they were both holding their breath, waiting for something to happen. Morgan frowned, "Danny? Are you guys okay?"

Brantley didn't take his eyes off the screen. Morgan heard the breath catch in his throat. "There!" he hissed, glancing at Danny. He pointed at the screen, "Look, they're all connected."

Morgan frowned and walked towards the boys, Amber trailing behind her. Morgan leaned over Brantley. On his display, she could see what looked like a genealogy, a single line jutting up out into multiple layers. What wasn't on the screen were the fake screen names the people had used to sign up for the encrypted messaging app. Instead, there were real names, including Katrina DeLuca. "You got through!" Morgan said, her eyes wide as she leaned her palms on the kitchen table. "You figured it out!"

"Yeah," Brantley sighed. "I got through all the people that are connected in this group, but not the person who invited them. There seems to be an extra layer of security that's got us stuck," Brantley frowned.

"Tell me the names you can see?" Amber said.

Danny cleared his throat, leaning towards Brantley, "Sarah Poole, Maisie Hill, Katrina DeLuca, Courtney Reese, and Ava Banks. Looks like there are a couple pending invitations too, but those haven't been unlocked yet."

Morgan stared at Amber, sucking in a breath, "That's all the girls from the high school. All of them. Whoever targeted them must have used the GenChat app to communicate."

Amber glanced at Morgan and then at the front door, "You might be right, but we've got to go meet my source." Amber looked at the boys, "Danny, can you and Brantley screenshot that and send it to me?"

Danny nodded.

"And if you're able to unlock the source person, get that to me right away, okay?"

"For sure. We'll keep working on it," Danny said, the words tumbling out of his mouth.

"Good. Come on, Morgan, we gotta go."

Morgan took a last look at the boys. They'd already turned their attention back to what was going on with the GenChat app, the two of them mumbling underneath their breaths, both of their fingers running across their individual computers in a blur. How exactly Danny was able to help Brantley, Morgan wasn't sure, but it didn't matter. They'd managed to find all of the victims' names in one spot. There had to be a connection. She stared at Bo for a second, wondering if she should take him with her, but she decided it would be better to leave him at home. At least if he was at the house and something happened, he might buy the boys valuable time in getting help.

As she walked towards the front door, following Amber, Amber glanced at her, "What is it?"

Morgan stared back at the kitchen, "I'm just concerned about the boys. What if GenChat notifies the attacker that he's been outed? What if the boys are tracked here?"

Amber nodded, "Say no more. I'll have a car sit on the house while we're gone."

Morgan jogged back to the kitchen and told Danny to expect a police car to be sitting outside in the next few minutes. As the words came out of her mouth, she noticed the color drained from his face a little bit. Brantley never looked up. She put her hand on top of his, feeling its warmth, "It's just until I get back, okay?"

He furrowed his eyebrows together, "Okay. But be careful."

"I will. Don't worry."

Danny frowned at her as if she was asking the impossible. After what they'd been through, maybe she was.

The drive to South Shore Beach only took ten minutes from Morgan's house, Amber turning from Gulf Shores Parkway down a couple of side streets to get to the water. There was a small trickle of cars and their headlights going both directions on the two-lane road, the dark having settled over the coastline only punctured by the occasional street light. While they drove, Morgan tried to imagine what the people in the cars around them were doing. Were they going home for a late dinner, driving to work the overnight shift, or maybe heading to the airport for a redeye flight? Her heart skipped a beat. She glanced at Amber, "Who did you say this guy is again?"

"I'm not sure I did," she grunted, glancing at Morgan as she drove. "His name is Nate Ambrose. He's the Chief of Security for some pharmaceutical firm in town. Bio-something. He said they're having issues with high-powered anesthetics leaving the building. The way he called, it was strange."

Morgan cocked her head to the side, "Why do you say that?"

"I don't know. He was very professional on the phone, but there was something in the way he talked that made it seem like he was more than just concerned. You know, if this was a routine theft issue, I'd expect him to call during working hours. But this late at night? The guy should be home putting his feet up."

The hair on the back of Morgan's neck stood up. The fact that Amber was concerned about the guy they were meeting twisted her gut into a knot. She stared straight forward as

Amber clicked the turn signal on to veer into the South Shore Beach entrance.

Morgan stared out the window. In terms of leads, they didn't have much, but they were getting closer. What they did have was an interview with someone who was talking about the same kind of drugs that could have incapacitated Katrina and Courtney. She chewed her lip. It was common to feel frustrated as a detective when leads wouldn't come together. The problem was she hadn't been a detective in years.

As Amber pulled into a parking spot next to the only sedan in the lot, Morgan touched the butt of the pistol on her side, double checking to make sure it was secure at her hip. She pulled her T-shirt and jacket down over it, zipping it up. Amber flashed the red and blue police lights letting the person in the sedan know they were police, or at least Amber was, Morgan thought.

Shutting the car off, Morgan got out of the car, following Amber as they stood behind the rear bumper. "Nate Ambrose?" Amber called, staring at the man who emerged out of the car.

"That's me," he said.

"Come towards me and turn around, please," Amber said. Morgan stood off to the side, watching as Amber patted him down. She pulled a loaded pistol from Nate's hip and handed it to Morgan. Morgan set it on the trunk of the police car, watching. "You have a permit to carry that, sir?" Amber said.

"Of course. It's in my wallet."

Amber nodded, "Okay, you can turn around." Staring at him, Amber said, "Sorry for the search, but police officers are targets these days. Better to be safe than sorry."

Morgan watched Nate Ambrose. He was well-built, with brown hair, attractive. He had on a button-down shirt, sport coat, and dress pants. He looked like he'd come straight from work. Whether that was true or not, Morgan didn't know. She leaned on the police car, her arms crossed across her chest, waiting.

"No problem as long as you give me my gun back."

"I'll be happy to do that before we leave," Amber said, shifting her weight onto one leg. "So, Mr. Ambrose, why are we here? You said something about drugs missing from your company?"

Morgan could see only the side of his face from the overhead lights in the parking lot. The other side was in shadow. He had scruff on his chin as though he needed to shave. Paul DeLuca looked the same the last time she saw him at the hospital. Was Nate just tired or under a lot of stress? Morgan uncrossed her arms and took a couple of steps forward, trying to hear what Amber and Nate were talking about better.

"As I told you on the phone, Detective, I'm the Chief of Security for BioNova Pharmaceuticals. Our headquarters are here in Tampa. One of our chief research scientists, Dr. Andrew McCall, came to me earlier this week insisting that someone was stealing powerful drugs from the lab. Things like cyclohexanone, etomidate, and methohexital. To be honest, I looked at the evidence he had and didn't give it much of a second thought."

Nate spent the next minute describing the interaction he'd seen between Candace Shaner, the CEO of BioNova, and Dr. McCall, which ended up in his termination from the company. "Honestly, I wasn't sure what to do but my gut told me I needed to look into it." From his pocket, he pulled out a flash drive and handed it to Amber. "Since Dr. McCall was fired, it's pretty much all I've worked on. On that flash drive," he gave a nod toward it, "you have all the evidence I've been able to assemble. It's got the drug names, video footage, and fingerprints on the compound."

"Fingerprints?" Morgan mumbled.

He nodded towards her, "Yeah, the security team at BioNova

is pretty sophisticated. Everybody on it is either former military or former law enforcement. The formulas and information we protect are literally worth billions of dollars between the research and the production. That doesn't even begin to scratch the surface when it comes to corporate espionage. I can only speak in general terms without breaking my non-disclosure agreement."

"And your employees just have free rein to play with dangerous chemicals?" A frown spread wide on Amber's face.

Nate held up his hands, "I have been working for the last couple of years to get our CEO, Candace Shaner, to restrict and log the usage of those chemicals like they do in hospitals, with barcodes and such, but it's been an uphill battle. She feels that because the labs are secured — only the people working on an individual project can get access to them — that that's enough. She doesn't want that creativity of the researchers to be hampered by too many regulations. I get that, but..." His words trailed off.

"But?" Morgan said.

Nate shrugged, "But, as you will see on the video, it's one thing to only let a certain group of people into a lab. That doesn't mean they won't try to take things off the property."

"And is that what you are alleging happened?" Amber said, rolling the flash drive over in her palm.

"Yes. Without a doubt. When you watch the video, you'll see. We have an intern who kept accessing the drugs in the lab and then poured some into a vial and left our campus with it." He glanced at the two women, "It's not a breach of security unless they walk off our property. Technically, any of our employees could walk around on the campus with any chemical compound or drug we have in our possession without a problem. The regulations are set up that way so we can transport products between lab spaces. Once someone leaves our property, though, it's a whole different ball game."

"And that's why you called?" Amber said.

Nate nodded.

"What kind of drugs are these? And who do you think took them off the property?" Morgan said, frowning.

"The drugs that were taken were a combination of powerful anesthetics and opioids that are used during surgery. Dr. McCall's team was charged with creating a new anesthesia drug that could immediately put someone to sleep, keep them under for a couple of hours, and then wake them up again, all without having to use an anesthesiologist or any complex side effects. It's a tall order. Anesthesia is a tricky business, from what I hear, but as everyone at BioNova keeps reminding me, I'm just the security guy."

Morgan pressed her lips together. From the way Nate spoke, she knew he was anything but just a regular security guy. If she had to guess, he was probably former military. He held himself confidently and answered their questions to the point.

"And who do you think took the drugs off campus?" Amber said, pulling a notepad out of her pocket.

"Based on my research, I think it's Justin Shaner. He's the CEO's son, unfortunately," Nate said, shoving his hands in his pockets.

"The CEOs son?" Amber said, raising her eyebrows. "Are you serious?"

Nate nodded, "Yeah. The kid's brilliant. He's a senior in high school, but he doesn't really belong there. From what I can tell, he's pretty arrogant, feels like he's better than everybody else. It doesn't surprise me given the way his mom treats him. Gets whatever he wants without asking."

At the mention of the high school, the breath left Morgan's chest. She was standing in front of the Chief of Security for a major pharmaceuticals firm who had just accused a high school student of stealing the exact drugs that were killing the girls. She rubbed her palms on her pant legs, noticing they were getting sweaty. Glancing at Amber and then to Nate, she said, "You mentioned the intern is a senior in high school? Any idea which high school he goes to?"

"Not sure about that. It's someplace local. He goes to school until one o'clock in the afternoon and then is in the lab from two to five. It's a public high school, I think. If I remember correctly, Candace told me she wanted him to go away to some fancy boarding school for geniuses, but he wouldn't go."

"Could it be Palm Coast High School?" Morgan said, the words coming out of her mouth slowly.

Nate shrugged, "Maybe? I wouldn't be doing you any favors if I said yes. I honestly don't know."

Morgan looked at Amber, her eyes wide. Amber returned the stare. Amber glanced at the ground for a second and then back at Nate, "One more question and then I'll let you go. Did you talk to his mom -- you said she's the CEO -- about this?"

Nate didn't say anything for a second, just staring at the ground, his hands still shoved in his pockets. When he looked up, Morgan saw the anger cross his face, even in the shadows. "That was the other thing I wanted to tell you. Yes, I attempted to. That's why I'm here. A couple of hours ago, I went to her with the same information I just gave to you. She went nuts. Threw a crystal carafe filled with some sort of expensive booze in it against the wall. Barely missed my head."

Amber shrugged and then looked at Morgan, smiling, "Sounds like a typical response from a mom, don't you think?"

Before Morgan could answer, Nate interrupted, "It was a little bit more than that. She threatened to kill me."

Morgan narrowed her eyes, "Do you have any evidence of that?"

From the pocket of his pants, Nate pulled out another flash drive. He handed it to Amber, "I have no idea if this would be admissible in court, not that I want to press any charges, but I recorded our conversation. She doesn't know, of course. But yeah, I'd expect you'll be able to hear the whole thing."

Amber stared at the two flash drives for a second and then glanced at Nate, "How did you leave things with her?"

"She told me to get out, so I did. Based on the way the office looked when I walked in, it looked like she'd been drinking. The carafe and a crystal tumbler were sitting on the coffee table next to some takeout containers. In her defense, I know she's been under a lot of stress. It's a hard enough job being a CEO of a major firm, but being a female makes it even worse."

Morgan wanted to groan, but held it in, "It's nice that you're trying to give her a pass."

Nate shook his head, the muscles of his jaw rippling, "I promise you it's anything but that. I'll be surprised if I still have my job at lunchtime tomorrow. I'm not concerned about myself or my job. If you decide to follow up on this, you need to be careful around her. She doesn't seem it, but she's downright dangerous. She'll do anything to protect her reputation and her job. Anything." He shifted from side to side, "She even accused me of being a plant for someone on the Board who is trying to get rid of her, which by the way, isn't true. She's a little paranoid, if you ask me."

He pointed to the flash drives he'd given to Amber, "The reason I came forward is that the drugs Justin Shaner looks like he accessed are powerful. They could easily kill someone. I have no idea what the kid is doing taking them out of the lab. It's not even part of his job. He's there to go to meetings and to help the team with some of the data." He looked at the ground for second, "You can probably already tell, but I was in the military. The one thing I've learned is sometimes you gotta do something hard so you can sleep at night. That's what one of my commanding officers told me. That's why I called. I don't have any jurisdiction outside of the BioNova campus, but you do. I'd just hate to see somebody get hurt because of this kid."

Nate jingled his keys in his pocket, "Now, if you don't have any other questions for me, I'd like to head home. It's been a long day."

Amber nodded, "That's fine. I'll need you to come by the station in the morning and file a report, but I have enough to get things moving right now. And I appreciate the heads up."

Morgan handed Nate his pistol and watched him walk away. The brake lights flashed as he pulled out of the parking lot, leaving Morgan and Amber alone.

The two of them stood, the sound of the surf thrumming in the background, the waves crashing on the shore in an almost constant rhythm. Morgan looked at Amber. "Now what?"

Amber walked toward the driver's side door of the car and got in, "Now I go back to the office to see what's on these flash drives after I drop you off at home. If this Candace Shaner is as powerful as Nate says she is, I gotta get resources moving."

Morgan nodded, closing the car door. If Candace was as big of a fish as Amber thought she was, Morgan wasn't sure they had time to wait.

27

J ustin had been home from the lab for just over an hour. He'd messed around on his computer for a little bit, checking for any new messages. He drummed his fingers on his desk. There weren't any. He checked the time on his watch and then stared out the window, butterflies in his stomach.

When he got back from the lab, his mom still wasn't home. That worked to his advantage. Less questions to ask. He stashed his car on a side street, cutting through a couple of the neighbor's back yards. If his mom showed up, he could slide out the window in his bedroom. She'd never even know he was there. He smiled a little, liking the feeling of being able to escape from her.

Checking the time again, he realized he needed to get moving if he hoped to make it to the library in time for the study group. Ella Boyd was on his mind. He'd just slipped his feet into his tennis shoes when he heard the garage door clatter open on the other side of the house. Mom. He doused the light in his room, grabbed his backpack and wallet. Sliding open the window, he straddled the sill, his heart pounding. He felt like a character from one of the Jason Bourne movies, except that his enemy happened to be his mother.

As he swung his other leg over, he was able to stand up on the first-floor roof that was under his bedroom, sliding the window closed. If his mom came up and checked on him, she'd knock and when he didn't answer, would assume he was asleep.

He took two steps down the roof and sat, dangling his feet over. Twisting, he let himself down, hanging by his fingers on the edge of the roof and dropping the last four feet with his knees bent, landing on the ground. Taking off at a jog, he cut through their backyard and then the backyard of their neighbors, moving as quietly as possible, keeping his head down. A minute later, he emerged on the side street behind his house, striding toward his car, digging his keys out of his pocket. As soon as he got close to the sedan, he tapped the fob, watching the car light up.

Checking the time as he got in, he realized the study group was due to start in about fifteen minutes. The library stayed open late a couple of days a week to accommodate students. This happened to be one of those nights. And from her messages, he knew that Ella would be there. She always was.

Ella.

The library was a new, modern building with more glass on it than walls about three miles from the high school. It was close enough that if the students wanted to walk, they could, but far enough away that the library was not part of the shenanigans on the high school campus. Pulling in the parking lot, seeing the warm glow from the light still on in the building, Justin thought that was wise. High school kids could be so immature.

Grabbing his backpack from the seat, Justin locked up his sedan, a tingle running through him. Ella had been the one he was really waiting for. The other girls, they had all been the warm-up act, the ones he could use and discard as he tested his drug. Sarah, Maisie, Katrina, Courtney, Ava. They didn't matter. Ella did.

Justin ran through the calculations in his mind again, the ones he'd used to make the latest batch. The new compound he derived should work better. And then... Well, he had a plan for her. Just like Sarah, Ella loved the beach. If everything went according to his plan, the two of them would be spending the rest of the evening at a secluded part of the South Shore Beach and not sitting in the library studying.

Pulling the front door open, Justin was always surprised at how much glass encased the library. Tampa didn't get hurricanes as often as the East Coast of Florida did, but when they did, it was usually a doozy. One hundred plus mile an hour winds, storm surge, electrical outages -- the works. He stopped to stare at the glass for a second, noticing it seemed thicker than traditional windows. Probably hurricane rated, he thought, realizing he was likely the only person who noticed the heavy-duty materials. That was likely the only way they could have gotten the building commission to approve the permits for it. It didn't matter where you lived in Florida, everything had to be ready for what the weathercasters were always concerned would be the storm of the century. He smiled. His mind was always working. Always solving problems. He was sure Ella would notice it too.

Passing a woman sitting at the front desk, Justin walked into the main area of the library. The covered lobby opened up into a dramatic, three-story building. The room was open floor-to-ceiling, with comfortable couches and chairs situated at one end of the room, large conference tables and cubbies for private study at the other end. Books lined the walls, the warm glow of lights filtering throughout the building. Staircases took library patrons to the second and third floors, which were open to below, the books seeming to stretch up to the sky. Justin kept his backpack on, walking into one of the dark aisles where the books were housed. He knew Ella was there. He could feel her in the building, but he wanted to circle the building before he went to her table, taking his time, getting glimpses of her before he made his approach.

Passing the psychology section, Justin had the same thought that he always did — their local library looked a lot more like a heavily endowed library on a college campus than one in the middle of a suburban Florida community. No one really used books that much anymore, he thought, running his finger across one of the shelves as he passed down another aisle, watching the center seating area. Everything important was online.

Except for The Study Girls.

That's what they called themselves. He'd discovered it about six months before, at the end of his junior year. He wandered into the library one day when he had nothing to do, seeing a table of girls all huddled together leaning over their books. It was the week before finals. He recognized most of them, Katrina DeLuca, Sarah Poole, and Maisie Hill. He had classes with all of them. Trying to look nonchalant, he remembered wandering over to them, "Hey, what are you guys doing?"

Sarah Poole looked up at him, her face stony, "Can't you see we're trying to study?"

Justin ignored her attitude, "Really? I'd be happy to help."

"No." Maisie Hill had said without any explanation.

He stood there for a second, staring at them, his mouth hanging open. Why would they shut him down like that? He could take all of their tests at the same time and ace every single one of them without even studying. It didn't make any sense. He remembered the sinking feeling in his gut, the surge of embarrassment that ran hot through his system. All he could do was turn on his heel and walk away.

It was just a couple of days later he found out that they called themselves The Study Girls, an all-girls group that was focused on getting them into the top colleges. He'd overheard them chatting at a locker just outside of one of their classrooms before going in. When he walked by, they didn't even look in his direction.

And now The Study Girls were no more.

It wasn't that he was opposed to competition. He knew he was smarter than all of them put together. It was that they had rejected him and not even given him a chance. These were beautiful girls. They should have known he could have been useful to them. He could see himself paired off with one of them, sharing the struggles of college, using his mother's contacts to get his girlfriend a prestigious job as soon as she graduated from college, the two of them building a life together. High school sweethearts.

But the moment Maisie had said no without any explanation, he knew he needed to convince them otherwise or punish them for their actions.

Passing by another line of books in the library, he realized his methods had been a little unorthodox, but if he could manage to convince the girls that they needed him, solve a major problem at his mother's firm, and land himself a top spot at the lab, then what could be better?

He scowled, except that it hadn't worked out that way until now...

Turning the corner around the aisle that held the books on World War II, Justin spotted her. The breath caught in his throat. Ella had come, just like she always did. She was the only one of The Study Girls left. He could see her from the back, a long sheet of black hair shining in the overhead lights, the gentle waves cascading down her back. He stopped for a second, licking his lips, watching her. She was hunched over a book, two notebooks spread out in front of her, her neck craned in a graceful arch over the work she was doing. She had a pencil in her hand and was scratching notes on the pages. He could almost hear it moving on the page, but not quite.

Stepping out of the shadows, he started walking toward her table.

It was time...

28

Danny met Morgan at the door as soon as Amber dropped her off, "Mom! I think we figured it out!"

He grabbed her hand and dragged her toward the kitchen table. Brantley spun the computer towards her. "We finally got through the last bit of the encryption. The person that's in the center of this group, his name is Justin Shaner."

A wave of nausea crashed over Morgan. That was the same name Nate Ambrose had given at the beach. Glancing over her shoulder, she wished Amber hadn't dropped her off but had come into the house. She glanced back at the boys, "Okay, slow down and tell me exactly what you know. Don't skip anything."

Brantley cleared his throat, "What we know about this encrypted messaging app is that you have to be invited. Once you are invited, then the messaging app starts building a family. It looks like one of those genealogy charts you see on commercials. Then, as the people you've invited invite other people, it builds the chart out."

Danny pointed at the screen, "But the thing that's different about this program is that everything is built out from a single person. In this case, what it shows through Katrina's account is that she was invited by Justin Shaner. When we went back and looked at who Justin invited, it's all girls."

Morgan felt her heart start to race, "All of them?"

Brantley nodded, pointing at a piece of paper, "Yeah, except for one."

Grabbing the piece of paper, Morgan stared at it. It was exactly the same girls that had been targeted — Sarah Poole, Maisie Hill, Katrina DeLuca, Courtney Reese, and Ava Banks. "Who's Ella Boyd?"

"That's what we were trying to figure out when you walked in the door. She's the newest addition to Justin's family group — that's what the software calls it. Then we found this." Brantley pointed to a string of messages going back and forth between the two of them. "The most recent was just a couple of hours ago. Ella said she was going to be at the library studying tonight. Why she's doing that with school canceled, I have no idea, except that exams are coming up next week. I guess she was part of a study group with the other girls, but since they're all gone, she's all alone. Justin offered to meet her."

Morgan's mind was reeling. Ella Boyd had to be his next target. "What time did she say they would be at the library?"

Danny stared at the screen, and then back at Morgan, "Now."

Morgan's eyes went wide. If Justin was at the library and what Nate had said was true, then Justin likely had some new drug cocktail he was ready to try out on Ella. Why, they still didn't know. Being brilliant wasn't exactly a motive for murder, but Morgan couldn't take any chances. Scooping up her keys from the counter, Morgan called to Bo, "Come on, boy! We've got work to do."

Turning back over her shoulder as she ran towards the back door, she looked at Danny, "Listen, when I walk out of this door, I want you to lock everything up. There's a police car sitting out front. If anyone comes to the door that you don't recognize, call 9-1-1. Okay? I'll be back soon."

Danny nodded and closed the door behind her as she went into the garage. She could hear the locks sliding into place as she put Bo in the truck. Opening the garage door, she revved the engine and pulled down the driveway parallel to the police car that was still sitting in her front yard, nearly missing her mailbox. She rolled down her window, "I have to go meet Detective D'Amico. You're staying here, right?" The words came out fast.

The officer inside the cruiser, a young guy with an old-fashioned brush cut and small eyes nodded, "Yeah, my sergeant told me to stay here until I was told otherwise. Anybody in the house?"

"Yes. Two juveniles. Danny and Brantley. Danny is my son. Don't let anything happen to them, okay?"

The officer gave a curt nod, "Yes, ma'am. Don't worry. I've got them. Go do what you need to do."

As Morgan put the truck into gear and stepped on the gas, she wondered what that was exactly. If she could find Justin, she could confront him, but then what? Drag him to Amber's office by the ear? She shook her head, setting her jaw. She needed answers for Paul's sake.

Speeding toward the library, Morgan grabbed her phone, calling Amber. There was no answer. Heat flushed her face. She pounded her palm on the steering wheel, "Come on, Amber!"

Morgan tried dialing again, but still no answer. Frustrated, Morgan tossed her phone on the passenger seat and pressed the accelerator, gunning the engine toward the library. If Justin Shaner was there, she'd need to find him, and fast.

The drive to the library only took eight minutes, but it felt like the longest eight minutes of her life. The images of the girls from Sylvia's autopsy room, Katrina and Courtney lying flat on their backs in the hospital, and the grizzled, worn look on the face of Paul DeLuca floated in her mind. Morgan swallowed, hard. There'd been so much death around her since the Sons of Goliath took Peter and AJ, it was hard to believe that more death could be coming her way. But that's exactly how it felt.

Morgan gripped the steering wheel with both hands, her knuckles white as she pulled into the library, the truck tires squealing. The lights were still on. It looked like the building was still open. That was a good sign. Leaving Bo in the truck, she jogged to the front door, pulling it open. The smell of old paper filled her nostrils. The woman at the front desk glanced up at her and then back down again as Morgan strode through the lobby. The library was big. It could be a maze. Where Ella Boyd was, Morgan wasn't sure. She didn't even know what the girl looked like.

Morgan went down the side hallways off of the lobby first, checking to see if there were conference rooms where Ella was working. They were all closed up and dark. Circling back to the main entrance, Morgan walked through the lobby towards the center of the building. She'd never been inside before. It was new, built while she and Danny were living in West Virginia.

The ceiling opened up in front of her, the towering three stories filled with volumes stacked on top of each other almost as far as her eye could see. Behind the first lines of books, the library was filled with couches and tables and cubbies for people to study privately. She scanned the area. Back in the corner, she saw a young woman sitting by herself. Her back was to Morgan. Morgan's heart skipped a beat. Was that Ella? She stopped for a second, watching. From out of the darkness of the stacks of books behind her, a young man stepped forward. He had brown hair and glasses, carrying a backpack. He was approaching the table slowly, as though he was trying to sneak up on her. Morgan hadn't seen a picture of Justin Shaner. Was that him?

Morgan felt in her back pocket for her phone and then real-

ized she'd left it in the truck. It was a stupid mistake. She'd have
to go without it. Morgan swallowed, circling around to the left,
making her way between the stacks of books, keeping her
approach quiet. She didn't want to spook him. There was no
telling what he was capable of doing.

Glancing between the bookshelves, she could see the young
man walking slowly toward the table. Ella had books spread
out in front of her like she was studying. She barely looked up
at him as Morgan circled behind him, watching. Morgan stared
at him for a second, trying to see if he had any weapons at his
waist. She didn't see anything until she glanced at his hands.
The color was strange. It was almost as though he had on skin
tone gloves or something.

Whatever he had or didn't have, it didn't matter. Morgan
held her breath as she emerged out of the shadows behind him.
The girl sitting at the table saw Morgan before Justin did.
Morgan held her finger up to her mouth to tell her to be quiet,
but it wasn't enough. Justin wheeled around. Morgan held her
hands up, trying not to spook him, "Sorry, I didn't mean to
startle you. Are you Justin?" Morgan tried to make her voice
sound casual.

Justin narrowed his eyes and then walked behind where
Ella was seated, using her as a shield. "I am. Who are you?"

"My name is Morgan Foster. A friend of mine, his daughter
is in the hospital, I think you might know her. Katrina DeLuca?" As the words came out of her mouth, she watched him. His
entire body tensed. His right hand started moving slowly
towards Ella. He had gloves on, Morgan was sure of it. Sylvia
had mentioned blisters on the skin of the victims. Was he
dosing them with something on his hand?

"I don't know what you're talking about," Justin said, stammering. "I'm just here studying with Ella. She needs my help."

Morgan took a step forward, trying to close the distance
between her and Justin without aggravating the situation. She

felt all the muscles in her back tense up, but she tried to keep her voice even and calm, "I'm sure she does need your help. I'm sure all the girls needed your help, isn't that right?" Morgan knew she was on thin ice. She had no idea why Justin had done what he had. All she could do was make assumptions.

"Yes, they all needed my help. What, are you stupid? Why are you here, anyway?" His voice rang with sarcasm.

Morgan stood completely still, staring at him. She didn't have time to think. She needed to get him away from Ella. "Why don't you come outside with me and talk about it. Katrina's family has some questions…"

"No!" Justin shouted, his voice bouncing off the walls of the nearly silent library. Morgan froze. Justin lunged for Ella, wrapping his right hand around her arm. Ella looked up at Justin and then at Morgan, her eyes suddenly blank. Before she could say anything, she started shaking violently. A seizure. Morgan ran to her side, grabbing her as she collapsed as Justin bolted out of the library.

"Help!" Morgan screamed. The young woman behind the desk came running into the library. They eased Ella's body down onto the ground. Morgan jumped up, her heart pounding in her chest. White foam was pouring out of Ella's mouth, her eyes rolled up in the back of her head. "Call 9-1-1. Tell them you have a drug overdose and you need help here right away. Stay with her"

Morgan charged out of the library and into the darkness, searching right and left. The only cars left in the parking lot were her truck and one other. She ran to it. There was no one inside of it. Justin must have parked someplace else.

The screech of tires caught her attention. The blue and red lights of Amber's detective unit pulled right up in front of the library. "How did you find me?" Morgan yelled.

Amber jumped out of her car and slammed the door, running towards Morgan, "I saw you tried to call. When I couldn't reach you, I called Danny. He told me about the messages between Justin and Ella. Where are they?"

"Ella's inside. He dosed her. The librarian's with her. I told her to call the ambulance. She was having a seizure. Justin ran out of the building." Morgan pointed toward the back of the parking lot. "I think he went that way, but I'm not sure."

"Okay, you stay here and wait for the ambulance. I'm going after him."

"No!" Morgan shouted. "I'm going with you." She ran to the truck and opened it up, letting Bo out. "Come on, boy. Let's go to work."

"Morgan! No. You can't!" Amber yelled.

Morgan took off running, the hand on the butt of her gun. Bo was at her heels. She knew when she adopted him that he'd had some basic police dog training, but never managed to pass his classes. As they rounded the side of the building, Bo started to growl and bark, charging at a line of thick bushes. Morgan heard some rustling from next to the building, "Stop!" she yelled. She glanced over her shoulder seeing that Amber was behind her, her gun drawn, hanging low at her side.

From out of the shadows, Morgan saw a figure running between the line of shrubs and the side of the building toward the back parking lot. Bo had flushed him out. "Justin! Stop!"

He didn't. Morgan took off at a run behind him, following him to the back parking lot, Amber right behind. Bo caught up to him before Morgan did, growling and barking. Bo had Justin cornered at the back of the parking lot. He spun around, fear in his eyes, "Don't get any closer and call the dog off, or I'll do it!"

Morgan broke down to walk and stopped in front of him. He had a vial in his hand. It was uncapped. It must've been the same chemical he'd used to dose Ella. Morgan drew her gun, lining up the sights, looking at him, "Justin, you don't want to do this. Whatever happened, it can be fixed. I promise you. I want to hear your side of the story and I know Detective

D'Amico does too. Just put the vial down and take the gloves off and we'll talk, okay?" Morgan's heart was pounding in her chest. Her fingers gripped her gun more tightly. The toxin he had in his hands was deadly. If he threatened them with it, Morgan would have to take action. She'd have no choice. She swallowed, waiting to see what he would do.

"Morgan," Amber whispered behind her. "Let me handle this. You're not on duty anymore."

Rage filled Morgan. All she could think about was the life growing inside of Katrina DeLuca, the seed of a madman who'd impregnated a young girl. "No way, Amber. I'm sorry. You can arrest me later if you want, but there's no way I'm letting this guy get away."

Hearing the two women argue must've been just the opening Justin needed. He took off at a run, jumping the curb, Bo at his heels. He plunged into the darkness. Morgan took off behind him, chasing the barks and growls of Bo. She heard a couple of steps behind her and then a grunt. She turned to see Amber sprawled on the curb condo, holding her leg. "I tripped. Get him!" Amber yelled.

Morgan nodded and took off at a run. She could hear Bo ahead of her. Certain that he had locked on Justin's scent, Morgan held her gun with her two hands, low in front of her as she made her way through the brush behind the library. She jumped over a fallen log and pushed tree branches aside just in time to see Justin and Bo run across the street, headed for the beach. It was the same beach where they'd met Nate Ambrose just a couple of hours earlier.

Morgan holstered her gun so she could run faster, using every bit of her strength to catch up to them. The back of her throat was burning, her lungs struggling to keep up with the demand on her body. She ran down the hill and through the parking lot trying to get to the water's edge.

By the time she caught up to them, Justin was standing on

the shore. In the darkness, Morgan could barely make out the waves behind him. She moved slowly, approaching him with one hand up and the other one on the butt of her gun. She called to Bo, "Come, boy." The big dog looked at her and then turned and walked slowly to her side where he sat and waited, his lips pulled back from his teeth. Before she could say anything, Justin started to yell.

"Stay back," he screamed. His voice was high, cracking with anxiety. He held the vial in front of him. "You don't know what's in here. The stuff is deadly." He reached into his other pocket and pulled out another vial, uncapping it. He held his right hand out toward her and kept his left one closer to his face, as though he was going to drink it.

Morgan lifted her gun, lining up the sights, aiming it at him. Justin eyed it suspiciously. Morgan spoke slowly, her finger on the trigger, "You've hurt a lot of people, Justin."

"You won't shoot me. You're police. You can't shoot me! I don't have a gun."

"That's where you're wrong. I'm not police..."

He narrowed his eyes, taking a step towards her absorbing the information. Without warning, he flung the vial of toxin in his hand towards her. Morgan jumped out of the way at the last second, the stream of drugs glistening as it spilled out of the vial, soaking into the sand. Justin started backing up towards the water. "None of this was supposed to happen," he muttered, stepping into the waves. "None of it!"

Without saying anything else, Justin poured the other vial of toxin in his mouth and turned running towards the water. He'd barely gotten three or four steps into the surf when Morgan saw him collapse.

Morgan stood for a second, staring at him. Part of her wanted to let him go, let the life seep out of him like it had for the girls, watching as his body was washed out to sea, but part of her knew he was just a kid, the same age as Danny. Morgan ran into the surf, the water filling her shoes and drenching her pants, dragging him back by his ankles. She turned him over, in time to see his mouth foaming the same way Ella's was. "Come on, Justin. Stay with me."

BY THE TIME the ambulance had arrived, Morgan's arms were burning from giving Justin CPR. Whether it had done any good or not, she wasn't sure. Amber came limping through the parking lot as the paramedics ran towards Morgan. They took over, pushing her aside. Morgan collapsed into the sand, next to Bo, exhausted. Her heart was still pounding in her chest as she watched the paramedics work.

"Is he alive?" Amber said, sitting in the sand next to Morgan, Bo between them.

"I don't know. Maybe? I gave him CPR but he drank the whole vial. Threw one at me, too. I probably would've shot him if he'd hit Bo with it." Morgan reached over and scratched her dog behind the ears.

"I'm glad you didn't. Too much paperwork."

"I know," Morgan said, staring at the ground. "You're right, too much paperwork."

Amber elbowed Morgan, "You miss it though, right?"

"The paperwork? No. Nobody misses paperwork."

29

M organ and Bo rode in the ambulance with Amber. She'd managed to limp to the beach, but after that, the damage to her knee was too bad. They'd had to send a separate ambulance to take her to St. Anne's. Ella was already there and Justin was on his way.

They'd only been in the emergency room for a couple of minutes when Nate Ambrose and another man came running in, holding a vial that looked similar to what Justin had poured down his own throat. "Morgan! Where are the girls?"

Morgan shook her head, feeling confused. "The girls? What are you talking about? And how did you find me?"

"I called the department looking for Detective D'Amico. They said you were all here."

"Yeah, Amber got hurt when we were chasing Justin Shaner. She's having an MRI done on her knee right now. What's this about? And who's this?"

"Sorry. This is Dr. Andrew McCall. He's Justin's supervisor. After I left you, I took another copy of the information I found to his house. Based on the drugs we found the fingerprints on,

Dr. McCall has crafted an antidote that he thinks will help the girls. Where are they?"

"Upstairs. In the intensive care unit."

The three of them ran the steps up to the third floor, racing down the hallway. Morgan slammed her hand against the button to get admitted to the intensive care unit. She ran to the first nurse she found and explained the situation. The nurse yelled for one of the doctors. Morgan and Nate stood back for a second, watching Dr. McCall and the doctor in charge of the PICU conferring. Chills ran down Morgan's spine as she saw Andrew hand over the vial of medication to the doctor. Would it work? The doctor yelled for a team to join him. Three nurses followed, flanked by two more doctors. Morgan stood for a second and then ran to Katrina's room.

Paul turned and looked over his shoulder as he saw Morgan come in. "Morgan? What are you doing here?" he said, just as the doctor arrived in the room with the rest of the staff. Using a needle, the doctor drew out a small amount of the serum that Dr. McCall had provided, injecting it into the fleshy part of Katrina's shoulder. It seemed like everyone in the room was holding their breath. If Morgan was right, she'd been in a coma for almost two weeks. Was there any chance she would wake up? Morgan couldn't breathe, the room crashing down on her, the rush of blood in her ears. She fought it off. She had to see what happened.

A minute passed and then another. The doctors and nurses stood back from Katrina's bed, staring at her and then looking up at her monitors. Katrina flinched and then rolled her head to the side. She blinked, opening her eyes.

Paul stood up, tears streaming down his face, "Katrina, it's okay, sweetie. It's Grandpa. I'm here. You're okay. You're in the hospital."

EPILOGUE

"I don't know, Duncan," Morgan said. "The trigger, it still feels a little sticky. Anything you can do about that?"

"I can look at it again. Why do you have to be so picky about your equipment?" Duncan chuckled.

"Oh, don't give her a hard time, Duncan," a low voice said from behind them. Paul walked into the range, carrying his gear bag.

Morgan turned around, her ponytail brushing against her shoulders, "How's Katrina doing?"

"Good. Good. She's getting some physical therapy at home, but should be able to go back to school at the start of the next semester, if not sooner."

"And the other girls? Any news on them?" Morgan sighed, leaning against the counter.

"Thanks to that Dr. McCall, Courtney and Ella are okay, too." He paused. "The other ones – we were too late to help them.

. . .

MORGAN HAD GOTTEN a call the day after Justin had been admitted to the hospital that Sylvia had found the same toxin in Sarah and Maisie that Justin had used to dose all of the other girls. Using Dr. McCall's antidote, the doctors had managed to save Justin, although he seemed to have some paralysis on the right side of his body. They weren't sure why that was. Probably from a lack of oxygen when he overdosed. Morgan wanted to feel bad, but she didn't.

Amber had been released from the hospital later on the night they'd captured Justin with a torn MCL in her knee. She was due to have surgery the following week to get it cleaned up. She promised to come to the range and meet Duncan while she was recovering.

Paul set his bag down on the ground, "What happened to the kid and his mother?"

"Well, last I heard the mom was arrested and lost her job. The Feds discovered she'd been pushing drugs without full FDA approval. Made a heck of a scene. Got dragged out of her office in front of a ton of television cameras. Her company stock tanked. It's been all over the news. She's being held at some federal jail awaiting trial. Last I heard she's trying to get out on bail, but the judge is worried she's a flight risk."

"Yeah, well I've been trying to stay off the news, if you know what I mean," Paul said, staring at the floor. "And what about the kid? Justin? He didn't get out, did he?"

Morgan narrowed her eyes. Two days after leaving the hospital, Katrina had a miscarriage. Paul had confided in her that it was a relief. The poor child had been through enough.

Morgan looked at the ground and smiled. Knowing Paul, he probably would have killed Justin with his bare hands if he had the chance. "You don't have to worry about that. They've got him locked up at a mental hospital for the criminally insane. I talked to Danny's therapist the other day. Dr. Solis doesn't think that Justin will ever see the light of day again."

"That's good." Paul put his hand on Morgan's shoulder, "Listen, my whole family, we wanted you to know..."

Morgan stared at Paul for a second, seeing his eyes were filled with tears. "Don't say anything more. We're family now." Morgan looked back at Duncan, "Now, about that trigger..."

More trouble comes Morgan's way in Deep Deceit.
Click here and get it now!

A NOTE FROM THE AUTHOR

Thanks so much for taking the time to read *Blister*. I hope you've been able to enjoy a little escape from your everyday life while joining Morgan on her latest adventure.

If you have a moment, would you leave a review? They mean the world to authors like me!

If you'd like to join my mailing list and be the first to get updates on new books and exclusive sales, giveaways and releases, click here! I'll send you a prequel to the next series FREE!

Enjoy, and thanks for reading,
KJ

MORE FROM KJ KALIS

Ready for another adventure? Check out these series!

Investigative journalist, Kat Beckman, faces the secrets of her past and tries to protect her family despite debilitating PTSD.
Visit the series page here!

Disgraced Chicago PD Detective, Emily Tizzano, searches for a new life by solving cold cases no one in law enforcement will touch.
Visit the series page here!

Intelligence analyst, Jess Montgomery, risks everything she has — including her own life — to save her family.
Visit the series page here!